Yule Be Mine

LORI FOSTER'S BOOKS

From Kensington

Too Much Temptation
Never Too Much
Unexpected
Say No to Joe?
The Secret Life of Bryan
When Bruce Met Cyn
Just a Hint—Clint
Jamie
Murphy's Law
Jude's Law

Anthologies

All Through the Night
I Brake for Bad Boys
Bad Boys on Board
I Love Bad Boys
Jingle Bell Rock
Bad Boys to Go
I'm Your Santa
A Very Merry Christmas
Bad Boys of Summer
When Good Things Happen to Bad Boys
The Night Before Christmas
Star Quality
Perfect for the Beach
Bad Boys in Black Tie
Truth or Dare
The Watson Brothers

LORI
FOSTER

Yule Be Mine

ZEBRA BOOKS
KENSINGTON PUBLISHING CORP.
www.kensingtonbooks.com

ZEBRA BOOKS are published by

Kensington Publishing Corp.
119 West 40th Street
New York, NY 10018

All Kensington titles, imprints, and distributed lines are available at special quantity discounts for bulk purchases for sales promotion, premiums, fund-raising, educational, or institutional use.

Special book excerpts or customized printings can also be created to fit specific needs. For details, write or phone the office of the Kensington Special Sales Manager: Kensington Publishing Corp., 119 West 40th Street, New York, NY 10018. Attn. Special Sales Department. Phone: 1-800-221-2647.

ISBN-13: 978-1-4201-1143-9
ISBN-10: 1-4201-1143-4

First Zebra Trade Paperback Printing: October 2009

10 9 8 7 6 5 4 3 2 1

Printed in the United States of America

CONTENTS

Yule
Be
Mine

He Sees You When You're Sleeping

1

Booker Dean stood in front of his six-foot Christmas tree, gazing at the brightly lighted star atop and thinking of things that should be, but weren't. Yet.

The drive home had shown so many beautiful sights: laughing people laden with packages, store windows lavishly decorated, wreaths and lights and song. It was a magical time of the year, a time when anything seemed possible, a time when love became clearer, and he hoped, more attainable.

He'd only come in moments ago, had just hung his snow-dusted coat in the closet before going to the tree to think about her, to consider the task ahead of him. Resisting her was never easy, but in his present mood, it would be doubly hard. He was a man, and he wanted her, right now, this very instant. He wanted to share the magic of the holidays with her, today, tomorrow, for the rest of his life.

Did he dare approach her now, or should he wait until he was in better control?

Those thoughts got interrupted when his apartment door flew open without a knock. Booker strode to the entryway, saw his visitors and cursed. Damn it, he was too tired and edgy to have to put up with company from his brother tonight.

Axel hadn't come alone. He had his best friend Cary Rupert with him, and they both looked too serious.

Booker cocked one brow high. "Forgotten how to knock?"

"On my own brother's door?" Axel snorted, then shook himself like a mongrel dog, sending snow and ice around the foyer. It would be a white Christmas this year for sure, given the present weather and next week's forecast. "Besides," Axel continued, "I figured if you were doing anything private, you'd have the good sense to lock it."

"I just got in." Booker propped his hands on his hips and surveyed them both. Axel's dark brown eyes, much like his own, were strangely evasive. Cary unbuttoned his coat while casting worried glances toward Booker. Given the combined behavior of them both, misgivings surfaced. "All right. What's going on?"

Cary forestalled him by shivering and slapping at his arms. "You got anything hot to drink?"

Seeing no hope for it, Booker nodded. "Yeah sure." The apartment was dark except for the multicolored lights on the tree, blinking in random patterns. The scent of evergreen filled the air. When he walked through the living room, the musical mistletoe triggered on, playing a tinny "Jingle Bells." Frances had bought him the whimsical gift only last week—an early Christmas present she told him. More than anything, Booker had wanted to hold her under the mistletoe and give her the killer kiss of a lifetime.

But Frances was a friend and only a friend and he had commitments he hadn't quite ended. Yet. But he was working on that, and then he'd see to Frances. *Soon,* he promised himself. *Very soon.*

Cary pulled a wooden chair away from the table and straddled it, crossing his arms over the back, his gaze still watchful. Axel went to stand by the sink. He rubbed his face tiredly and Booker realized he hadn't shaved.

At thirty, Axel was one year older than Booker, but ten times more outrageous. Where Booker had always wanted to settle down, buy a nice house and start a family, Axel seemed hell-bent on sowing wild oats till the day he croaked. He took his residency as a gynecologist seriously—despite all the teasing he got from male friends and family. But other than that, other than his chosen profession, Axel was a complete hedonist intent only on having fun and indulging desires.

Booker opened the cabinet door and pulled out a strong coffee blend; it looked like he was going to need it. "While I fix this, why don't you tell me why you look so glum."

Appearing more morose by the second, Axel groaned. "That's why I'm here, so I suppose I should. But God knows I hate to be the bearer of bad news. It's just that I figured you should hear it from me, not anyone else."

Booker paused. "Mom and Dad—"

Cary made a sound of exasperation. "Your family is fine and no one died. Jesus, Axel, just spit it out."

Axel pointed a finger at his friend. "You're here for moral support, so how about showing a little?"

Cary just rolled his eyes.

"Out with it, Axel." Booker threw in an extra scoop of coffee for good measure. "What did you do now?"

"I said no, that's what I did."

"No to what?"

"Not what, who."

"All right. Who?"

Visibly pained, Axel blurted, "Judith."

"Judith?" And then, with confusion, "My Judith?" Even as he said it, Booker winced. He didn't want her to be *his* Judith anymore. She was a sweet woman, very nice and innocent, but he wanted Frances. Hell, he'd been with Judith for five months now and . . . there was nothing. Just fizzle. Once Frances had moved in next door two months ago, he'd figured out what he really wanted in a woman, and Judith wasn't it.

But Frances was.

Axel pushed away from the sink. "Swear to God, Booker, I was just there minding my own business, burning off a little tension after a really long week."

Because Axel had raised his voice, and because Cary was busy nodding hard in agreement, Booker's suspicions grew. "You were just where?"

"At the bar. Hell, I was hitting on a redhead two seats down. She was hitting back, things were looking good, then suddenly Judith was there."

"Judith was at a bar?" That didn't sound like the Judith he knew.

"I think she was drunk, Booker," Cary explained in a rush. "She, uh, wasn't acting like herself. Said something about being tired of pretending."

Axel's Adam's apple bobbed and he said in agonized tones, "She grabbed my equipment, Booker. She just . . . grabbed it. I know you've been seeing her for a while now, but she's not who you think she is."

"She grabbed his equipment," Cary reiterated, still nodding.

"It was like . . ." Axel opened his hand over his fly and held himself firmly, making sure Booker understood. "Then she pressed up real close and breathed in my damn ear that she wanted me. *Me*, Booker." He shook his head in apology. "Not you."

Booker was so stunned, he reached back for a chair. Cary acted quickly, sliding one underneath his ass so he didn't hit the floor. "She grabbed you?"

"Like this." Still holding himself, Axel gave his crotch a small shake. "I damn near swallowed my tongue and, well, hell, Booker. You can't hang onto a guy's equipment without getting a rise. I didn't mean to react. I even told her to let go. But she held on real tenacious like, even when I backed up. And backing up wasn't easy, I can tell you that. The place was jammed and that girl has a grip."

"He did say no," Cary assured him. "I was there, Booker. It

was sort of a strangled whisper, a little garbled, but he said it. Only Judith didn't want to take no for an answer."

Booker looked between them. Scenarios played out in his mind in rapid succession. "Did you sleep with her then?"

"No!" Axel pulled back, horrified by the mere suggestion.

"Booker!" In his friend's defense, Cary was equally affronted. "You know your brother better than that."

It was all Booker could do not to laugh at the two of them, squawking like hens. He rubbed his jaw, bit back a grin, and said, "Axel, you can let go of yourself now."

"Oh. Yeah." Axel released his crotch and shoved his hands into his pockets. He hesitated, his frustration bubbling up until he started squawking again. "You had to know, Booker. I didn't want to be the one to tell you, but you had to know."

"Yep. I had to know."

Cary leaned toward him, filled with masculine concern. He clapped Booker on the back of the neck, gave him a too-tight squeeze. "You okay, Booker?"

"I'm fine actually." He shrugged off Cary's stranglehold, glanced up and saw the coffeemaker give one final hiss and spit. "Good, the coffee is done. You can each have one cup. I'll even let you have a Christmas cookie. Then I want you gone."

Axel and Cary looked at each other helplessly. "You upset?"

"Not really." Surprised. Exhilarated. But not upset. Booker filled three mugs to the top. None of them used sugar or cream, though Booker kept it on hand because Frances liked her coffee with plenty of both, and there were many a lazy Sunday morning where they shared a cup and talked about upcoming sports, work, or just sat together, doing nothing.

Well, Frances did nothing. Booker spent his time surreptitiously watching her, thinking about getting her out of her clothes, basically doing all the fantasizing men indulge when with a woman they want. Bad.

He opened his cookie jar, took out a handful of the delicious, decorated cookies Frances had made for him, and set them on the table.

"What are you going to do, Booker?"

Booker shook off his musings. He noticed that Cary's brown hair was still damp from the sleet and snow. He pushed it back from his face while watching Booker with sympathy and concern. Hell, did they expect him to go ballistic? To be furious with Axel? To sit around and mope with a broken heart?

This time he did laugh.

Cary leaned forward, and as a doctor, gave his professional opinion. "Damn, he's hysterical."

Axel's eyes widened. "Booker. Man, I swear I'm sorry. Judith is sweet on the eyes, no way around that. But I would never go behind your back—"

Knowing he had to put them at ease before they started trying to hug him or something equally unsavory, Booker set down his coffee. "You want to know what I'm going to do? Okay, I'll tell you. First, I'm going to shower and change into clean clothes. Then I'm going to go next door to see Frances. And then . . ." He savored the moment, his voice dropping to a husky drawl without him even realizing it. "Then, I'm going to make up for lost time."

Silence filled the kitchen until Axel fell back against the counter. "Frances?" he asked with some confusion.

Cary drew an incredulous face. "Your neighbor?"

"Yeah." In extreme anticipation, Booker rubbed his hands together. Frances might think of herself as just a friend for now, but that was about to change. The sooner the better.

When he got her naked and kissed her from head to toe, she'd understand he wanted more than friendship. A lot more—like everything.

"You're talking about that tall girl next door?" Cary asked, apparently needing clarification. "The one who likes football and runs all the time?"

"She jogs, and yeah, she's the one." She'd been *The One* almost from the day he'd met her.

"I kinda thought she was gay," Cary confided.

Booker laughed. "No. She just doesn't date much because

she's always working." Frances was a very talented artist, though so far most of her work centered around commissions for commercial outlets, like window paintings and murals in pediatrician and dentist offices. Recently, however, the local galleries had started showing her work—with much success.

"You got a thing for her?" Axel asked.

"Yeah. A thing. A big thing. Like a hard case of *gotta have her.*"

"No shit?" Axel grinned and for the first time that night, he relaxed. "Well, hell, that's great news, Booker." Then he thought to ask, "Does this girl feel the same about you?"

"Woman, and no. At least, not yet she doesn't. But then, we've done that damned disgusting platonic thing because she thought I was permanently tied to Judith and I was waiting until I could figure out how to end things with Judith without breaking her heart."

Cary choked. "I think her heart will be safe."

"It seems so." Booker was so relieved to have that particular problem solved that he couldn't wait to get to Frances. He turned to his brother. "I suppose I owe you a thank-you, for helping things along."

Axel fell into a thoughtful silence while sipping his coffee. "So let me get this straight. You're not even the smallest bit upset that Judith was pawing me and licking on me?"

"Pawing you *and* licking you?"

Axel shrugged. "My ear and neck and stuff. She's got a hot little tongue on her, too. I thought for a minute there she was going to take a bite. And I had a helluva time getting her fingers off my zipper, but with the way she used that tongue, no way did I want my zipper down. She'd backed me damn near into the men's room and I swear, I thought the girl would molest me."

When Booker smiled, Cary added, "I've never seen your brother in such a panic, Booker. If I hadn't been worried about how you'd take it, I'd have been laughing my ass off."

"I'm not upset, Axel. This gives me the perfect out and I won't even have to be the bad guy."

Axel nodded, did some more thinking, then plunked down his coffee cup. "You know, Booker, I really wish you'd have let me in on all this *before* I told Judith no."

Cary snickered. "She was plenty pissed when you turned her down."

"Probably because she knows my brother never turns women down."

"Almost never," Axel specified. "But even I have to draw the line at women involved with my baby brother." He tipped his head at Booker. "Say, I don't suppose you'd care to give me her number?"

"God, Axel." Cary shook his head in disgust. "You're unbelievable."

Axel just smiled. "The way that girl held me was unbelievable. And since Booker doesn't mind, I figure why not?"

"I don't mind at all." Booker wrote down her number and handed it to Axel with his best wishes. "Good luck, and get out. I have things to do and they don't include the two of you."

"Given that look in your eyes, I should hope not," Cary said with a laugh.

Axel slung his arm around Booker on the way to the front door. He was twenty-five pounds heavier and an inch shorter than Booker, but other than that, the similarity in their appearance was uncanny. "So you think you'll be bringing Frances to Christmas dinner?"

With all his most immediate plans centered on getting her into bed, preferably tonight, he hadn't yet thought that far ahead. But it sounded like a hell of an idea. Frances was friendly, open, easy to talk to. If things worked out as he hoped, they'd be spending a lot of time together, especially during the holidays—and especially in bed. "I'll work on it."

* * *

Frances had paused in front of her tree to straighten a plump Santa ornament. The delicate glass reflected the white twinkly lights, looking almost magical. But there'd be no magic for her this year. What she wanted most, Santa couldn't put under her tree.

After working all day, she was hot and tired, and so when What-She-Wanted-Most knocked on her door, she almost jumped out of her skin. She knew it was Booker, because she knew his knock, just as she knew his laugh, his tone of voice when he was excited, and his scent. God, she loved his scent.

With her heart swelling painfully, she opened the door with a false smile. As usual, he looked dark and sexy and so appealing, her pulse leaped at the sight of him.

Hands snug in his pockets, his flannel shirt open over a white thermal and nicely worn jeans, he leaned in her doorway. His silky black hair was still damp from a shower and his jaw was freshly shaved. He had a rakish "just won the lottery" look about him and the way he murmured, "Hi" had her blinking in surprise.

Somehow, he was different. There was a glimmer in his dark eyes, a special kind of attentiveness that hadn't been there only the day before. His gaze was direct and almost . . . intimate. Yeah, that was it. And he wore a funny little half smile of expectation.

Expectation of *what?*

Uncertainly, Frances managed a reply. "Hey, Booker. What's up?"

He stepped inside without an invite, but then, they were *friends* and Booker visited with her a lot. Whenever he wasn't working—or with Judith—he came by to play cards, watch sports, or just shoot the bull. Like he would with a pal.

Maybe it was the holidays making her nostalgic, but when she thought of being Booker's pal for the rest of her life, she wanted to curl up and cry.

A stray lock of hair had escaped her big clip and hung near

her eyes. Taking his time and stopping her heart in the process, Booker smoothed it behind her ear.

No way in hell did he do that with his guy friends. She gulped.

In a voice low and gentle and seductive, he said, "What have you been doing that has you all warm on such a cold snowy day?"

Unnerved, Frances backed up out of reach. Booker stepped close again. "I, ah . . ." She gestured behind her. "I'm moving my room."

"Yeah?" He looked at her mouth. "Want to move it next door with me?"

She shook her head at his unfamiliar, suggestive teasing. "I'm switching my bedroom with my studio because the light is better in that room now."

As an artist, she liked to take advantage of whatever natural light she could get. In summer, she used her smaller guest bedroom for sleeping so that the larger room could be filled with her canvases and paints and pottery wheel. But now with winter hard upon them, the light was different. More often than not, long shadows filled the room, so she was switching. If nothing else, it gave her a way to fill the time rather than think of Booker and Judith snuggled up in front of a warm fire, playing kissy-face and more.

Booker stepped around her and closed the door. "Maybe I can help. What else do you have to move?"

Now that was more like the Booker she knew and loved. "Just the bedroom furniture. I already moved the small stuff and my clothes." She turned to meander down the hallway and Booker followed. Closely. She could practically feel him breathing on her neck. Neil Diamond's Christmas album played softly in the background, barely drowning out the drumming of her heartbeat.

Today, even Neil hadn't been able to lift her spirits.

As they passed the kitchen, they walked beneath a sprig of mistletoe hung from a silver ribbon. Because she was a single woman without a steady date—without any date really—Frances had put it up as decoration, not for any practical use. She paid it little mind as she started under it, until Booker caught her by the upper arm.

Turning, she said, "What?"

Gently, he drew her all the way around to face him. He looked first into her eyes, letting her see the curious heat in his, then he looked at her mouth. His voice dropped. "This."

In the next instant, Frances found herself hauled up against his hard chest while his hands framed her face.

Startled, she thought, *He's going to kiss me.*

Just as quickly, she discounted that absurd notion. Booker was a friend, nothing more. He was involved with Judith. He didn't see her as a—

His mouth touched hers.

She went utterly still outside, but inside things were happening. Like her heart hitting her rib cage and her stomach fluttering and her blood taking off in a wild race through her system . . .

"Frances?" He whispered her name against her mouth.

Dazed, her eyes flickered open. "Hmm?"

Booker held her face tipped up, brushed her jaw with his thumbs, and kissed her again. It was a gentle, closed-mouth kiss, but there was nothing platonic about it. His mouth was warm, soft, moving carefully over hers. His tongue traced the seam of her lips with such enticing effect that her toes curled and her hands lifted to his hard shoulders. Booker groaned, tightened his hold—and Frances came back to her senses.

"Booker." She shoved him away, suffused with indignation and hurt and an awful yearning. "What do you think you're doing?"

Because she was nearly as tall, her push had thrown him off-balance. He caught himself, grinned at her, and said, "Something I've been thinking about doing for a long time."

Frances touched her mouth, equally doubting and flustered. She could still taste him. "You have?"

"Yeah. I have." He closed the space between them again. Frances inhaled the clean scent of his aftershave and the headier scent of his body. She could practically feel the heat in his unwavering gaze. He touched her chin, tipped up her face, and asked, "Haven't you, Frances? Ever?"

2

Frances swallowed hard. Think of him? Of course, she had. There were nights when she couldn't sleep at all, fantasizing about Booker, about kissing him and touching him, feeling his weight on top of her, naked flesh to naked flesh. But all she did was fantasize because he was already with someone else and she would never, ever be blamed for breaking up a couple.

She couldn't lie to him, but she wouldn't be a party to him cheating either. "Yes, I have."

His expression tightened, his voice went deep. "Tell me."

God, he was potent in seduce-mode. "No. Because I'm not going to do anything about it."

"Wanna bet?"

Oh, the wicked way he murmured that. "Booker Dean, have you forgotten that you're already involved? Have you forgotten about *Judith?*" Damn, she hadn't meant to sneer the woman's name. It wasn't Judith's fault that Booker had fallen in love with her long before Frances had even moved into his apartment complex. She scowled. "You know you don't really want to do this."

"Oh, I want to all right." He kept inching toward her, forcing her to back up. "You probably have no idea of all the things I want to do to you."

Her mouth fell open, then snapped shut. "Let me rephrase that. I won't let you do them."

He reached out and brushed her cheek with the back of his knuckles. His voice was soft, mesmerizing. "Even though Judith and I aren't together anymore?"

"You aren't . . ." Her eyes narrowed. "Since when?"

With a load of satisfaction, Booker said, "About twenty minutes ago."

Forget indignation. Frances was outraged. She stopped retreating and took a stand. Through stiffened lips, she said, "Judith breaks up with you twenty minutes ago and so you come tripping over here expecting . . . what? You want me to comfort you, Booker? Is that it? You want to use me to forget about her?"

Booker looked momentarily nonplussed, then annoyed. "No, damn it. That's just dumb. Besides, she didn't break up with me."

That surprised Frances. "You're the one who broke things off?"

He worked his jaw. "Well, not yet. Not officially. But see . . ."

Frances threw up her arms. "I don't believe this. Go home, Booker." She turned and stomped down the hall to her bedroom. *Not officially,* she mimicked in her mind. Damn. She hit a pillow, but it didn't help. She'd wanted Booker too long to play games like this.

Conflicting emotions wreaked havoc with her heart. She'd dreamed of Booker seeing her as more than a friend, but never would she allow him to use her to get over another woman.

She started to hit the pillow again, then Booker slipped his arms around her from behind. All along the length of her back, she felt him, hot, hard, most definitely male. Because he held a physical job, Booker's strength was evidenced in lean, hard muscles. When Frances started to jolt away, he carefully restrained her, gathering her close against his body, enfolding her in that delicious scent. "Just hold on and let me explain."

She'd melt if she stayed pressed to him like this. In a rasp, she whispered, "Let go."

"No."

His refusal gave her pause, then renewed her temper. She'd never known Booker to be a dominating-type man. "What do you mean no? I said to let me go."

Instead, he immobilized her by kissing the side of her neck. Stunned, Frances registered the heat and firmness of his mouth, the soft touch of his damp tongue—and she registered his smile. "Honest to God, Frannie, you make me nuts. You've been making me nuts for a while now." His arms tightened in a bear hug and he rocked her side to side.

Holding herself stiff against the urge to relax in his embrace, Frances said, "Well it wasn't on purpose."

"I know," he soothed. "You can't help it."

"Booker—"

He interrupted her warning with another soft smooch, this one behind her ear. That small kiss, accompanied with the sigh of his breath, had her breathing accelerating and her temperature on the rise. She shivered.

"There, you see? You do it without even trying."

"Do . . . what?"

"Make me crazy." He pressed his nose into her hair. "With the way you smell—"

Smell? She tried for sarcasm to save her. "You mean like paint thinner and clay?"

"And woman and sex and *you,* Frannie Kennedy. I love how you smell." He took another deep breath, then growled to show his sincerity. "And the way you dress."

Now she rolled her eyes. "In paint-stained work clothes? C'mon Booker." Since they couldn't be more than friends, she'd made a point of *not* primping with him. In the last few weeks, he'd started coming over more often, staying longer when he did, and she'd come to appreciate how nice it was to be totally herself with someone. She could forget makeup and uncomfortably stylish clothes. She could laugh out loud without worrying if he found her inelegant. She could blow her nose when she had a cold or sniffle and cry at sad movies. She could cheer as loud as any guy when her favorite football team won, and she could even share a few dirty jokes with him without blushing.

Now he wanted to throw a kink in the works.

Booker's hands opened over her middle. He had large hands, rough from working in his lumberyard and doing custom millwork. With his fingers splayed, he was only a millimeter from her breasts with one hand, and closer than that to her left hipbone with the other.

Anticipation held her in thrall. Would he touch her? Would she let him?

His warm breath brushed her ear. "In soft loose smocks that tease because they hide your breasts, making my imagination go wild."

She didn't know Booker had ever noticed her breasts. They certainly weren't big enough to automatically draw attention.

". . . and snug leggings that make your ass look great."

Her *ass?* She tried to twist to see him, but he wouldn't let her.

". . . and thick socks that look so cute on your feet."

Being almost as tall as him meant her feet were proportionate—and not in the least cute. "Now you're just being ridiculous."

"Frannie, Frannie, Frannie. You'd be amazed at what appears sexual to the male mind, especially when it's been deprived. Like the funny way you always pin up your hair." He teased a twisted lock with his nose. "It's sort of sloppy and casual, but I can see your nape and those baby-fine curls there and it makes me horny as hell." To emphasize that, he took a gentle love bite at the side of her throat.

Frances swallowed down a gasp, both of shock and sexual spark. Against her behind, she felt the start of an impressive erection. She gave a small, nearly silent moan. It took all her willpower not to nestle up closer to that purely male reaction—*to her.*

But willpower was something she'd cultivated since moving next door to Booker Dean. When she'd first met him, she'd panicked because he was so appealing and she'd been a complete wreck, a typical state for her when she worked, and she worked almost all the time. But when she'd realized he was already taken and so off-limits, she'd given up and been herself and found a wonderful friendship that no matter how she tried wasn't quite enough.

It still wasn't enough, but she'd be damned before she got him on the rebound.

"So," she said, forcing the word out while closing her hands around his wrists to ensure he wouldn't move them up or down. "You're not officially over with Judith, but you expect me to just say, 'Hey, okay, let's go to bed'?"

He shuddered against her, asking roughly, "Would you?"

"No." She again started to lunge away but Booker held on and they stumbled into the wall.

"If you'll just settle down and listen, I'll explain." Cautiously, he turned her around so she faced him. Then, before she could protest, he looked at her mouth, appeared drawn there and he started kissing her again, light, teasing kisses. "I swear, Frannie, you have the sexiest mouth."

"In about two seconds, I'm going to unman you with my knee." He released her and stepped back so quickly, she almost smiled. "Now, if you insist, you can explain while you help me move my stuff." If he kept his hands busy moving her furniture, he couldn't have them busy feeling her up, and she wouldn't have to worry about resisting him.

He followed her to the bedroom, reacting to her antagonism with inexhaustible good humor. "Sure thing, Frannie." Muscles flexed and his shoulders strained when he hefted a nightstand high and started out the door with it. "Hey, do you realize your room will be right next to mine now?"

Frances froze in the process of lifting a plant. Good God, he was right. Only a thin apartment wall would separate them now. He came back into the room, saw her stunned expression, and clicked his tongue. "What are you thinking, Frances Kennedy? Can I trust you not to put your ear to the wall? Will you drill a hole and peek at me at night? I sleep naked you know."

Heat pulsed in her cheeks. "Booker . . ."

"In fact, if you actually want a peek, I'd be more than happy to—" He reached for the snap on his jeans.

Frances shoved the plant into his arms. "I was just wondering if I'd have to listen to you and Judith."

He chided her with a look. "Nope. I told you, that's over. Actually, it's been over for a month. I just wasn't sure how to finish it off."

She desperately wanted to believe that. "So what changed?"

With great relish, he confided, "She wants Axel."

"She *what?*"

Booker laughed. "Don't sound so shocked. I haven't met too many women who don't want Axel."

"Well, I certainly don't." Axel was a nice enough guy, and she could see why he'd be popular with the females. But it was this particular brother who pushed all her buttons. Not Axel. Not any other man.

"I'm really glad to hear that. He can have Judith, but I don't want him to even look at you funny."

Like a zombie, Frances moved to the end of her mattress and helped Booker lift it. Her thoughts were churning this way and that. "You don't seem upset that she might want your brother."

"No 'might' to it, and no, as I told Axel, I'm relieved." He winked at Frances. "Leaves me free and clear for other . . . pursuits."

Frances ignored that bit of nonsense for now. "Did Judith tell you she wanted Axel?"

"No." Booker wrestled his end of the mattress into the other room. "From my understanding, she just caught Axel alone and tried to molest him."

Frances snorted. "Yeah right. Like Axel ever needs to be coerced."

Booker paused to give her a long look around the side of the mattress. "He's my brother, honey. Whatever else he might be, he's loyal to family."

Somewhat chastened, Frances dropped her end of the mattress. "Meaning he wouldn't go behind your back with Judith?"

"That's right. She came on to him, he turned her down, but felt he had to let me know. Rightfully so because what man wants to tie himself to a woman who's after his brother?"

"Only an idiot."

"And I'm sure we'll both agree I'm not an idiot." He didn't wait for her agreement at all. "But as it turns out, I'm pleased to have the perfect opportunity to end things." He, too, let his end of the mattress rest on the floor. "I'd been working on that anyway."

Frances bit her lip and tried not to sound too hopeful. "You have?"

"Yeah, I have. Only I'm a nice guy and I didn't want to hurt her." His voice lowered. "We haven't been . . . close for a month anyway."

It had been about a month that he'd been coming around more often, staying longer, teasing her more. But did he mean he hadn't slept with Judith in a month? Her brows drew down in disbelief.

"Now Frannie, don't look at me like that. Have I ever lied to you?"

"No. But you've never acted interested either."

He sighed, lifted the mattress again and dragged it the rest of the way into the room. Frances thought he was going to let the subject drop until he said, "I've always been attracted to you, Frannie. From the first time I saw you, I knew I wanted you."

She swallowed hard, frowned, then turned away. Booker followed her back into the bedroom where they tackled the bedsprings next. Unable to keep it in, she finally grumbled, "You hid it well."

He grinned. "Really? Maybe I should have been an actor." They both strained to get the cumbersome bedsprings through the doorway. Once it was in place with the mattress, Booker dusted off his hands. "I must be more accomplished than I realized. I mean, I know I didn't come right out and tell you, but if all the attention didn't clue you in, then I thought for sure the occasional boner would be a giveaway."

Frances silently cursed herself for blushing again. She retreated back to her room to dismantle the bed frame.

Booker knelt beside her. "Frances?"

"I never noticed."

"Never noticed what?"

Keeping her attention on the task at hand, she blindly gestured toward his lap and gave a whopper of a lie. "Any . . . boners."

Booker clutched his heart theatrically and toppled back on his rear. "God, I'm wounded. You really know how to damage the old male vanity, hon."

Laughing, Frances lifted one half of the frame and stood. Truth was, she'd noticed a few erections here and there, but had always discounted them as some strange male phenomenon. Guys got hard for the most ridiculous reasons.

Booker came to his feet to face her. Losing his smile, he stared at her with beguiling seriousness and seductive charm. "How about now?"

"Now?"

Without looking away from her eyes, he took her wrist and carried her hand to his fly where a thick ridge had risen beneath his denims. The second her fingers touched him, he caught his breath and his voice went hoarse. "Can you notice this one?"

A rush of giddiness nearly took Frances's knees out from under her. He was long, thick and hard . . . how could she not notice? She thought of him naked, thought of him pressing inside her, filling her up, and her fingers curled tight around him. Booker's eyes closed and she heard the roughness of his breathing.

Filled with curiosity, she traced his length upward, then back down again, measuring him, teasing herself. Booker locked his jaw. "Keep that up and I'm going to lose it."

She barely heard his words. Lifting her other hand, she covered him completely, stroking, squeezing, reaching lower to feel the heavy weight of his testicles. His teeth clenched. "Frances, I've wanted you too long to have any patience. Add that to month-long celibacy, and I'm working on a hair trigger here."

So, it really had been a month? That meant something, didn't it?

He stood rigid before her, letting her do as she pleased. Or rather, as she dared. She wanted to push him to the floor and strip him naked, but everything had happened too quickly . . .

Releasing him, she stepped back. It took him a moment, but Booker finally got his eyes open. He looked in pain. He looked ready to jump her bones. Suggestively, he said, "Why don't we finish putting the bed together?"

"All right."

His eyes flared at her agreement.

Damn it, she hated her conscience sometimes. "But Booker, I can't . . . we can't, do anything until you've officially broken things off with Judith. You said you're a nice guy. Well, I'm a nice woman. And like your brother, I want no part of poaching."

Booker frowned. "Speaking with her is just a formality at this point."

"It's a formality I'll have to insist on." In the darkest part of her soul, Frances was afraid that Judith would beg him not to leave her, and he'd agree. She knew it was wrong to hope things would be over between them, especially if Judith would be hurt. But she wished it just the same.

Booker hesitated a long moment before agreeing. "All right. Let's get done here and I'll go call her. But it won't matter, Frannie, not to me."

Hoping that was true, Frances nodded. They spent the next hour setting up her bedroom. Booker even helped her remake the bed, then rearrange everything in her new studio so that the job was complete. The busy work afforded Frances a little time to think about the new turn of events.

When they'd finished and the last item was in place, Booker caught both her hands and bent to kiss her. "If Judith is home, I could be back here in no time."

Booker Dean was more temptation than any woman should have to endure. Regretfully, Frances shook her head. "Booker, I need some time to adjust to this. You can't just expect me to take it all in stride."

"Do you want me, Frances?"

"Yes." She didn't mind admitting that much. "I have for a long time."

His triumphant smile was sexy and pure male.

"But I still need some time to think things through."

"How much time?"

"I don't know. At least until tomorrow."

Disappointment showed in the drawing of his brows, the darkening of his eyes. "Tomorrow, huh?"

Unable to continue meeting his gaze, Frances looked down at her feet. "You need time to think about this too, you know. You could still change your mind. You might be here on the rebound or because you want validation because Judith tried to cheat on you." Frances shrugged, feeling a little helpless, caught between wanting to say *yes* and having enough common sense to say *not yet*. "I want you, but I don't want to be used and I don't want regrets and even more than that, I don't want things to get weird between us if we do this, and then tomorrow or the next day or a month from now, you're back with Judith."

Booker said nothing to all that, and Frances had the feeling he waited for her to look at him. Finally she did and got trapped in the mesmerizing intensity of his dark gaze. She had the bed at her back, Booker in front of her, and a whole lot of desire crackling in the air between them.

One side of Booker's mouth tipped in a sensual smile, then he stepped up against her and toppled her onto the mattress. Before she could catch her breath, he came down over her. His solid chest crushed her breasts, his hard abdomen pressed into her stomach. Like a tidal wave, desire rolled through her.

Booker cupped her face, kissed her nose, her forehead, her chin. "I don't want Judith. I haven't wanted Judith since I got to know you. But I'll wait. I'll give you some time. And while you're thinking things over, Frances, think about this."

His earlier kisses had been teasing, tentative.

This one scorched her.

Using his thumbs, he nudged her chin down so her lips parted. He sank his tongue in, leisurely exploring while giving her that full-body contact she'd craved for so long.

Her hands gripped his shoulders, holding on. His hips moved in a carnal press and retreat, mimicking how he'd take her if only she'd say yes. Frances moaned, then moaned again when his fingers found her breast, gently cuddled her, traced her nipple—and then he was gone.

It wasn't easy, but she got her eyes open to see Booker standing between her legs at the side of the bed. He stared down at her, his face flushed, his chest heaving, his dark gaze fierce.

Frances pushed up on one elbow. "Booker?"

"If I don't go now, I won't go at all. But I want more than just a quick tumble, Frannie. You'll figure that out on your own, without me pushing you. So . . . good night." He took one step back from the bed. "Think about me tonight. And try trusting me just a little."

She watched him leave the room, then dropped back down to the mattress with a long groan. Good gracious, Booker on the make was even more exciting than she'd ever imagined. And if he was like this when she said no, how tantalizing would he be when she finally said yes?

3

No way was she going to be able to sleep. It was midnight, but her body hummed and her mind was in turmoil. Had he called Judith yet? What had happened?

Frances punched the pillow, moaned in frustration, and rolled to her side. She'd asked for tonight to think. But all she could think about was whether he'd called Judith, what might have happened, if it was really over. Why didn't he call and tell her?

She moaned again. When she saw him tomorrow, she'd . . .

"Frances?"

She froze at the muffled call of her name. Eyes wide in the dark, she peered around but saw nothing. No one.

A knock sounded on the wall right behind her head. "C'mon Frannie. I hear you in there." The squeak of his bed resonated through the wall.

Frances jerked upright. "Booker?"

"Of course, it's Booker. I told you we'd be sleeping right next to each other." Silence, then: "Why did you moan?" And sounding a little wishful: "Thinking of me?"

"Yes."

Throbbing silence. "What *are* you doing over there, Frannie?"

The way he said that, she knew exactly what *he* thought she was doing. She punched the wall, heard him curse softly, and smiled. "Get your mind out of the gutter, you pervert. I was beating up my pillow."

"How come?"

Because you made me all hot and bothered and then walked away. "Because I can't sleep."

"And? You can't sleep because . . . ?"

Through her teeth, Frances snarled, "Because I'm wondering if you spoke with Judith and how it went, but you didn't bother to call and tell me."

"Oh."

A few seconds later, her phone pealed loudly, giving Frances a horrible start. She stared toward the nightstand in the dark, then groped across the bed until she found it. She lifted the receiver. "Hello?"

"I called her."

Her fingers curled tightly. "And?"

There was a definite shrug in Booker's tone. "Axel answered."

"*Axel* answered?" Frances collapsed back against the headboard. Man, Booker's brother hadn't wasted any time. Of course, where women were concerned, he seldom did.

But Booker didn't seem perturbed by his brother's rush into his ex's bed. "Yeah. He sounded winded, too, so I'm thinking I interrupted things."

Her eyes flared wide again. "You interrupted things?"

Laughing, Booker asked, "Are you going to repeat everything I say?"

"Maybe." She couldn't believe how cavalier he was about the whole thing.

"I want you."

Frances gripped the phone, swallowed hard.

"Not going to repeat that, huh?" He sighed, very put out. "Anyway, Axel put Judith on the line, she apologized, said she was drunk. Then I heard Axel grousing at her and pretty soon, she was giggling, then panting. I don't know what he did to her, but she liked it because she finally admitted that she'd been thinking about Axel for a long time, and because of that, she knew she wasn't ready to settle down."

"Um . . . wow." Frances cleared her throat. "I don't know what to say."

"I say all's well that ends well. At least with those two. Now to work on you." His voice dropped. "I need your trust, Frannie."

Knowing she'd never get to sleep now, Frances flipped on the lamp and got out of bed. A peek out the darkened window showed drifting snow and ice crystals covering every surface. It looked magical, perfectly picturesque for Christmastime, and perfect to help clear her mind.

With the phone caught between her shoulder and ear, she pulled on thickly lined nylon jogging pants. "It's not a matter of trust, Booker. You've just done a hundred and eighty turn, and we both need time to adjust."

"What are you doing?" He sounded suspicious.

"Nothing." She sat on the bed to pull on two pairs of socks and her all-weather running shoes.

"Frances Kennedy, are you getting dressed?"

A new alertness had entered his tone, so she hesitated before finally saying in a small voice, "Yes."

The phone clicked in her ear. Well. In a huff, Frances put the phone back in the cradle and stood. Over her T-shirt, she layered on a thermal shirt and finally a sweatshirt. After wrapping a muffler around her throat, pulling a wool hat low over her ears and grabbing up her mittens, she headed for the apartment door.

She opened it only to find Booker standing there in hastily donned jeans and nothing else. He pushed his way in, forcing her back inside.

"Oh no, you don't." He flattened himself against the closed door, arms spread, naked feet braced apart, blocking her from leaving. The sparse sprinkling of dark hair over his chest drew Frances's attention. She'd seen his bare chest before, but always with the awareness that she couldn't, shouldn't stare. Now she could. And she did.

His chest hair was crisp, spreading from nipple to nipple, and a line of silkier hair trailed happily from his chest down his abdomen. Fascinated, she visually traced it as it twirled around a tight navel, then dipped beneath his unsnapped jeans. Lord have mercy.

It wasn't easy, but Frances got her attention back on his face—and caught his indulgent look of satisfaction. "What are you doing here, Booker?" *Besides looking like sin personified.*

"Supplying some common sense, apparently." Vibrating tension brought him away from the door until he stood nose to nose with Frances. "It's too cold, too late and way too damn dark to be out running around by yourself."

"Wanna go with me?" She wouldn't mind the company.

"Hell no." He shivered for emphasis and began unwinding her muffler. "We'd both end up with pneumonia."

"I can't sleep. Running helps me relax."

Eyes twinkling, he opened his mouth and Frances, knowing good and well what his alternate suggestion would be, snapped, "No, don't say it, Booker. I told you I wanted time and damn it, I'll get time."

His grin sent a curl of heat through her stomach. He whipped off her hat, kissed her nose. "Okay. Then let's make cookies." Eyebrows bobbing, he added in a growl, "I *love* your cookies."

Well, that was nothing less than the truth. She'd already made him several batches of frosted Christmas cookies and they never lasted him long. She supposed baking would be as distracting as running. "All right. But you have to help."

Using both hands, he pushed his bed-rumpled hair away from his face. "My pleasure. Lead the way."

This time she dodged the mistletoe as she headed to the kitchen, making Booker laugh. She pulled out flour and sugar, eggs and other ingredients, and he got her big glass bowls off the top shelf.

"You know," Booker said thoughtfully, "while you're getting used to the idea, I could detail all the benefits of a more intimate relationship between us."

Frances bit back a moan. The intimate benefits were already more than apparent to her. She didn't need them detailed. Keeping her back to him and carefully measuring in vanilla, she said, "I have a good imagination, Booker. I don't need any help."

"But I want to tell you." He came up behind her, caught her hips in his hands and kissed her ear. "It occurred to me that there may be nuances involved that you haven't considered."

Her right hand held an egg suspended over a bowl. "Yeah? Like what?" She leaned into him, tilted her head to give him better advantage, and sighed when his kisses trailed to her throat. She'd dated plenty of times, even semiseriously once or twice, but she'd never known the side of her neck was that sensitive.

Then again, maybe it was just Booker. Everywhere he touched her made her senses riot.

She knew she should resist him, but it just wasn't possible.

"Like tonight," he whispered huskily. "When you're restless, I'll be right there to help." He smiled against her throat. "But if you insist on jogging at night, I can go with you. Or we can make more cookies."

"Sounds . . . interesting." Truth was, she couldn't clear her thoughts long enough to decide what made sense and what didn't. Not with Booker touching her.

"You wouldn't have to worry about finding a date."

"I never worry about that anyway."

The squeeze he gave her nearly took her breath. "I know. How come you never go out much?"

Because she loved him and he'd been with Judith. "I dated a lot before I moved here. But since then, I've had one job after another. Especially with the holidays." Recently, with her growing popularity, every small gallery around had wanted to put on a show with her work.

Booker stepped away from her, enabling her to draw a deep, fortifying breath. "That's another thing," he said. "When you're working nonstop the way you do sometimes, I can help with your dinner and chores."

Slowly, Frances turned to face him. What he suggested sounded a whole lot more involved than an affair. Because everything was so new, she didn't have the nerve to ask him to spell out his intentions. Instead, she said, "I can take care of myself."

His expression warmed with tenderness. "You're the strongest woman I know. I admire you a lot, Frannie."

He admired her.

"You're also smart and funny, and I love how I can be myself with you."

He'd said the *L* word, and it nearly stopped her heart. She watched him with wide eyes and growing tension.

"But Frannie, wouldn't it be nice to have someone to cuddle with at night? Wouldn't it be nice to go Christmas shopping together for gifts? To wake up Christmas morning and share all the magic and fun?"

It felt like her tongue had stuck to the roof of her mouth. He implied that he wanted to . . . move in?

"I'd like you to meet my folks. They're great. You can't judge them by Axel," he teased. "He's the black sheep of the family. Were you planning to go home on Christmas?"

He ran that all together too quickly, leaving her dazed. "Christmas Eve," she murmured, still trying to mentally catch up with him.

"Great. Then I could go there with you and we could hit my folk's place Christmas morning. Gramps and Gramma will be there. Hell, they're ninety now, but still have a wicked sense of humor. There'll be some aunts and uncles, too. Do you have big get-togethers? How many of your relatives will I get to meet?"

Her head spun. She almost dropped the stupid egg but caught herself in time. Turning back to the large bowl, she began adding ingredients. "There's, uh, about twenty of us. Lots of kids. My two sisters are already married."

"I bet they all tease you about being single."

Her chin lifted. "Actually, they consider me the strange artsy one in the bunch. They never know quite what to expect from me." For certain, they wouldn't expect Booker.

"Strange? Really?" He said it with amusement.

"And why not? Look how different I am from Judith."

"Yeah." She felt his gaze tracking over her body, pausing in prime places until she almost squirmed. "You're different all right."

Just what the hell did he mean by that? Flustered, she dumped in too much sugar. "Set the oven on three-fifty."

"Yes, ma'am." He took care of that before leaning beside her against the counter. Without a shirt and his jeans undone, he proved a mighty distraction. "Now, about these differences."

Frances stirred the batter with single-minded ferocity. "Judith is beautiful."

With a snort, Booker leaned around to see her face. "You're an artist, Frannie. You know you're easy on the eyes."

"I know I'm not a hag," she specified. "But I am too thin and probably too tall."

"You're damn near the same height as me."

"Exactly. And judging by Judith, you like women who are elegant. Judith always had her hair just right, her makeup perfect and her nails freshly painted."

Indulgently, Booker tucked her hair behind her ear. "And the only paint I see on you is often on your nose."

Rolling her eyes, Frances said, "Or under my nails, rather than on them." She hesitated a moment, unsure how many comparisons she wanted to make. "Judith has bigger boobs, too."

His grin came and went quickly. "She's got a nice rack on her, true. But Frannie?" When she glanced up at him, he said,

"She's not you." He stroked the side of her throat. "You make me laugh, almost as much as you make me hot. I enjoy being with you, talking to you. I knew things were over with Judith when I decided I'd rather watch football with you than sleep with her."

Frances paused in her stirring. "Has it really been a month?"

"At least. It feels longer because I've wanted you more every damn day." When she stood there, just staring at him, he gently nudged her aside and began scooping the cookie dough into the press he'd taken from her cabinet. "I should have realized Judith felt the same when she didn't protest my lack of interest. But everyone kept talking about us being an item, hinting that we should get married. And it was the holidays, a bad time to dump someone. And so, like an idiot, I tried to figure out a way to end it without causing a big scene—so I could be with you."

He began turning the crank on the old press and a tree-shaped cookie appeared on the baking sheet. "You," he told her with a sideways glance of accusation, "kept treating me like some asexual buddy."

Frances gasped in affront. "That's how *you* treated *me*."

"Not by choice. I just wanted to make sure I didn't scare you off until I could tell you how I really felt."

The baking sheet now held two dozen small trees. Frances took it from him, opened the oven and bent at the waist to slide it in.

"Oh, sweetheart," he said from right behind her, "you don't know what you're advertising there."

Frances glanced around to see him staring at her behind. She jerked upright, her face flushed from his attention and the heat that wafted from the oven.

Booker reached out, caught her elbow and dragged her close. "You're too warm." So saying, he caught the hem of her sweatshirt and pulled it up and over her head. "Damn, how many layers are you wearing?"

"Enough to jog outside without freezing."

"Well, maybe you can be an early present and I'll just keep unwrapping you." He removed her thermal shirt too, leaving her in an oversized blue T-shirt and gray nylon jogging pants. He stared at her breasts and said, "I don't suppose you'd want to do a little making out? We could sort of ease into things with a lot of kissing, maybe a little petting. Then tomorrow when you've made up your mind—"

Frances threw her arms around his neck. "Yes."

4

Surprised by her sudden acquiescence, Booker lifted her to the countertop and moved her knees apart to stand between them. Frances's eyes widened, but he didn't give her time to change her mind. He kissed her.

God, he'd never get used to her taste, her softness. The T-shirt hugged her small breasts, showing the strained outline of her puckered nipples. He slid his hands down her sides, enthralled by her narrow waist, the firmness of her supple muscles. As a runner, she stayed toned and trim. He couldn't wait to feel her legs around him, squeezing him tight.

But she wanted a day to think about it, so by God, he'd give her a day. Tonight he'd only tease, show her what they could have together in an effort to hedge his bets. It was a ruthless move, but then, he'd wanted her too damn long to play fair.

He took her mouth in a long drugging kiss, meant to distract her while he slipped his hands beneath her shirt. She felt warm and firm and soft and he knew he'd bust his jeans if he prolonged this too long. The silky skin of her back drew him first. She was so slight of build, so narrow that with his fingers spread, he could span her width. He rubbed back down her sides, then up to her breasts, just under them, not touching her yet despite the urge to weigh her in his palms, to learn her.

"Booker . . ." she groaned, and the way she said his name pushed him that much closer to the edge.

Using his thumbs, he stroked her nipples, felt them stiffen, and he couldn't take it. He leaned back, pulled the shirt up to bare her and inhaled sharply at the sight of her.

"Frannie." He could feel her hesitancy. Her breasts were small, perfectly shaped with dark pink nipples. He bent to take one puckered nipple into his mouth, drawing gently, flicking with his tongue.

Her reaction was electric. She stiffened, lacing her fingers tight into his hair, pulling him closer. Her legs opened wider around him and Booker used one arm to pull her to the very edge of the counter, in direct contact with his hips.

Her groan was long and gratifying.

Earlier, he'd been on the ragged edge, damn near ready to come in his pants. But now he had her where he wanted her. Almost. Naked would be better, but he'd make do.

"I'm going to make you come, Frannie."

Her eyes snapped open and she stiffened, but Booker didn't let her gather her wits enough to retreat. Carefully, he laid her back on the counter, kissing her deeply again until she sighed and clung to him. Stroking her, he smoothed his hand over her shoulder, down her side, and to her hip. The elastic waistband of her jogging pants proved accommodating.

Her stomach sucked in and she gasped.

"Shhh . . ." he told her, then groaned when he found her panties damp. "God, I've dreamed of touching you like this."

He heard her fast shallow breaths and lifted his head. Eyes wide, she stared at the ceiling. Her face was warm, her breasts rising and falling as she panted, her nipples achingly tight.

Booker gently pushed one finger inside her, gritting his teeth against the instant clasp of her body. Her lips parted on a deep inhalation. "How's that feel?" he asked her, slipping his finger in and out, his voice so low and hoarse he barely recognized himself.

Rather than answer, her neck arched and her eyes closed. With his heart slamming hard enough to shake his body, Booker went back to her breasts—at the same time working in a second finger. She was tight, but so wet and hot he knew she would enjoy the slight stretch of ultra-sensitive flesh.

Her legs opened wider.

Nipping gently with his lips, he teased her nipple. He circled with his tongue, held her with his teeth and tugged until she cried out, rolling her hips against his hand, bathing his fingers in slick moisture. He found her clitoris with his thumb, pressed, and then let her set her pace.

"Booker," she whispered, then again, a little louder, a little more shrill, "*Booker.*"

God, yes, he thought, thrilled with her response. He held her closer to still her movements. While thrusting his fingers harder, faster, he sucked strongly at her nipple. In a sudden rush of sensation, she climaxed, her body bowing on the countertop, her cries loud and sweet. Booker had to fight back his own orgasm so he didn't embarrass himself by coming in his pants.

Slowly, Frannie subsided, her body going limp by small degrees. She'd managed to knock the clip out of her hair and it tumbled around her face, a little tangled, a little sweaty. Booker leaned over her, smiling, feeling pretty damn good except for a straining, painful erection.

He touched her lax mouth, brushed a pale blond lock away from her forehead. "I love you, Frannie."

Her eyes snapped open—and the oven dinged.

Good timing, Booker decided. He knew he could take her now and all her protestations wouldn't mean a thing. She was soft, limp, open to him in body and emotions. Her gently parted lips told him so. The flush of her skin told him so. Her heavy, unfocused eyes told him so.

But he'd promised her and because he loved her, because he

wanted her for the rest of his life, not just tonight, he slid his arms under her shoulders and lifted her off the counter. She was unsteady on her feet, weaving until he steadied her.

Her T-shirt fell into place. He helped readjust her displaced jogging pants. After a teasing flick on her nose, he said, "The cookies will burn," and went to fetch a potholder to remove the tray from the oven. The air filled with the humid scents of sugary cookies, and the more subtle scent of aroused woman.

When he turned to face Frances again, she hadn't moved. She was still staring at him, mute, but also drowsy with satisfaction.

Booker sighed. "I'm going to go now. If I don't, you won't get that time you need to think about things."

That brought her around, her eyes blinking and her shoulders straightening. "You need time to think too, to make sure—"

"No." He reached out and brushed one fingertip over her left breast, making her shudder anew. "I know what I want."

"You mean right now?" She swallowed. "Or tomorrow?"

Smiling, Booker told her, "I already got what I wanted right now. Thank you."

She blinked rapidly again. "You're welcome."

"Tomorrow I'd love to have you naked, so I can really love you proper. So I can come with you. Inside you."

She rolled her lips in on a soft moan.

"After that," he said, looking at her directly, making sure she understood, "I want *everything*. Every day, every night, the rest of our lives."

She drew a shuddering breath, opened her mouth to speak, and Booker put a finger to her lips. "No, honey. Just do your thinking, okay? We'll talk in the morning."

"But—"

"Can you sleep now? I don't have to worry about you slipping outside?"

"I can sleep."

She already looked halfway there, amusing him and blunting the lust with tenderness. He cupped her jaw. "I love you, Frannie," he stated again, then he went to her door and walked out.

Frances woke slowly, a smile on her mouth. He loved her. Her Christmas wishes had come true. Feeling energized despite the fact she'd only had a few hours sleep, she threw off the covers and went to the window. More snow had fallen, blanketing the world in a dazzling display of silver and white. It was so awe-inspiring it took her breath away.

A tap sounded on her bedroom wall. "G'morning, beautiful."

Almost dancing in her happiness, Frances dashed back to the bed and laid her hand on the wall. "Good morning, Booker."

"I miss you."

She hugged herself in giddy pleasure. "It hasn't been that long. Why are you up?"

"Because a sexy broad turned me inside out last night, then sent me to my lonely bed. Oh wait. Do you mean why am I out of bed?"

She chuckled. "Booker Dean, you know exactly what I meant." He *had* gone home alone, all because he was so considerate and wonderful . . . and he said he loved her. She wanted to stand up and sing.

"Well, as to that, I was hoping that same sexy broad would have something special to say to me today. I've been laying here just waiting."

Frances fell back on the mattress, arms wide, heart full. Oh, she had things to say to him. Lots and lots of things. What he'd done to her last night, how he'd made her feel . . .

She sat back up and spoke close to the wall. "She just might." Booker said today he wanted her naked, then he wanted her for the rest of their lives. She badly wanted to give him whatever he wanted. Struck with sudden, very daring inspiration, Frances glanced at the clock. She bit her lip, hesitated, then forced herself to say, "I'll need an hour, okay?"

"Right. One hour. But keep in mind I'll be holding my breath." He tapped on the wall, and Frances knew he'd left the room. She jumped up and dashed into the shower. This was going to be the most magical Christmas ever—one that would start her on a new life with the man she loved.

Booker got out of the shower at the sound of knocking on his door. Frances? Damn, he hoped so. He pulled a towel around his hips and went to greet her.

Unfortunately, it was Axel and Cary, not Frances. They sported a box of doughnuts, beard-shadowed cheeks, and red-rimmed eyes.

"Morning, Booker," Axel said as he walked in, then nudged the door shut behind him. "Did you lock me out on purpose?"

Booker headed to his bedroom to dress. "It's only seven in the morning. I always lock my door at night when I sleep."

Cary said, "See? It wasn't personal." Then to Booker, "I'm going to put on coffee."

Booker emerged wearing jeans and carrying a shirt and sneakers. "No. Your coffee sucks. I'll get it." Feeling a touch of déjà vu, Booker pulled his shirt over his head, pushed his feet into his sneakers, and began coffee preparations. "All right. Why the early-morning visit?"

Cary grinned. "You are so damn suspicious, Booker. Hell, we're just heading home after pulling an all-nighter."

"Together?"

"No." Axel fished out a fat jelly doughnut and took a large bite. "We hooked up for breakfast, then decided you might want doughnuts, too."

"You were with Judith all night?"

Axel paused in the middle of chewing. "Is that okay?"

"I keep telling you that it is. Just don't ever try it with Frannie. I don't even want you looking at her. Got it?"

"I'll wear blinders when the girl is around."

"See that you do." He finished the coffee. "I'm kind of amazed at your speed with Judith, though."

Grinning, Axel said, "Yeah, well, she's been converted."

"Axel-fied?" Cary asked.

"Exactly. And who can think of marriage when having so much fun being single?"

Booker's front door opened again and Frances called softly, "Booker?"

Knowing he grinned like a sap and not caring in the least, Booker saluted his brother and Cary. "I'll be right back." He would allow his brother one cup of coffee, and then he'd oust him for some alone-time with Frannie.

She stood uncertainly inside his door, her bare feet shifting on his carpet, her hands playing with the belt to her robe. She hadn't dressed yet? Excellent.

For once, she had her hair loose too, freshly brushed and hanging past her shoulders. She chewed on her bottom lip. Her continued shyness charmed him.

Booker looked her over, realized she appeared naked beneath the robe, and all kinds of delightful possibilities rolled through him. "Good morning," he murmured, already thinking ahead to how quickly he could get rid of his brother and get Frannie into bed.

Her smile trembled. "Do you remember what you said yesterday, Booker?" Her hands continued to fidget with her belt.

He walked closer. "I said a lot of things."

"You said you wanted me naked."

Heat raced up his spine. "Yeah, I—"

She jerked the belt loose and dropped her robe. It pooled around her slim ankles leaving her gloriously, beautifully nude.

Booker froze, his eyes going wide, his cock leaping to attention. Lord, she devastated his senses. He couldn't blink, couldn't move.

And then from behind him, Axel said, "I don't suppose I should be witnessing this?"

Frannie's screech was shrill enough to shatter glass. The damn robe was on the floor and she dropped down to grab it, twisting at the same time so that her rump faced them instead of her front. And good Lord, the view . . .

Cary coughed. Axel choked.

Belatedly, Booker reeled on his brother. He blasted him with a look and gave him a hard shove that sent him stumbling back into Cary, toppling them both into the kitchen. Neither Axel nor Cary seemed to mind the attack. They were both too busy laughing.

Booker slugged his brother hard in the arm.

"*Ow.*"

"Damn it, Axel, I told you I didn't want you looking at her."

In his defense, Axel said, "I didn't know I'd get to see her in the buff, now did I?" and he rubbed at his shoulder where Booker had hit him. "It's a reflex. Naked woman equals staring. Any man still breathing would look at that, and you damn well know it."

"I would," Cary said, and Booker slugged him, too. But Cary just continued to snicker and grin.

Booker's front door slammed shut.

Damn it! He rounded on his brother again. "Now see what you two have done?"

"Us? We're innocent bystanders. In fact, I think I may have wounded myself when she dropped that robe. My eyeballs hit the floor."

Cary nodded. "Coffee came straight out my nose. Hurt like hell."

Booker pointed a finger at them both. "*Leave.*" Then he went into his bedroom and sat on the bed nearest to the wall. He could hear funny noises in Frances's room. Probably her thumping her fists on the bed.

"Frannie?"

The noise stopped, then in an agonized whisper, "I'm going to kill your brother, Booker."

"Not if I kill him first." He smiled. At least she was still talking to him. "Mind if I come over?"

"Yes!"

He rose from the bed, turned—and ran into Axel. After they'd both regained their balance, Booker scowled. "I told you to leave."

"I thought I'd apologize."

Frannie yelled, "Go to hell, Axel!"

Axel grinned. "She's got a temper, doesn't she?"

Booker pushed past him. "Go home, okay?" He went through his apartment and next door to Frannie's. Her door wasn't locked, so he walked on in, but made a point of locking it behind him.

He found Frances on her bed, facedown, a pillow over her head. She'd pulled the robe back on, but when she'd flung herself on the bed, it had fluttered up to her knees. Her smooth calves and bare feet drew him.

God, he had it bad. "Frances?"

She went utterly still, then gripped the pillow over her head more firmly.

"Are you trying to smother yourself, honey?"

"Maybe," came her muffled reply.

Booker sat on the bed beside her. "I'm sorry you got embarrassed." He was so damn horny, he could barely speak. He wanted to soothe her, to make her feel better, but more than that he wanted to dispense with the robe, turn her to her back and look at her some more. That flash peek at her naked body had only whet an already ravenous appetite.

"Embarrassed?" she repeated with incredulity. "I'm *mortified*. I'll never be able to face your brother again."

Through the wall, Axel said, "That's okay. The rear view was pretty spectacular, too."

Frannie lifted the pillow and stared at the wall with the meanest look Booker had ever seen. Before she could say anything rash, he touched her shoulder. "Ignore Axel. He's an idiot."

"I am," Axel agreed. And then, more sincerely, "I'm sorry I embarrassed you, hon. Booker will beat the hell out of me later, I'm sure, because I bumbled into his fantasy. And I've no doubt you *are* his fantasy. You only have to look at his face when he talks about you."

Frannie twisted about, her narrowed gaze colliding with Booker's heated expression. "Really?"

"Cross my heart."

Axel sighed. "There. All's well that ends well?"

Booker growled. "Will you *go away,* Axel?"

Cary said, "I'll drag him off, Booker. You two just go about your business."

Frannie's expression said, Yeah, right. They both knew Cary and Axel probably had their ears pressed to the wall with no intention of budging.

She was still red-faced, Booker noted, but at least she appeared less murderous. Tired of waiting, Booker scooped her up into his arms and carried her into her living room, away from prying ears. He settled onto the sofa with Frances on his lap. She hadn't turned any lights on yet, so the Christmas tree provided the only real glow in the room. The lights blinked behind her, forming a soft halo against her fair hair.

"I love you, Frances."

She curled into him, hiding her face in his neck. "Even though I just made a gigantic fool of myself?"

"You didn't. You pleased the hell out of me." He smoothed her waist, enjoying the feel of her beneath the terrycloth, the dips and hollows and swells of her body—soon to be his for the taking. Maybe even his forever.

"Axel's right, you know. You are my fantasy, and knowing what you likely intended when you came over to my place has me fully loaded and ready to go." He nibbled on her ear, kissed her temple.

"Yeah?" She wiggled against his erection, letting him know she understood his meaning.

"Damn right. Now if I could just get you to let loose of this robe . . ."

Wearing a beautiful smile, she did, and Booker spread it

open so he could look at her to his heart's content. Curled on his lap, every part of her was within reach. Her breasts, her soft belly, her smooth thighs. Those dark blond curls over her mound.

Booker drew a shuddering breath. Physically, he didn't know where to start, where to touch or taste her first.

Emotionally, he knew exactly what he wanted. Gaze glued to her breasts, voice gruff with tenderness, he said, "As long as you're being agreeable, do you suppose you could tell me that you love me, too?"

"I do." He glanced up to find her face rosy with pleasure, anticipation and . . . love. "I have for such a long time."

He hadn't realized he was so tense until her quick agreement sank in. He let out a long breath. "Do you suppose you could agree to marry me?"

"Yes."

She squeaked from his sudden tight embrace, but Booker couldn't seem to loosen his hold. She pressed her palms against him until she could turn on his lap, facing him. She shrugged off the robe, opened his shirt and pressed herself to him chest to chest—heart to heart.

Booker's hands roamed freely down her back to her bottom, along the sides of her thighs. Again, he scooped her up, keeping her tight to his chest until he laid her gently on the floor beneath the tree.

As he shrugged off his clothes, his hands already shaking with anticipation, he smiled. "Christmas dinner is going to be interesting." He pulled a condom from his wallet and tossed it to the floor beside her.

"If your brother says one word to me, if he even looks at me funny, I'll clout him."

Booker came down over her. She hadn't refused dinner, and that was all he cared about. He wanted his family to meet her. They'd love her as much as he did. "As I said, interesting."

For several minutes, he simply enjoyed kissing her, touching her. There was no music in the background this time, but Frannie's soft moans and small whimpers were better than any holiday tune.

When he slipped his fingers between her thighs, she arched up. Wet, hot. He stroked two fingers deep, working them in and out of her at a leisurely pace, feeling the grasp and release of her body. Her eyelids sank down, her lips parted.

"Come for me, Frannie." He brought his thumb into play, using her own wetness to glide over her clitoris, softly, easily, repeatedly.

"Booker."

"That's it." He kissed her mouth hard, swallowing her cries, drowning in satisfaction. When she quieted, he rolled the condom on in record time, held her knees high and wide, and pushed into her.

They both groaned.

To Booker's delight, he felt Frances begin tightening all over again. Her short nails stung his shoulders, her runner's thighs held him tight to her. He pumped into her fast, deep—and as she arched high, her mouth open on a raw cry, he came.

Though it was frosty and cold outside, they were both now warm and sweaty. Frances's heart continued to gallop under his cheek. He remained deep inside her, and he never wanted to move.

She was quiet so long, he finally forced himself up to his elbows. Looking at her, at her sated, sleepy contentment, filled his heart to overflowing. "What are you thinking about?"

Lazily she smiled, her eyes opening the tiniest bit. "I got what I wanted for Christmas."

"Me, too."

"But Christmas morning isn't for several more days. I'd like to know just how you plan to top this, Booker Dean. Because I can tell you, it isn't going to be easy."

The grin tugged at his mouth, then won. He laughed out loud. "Oh, I dunno. I think I can come up with something."

"Yeah?"

"Yeah." He lowered himself to kiss her throat, her flushed breasts, each and every rib. Little by little, he scooted down her body. When he reached his destination, he whispered, "Now this is a gift I won't mind getting every morning for the rest of my life."

With a small moan, Frannie agreed.

WHITE KNIGHT CHRISTMAS

1

With the sluggish winter sun hanging low in the gray sky, Detective Parker Ross dragged himself out of his salt-and-slush-covered car. Howling wind shoved against him, jerking the car door from his hand to slam it shut. His dress shoes slipped on the icy blacktop and he almost lost his footing. The frozen parking lot echoed his muttered curse.

Cautiously, he started forward, taking in the depressing sight of his apartment building. The landlord's attempts at decorating had left bedraggled strands of colored lights haphazardly tossed over the barren, neglected bushes that served as landscaping. Some of the bulbs had blown, while others blinked in a drunken hiccup.

On the ground near the walkway, a dented plastic snowman lay on its side, half-covered in brownish slush, cigarette butts, and scraps of garbage.

Damn, but he'd be glad when the holidays passed and life returned to normal.

Slinging his soiled suit coat over his shoulder, his head down in exhaustion, Parker trudged along the treacherous, icy walkway. He didn't have an overcoat with him because the last perp he'd tangled with had destroyed it. Weariness and disgust kept him from noting the frozen snowflakes that gathered on the back of his neck; after such a bitch of a day, even the frigid December weather couldn't revive him.

A hot shower, some nuked food, and sleep—that's all he needed, in that exact order. Once he hit the sheets, he intended to stay there for a good ten hours. He had the next week off, and he didn't want to do anything more involved than camping on his couch and watching football.

God knew he deserved a rest. The past month of holiday-evoked lunacy and criminal desperation had left him little time for relaxation.

Parker saw Christmas as lavish, loud, and downright depressing. With his planned time off, he intended to hide out and avoid the nonsense.

Now, if he could just slip into his apartment without Lily Donaldson catching him . . .

Thinking of Lily sent a flood of warmth through his system, rejuvenating him in a way the frozen weather couldn't. He was old enough to know better, but no matter how he tried, Lily tempted him. She also infuriated him.

She aroused his curiosity, and his tenderness.

She made him think, and she made him hot.

She had trouble written all over her. *He* wanted to be all over her.

In the ten months he'd known her, Lily had influenced his life far too often. Smart, kind, gentle. She carried food to Mrs. Harbinger when the old lady fell ill. She argued sound politics with fanatical Mr. Pitnosky. Both intelligent and astute, Lily smiled at everyone, never gossiped, and had a generous heart.

She *loved* Christmas, which rubbed him raw.

And she had a terrible case of hero worship. That was the hardest thing to deal with. Parker knew he didn't possess a single ounce of heroism. If he did, then resisting her wouldn't be so damn difficult.

In a hundred different ways, Lily made it clear she wanted to be more than friends. But her age made him wary, her enthusiasm scared him to death, and her love of a holiday he scorned showed they had little in common.

On top of all that, he had serious doubts about her occupation.

Yep, a conundrum for sure. Parker hated to think about it, yet he thought about it far too often. Not once had he ever noticed any work routine for Lily. Sure, she left her apartment, but not dressed for anything other than a real good time. Always made up. Always decked out, dressed for seduction.

Sometimes she left early, sometimes late.

Sometimes she stayed gone for days, and some days she never left the apartment at all. But that didn't stop a steady stream of admirers from calling on her. The only reason Parker could tolerate that situation was because the guys seldom lasted more than a few hours, never more than a day.

Whatever Lily did to support herself, she sure as hell didn't punch a time clock.

He'd tried asking her about her job a couple of times, but she always turned evasive and changed the subject, leaving Parker with few conclusions to draw.

He was a selfish bastard who refused to share, so even if the other roadblocks didn't exist, no way could he let their friendship grow into intimacy.

That didn't mean he could keep his mind off her. Throughout the awful day—hell, the awful *month*—thoughts of Lily made the hours more bearable. He imagined her sweet smile, the special one she saved for him. He imagined that deep admiration in her eyes whenever she looked at him.

He imagined her lush bod, minus the sexy clothes she wore.

Seeing her now would shove him right over the edge. Avoiding her was the smart thing to do.

He planned to duck inside as fast as his drained body would allow. If she knocked, and he knew she would, he'd pretend he wasn't home.

After rubbing his bloodshot eyes, he opened the entrance door to the apartment building and stepped inside. Whistling wind followed in his wake—and still he heard her husky voice, raised in ire.

Shit. With no way to reach his front door, Parker paused by the mailboxes and listened. Lily's usually sweet voice held a sharp edge of annoyance. She probably had another smitten swain who didn't want to take no for an answer.

Peering out the glass entrance doors, Parker considered a strategic retreat. Maybe he could drop by a bar and get a beer. Or visit his mother—*no, scratch that.* His mom would start trying to rope him in for a big family get-together, caroling, or God-knew-what-other holiday function.

Maybe he could . . .

Lily's voice grew more insistent, and Parker's protective instincts kicked in. Damn it, even if it fed her goofy misconceptions about him being heroic, he couldn't let some bozo hassle her. Giving up on the idea of escape, Parker trod the steps to the second floor. Halfway up he saw her, and he forgot to breathe.

A soft white sweater hugged her breasts. Dangling, beaded earrings in a snowflake design brushed her shoulders. Soft jeans accentuated a deliciously rounded ass.

Previously spent body parts perked up in attention. Nothing new there. No matter what Parker's brain tried to insist, his dick refused to pay attention.

Lily's pale blonde hair, pinned up but with long tendrils teasing her nape and cheeks, gave the illusion that a lover had just finished with her. Heavily lashed brown eyes defied any innocence.

And her bare feet somehow made her look half-naked.

His heart picked up speed, sending needed blood flow into his lethargic muscles. Predictably enough, he went from exhausted to horny in a nanosecond.

Vibrating with annoyance, Lily stood just outside her apartment. A fresh, decorated wreath hung from her door, serving as a festive backdrop.

Lily loved the holiday. And he loathed it.

But for now, he couldn't let that matter. Lily had a problem. She had a dispute.

She had . . . *a guy on his knees*?

Parker blinked in surprise at that. Lily's confrontations always involved men. More specifically, they involved Lily rejecting men. But a begging guy?

That was a first.

Glued to his spot on the stairs, Parker stared, and listened.

"It was *not* a date, Clive. Not ever. No way. I made that clear."

"But we had lunch," Clive insisted, reaching out to grasp her knee. "Just the two of us."

While stepping back, out of reach, Lily exclaimed, "I picked up the bill!"

Clive crawled after her. "But I would have."

She slapped his hands away. "I didn't let you—*because it was not a date*."

"Lily," he moaned. "I thought we had something special."

"Tuna fish on rye is not special, Clive. Now *get up*."

At her surly reply, Parker bit back a smile. Lily excelled in brokenhearted boyfriends, and this guy looked very brokenhearted. Poor schmuck.

As Clive obediently climbed to his feet, Parker looked at Lily—and met her gaze. The surprise in her brown eyes softened to pleasure; she gave him a silly, relieved smile—expecting him to heroically save the day.

And Parker supposed he would.

He'd taken one step toward her when good old Clive threw his arms around her. "I love you!"

"Oh, *puh-lease*." Lily shoved against him, but Clive wouldn't let go.

"I do," he insisted. "Let me show you how much."

Glancing toward Parker, Lily said, "Don't be stupid, Clive. I know why you're here."

Parker knew why, too. Lily was sexy and sweet, and Clive wanted in her pants.

"You're after my money," Lily stated, causing Parker to do a double take.

"Lily, no!" Clive cried.

"You're broke, Clive. I know all about your business going under, the losses you've sustained."

"Temporary setbacks, I swear."

"Right. Temporary, because you figured I could shore you back up." She leaned away from Clive's hold.

"*Noooo.*" Clive tugged her close again.

Straightening her arms to hold Clive off, Lily looked at Parker. "Well, don't just stand there."

Smirking, Parker took the remaining steps to the landing and caught Clive by the back of his coat. Because he was tired and annoyed—and damn it, he didn't like seeing other men slobbering on Lily—Parker rattled him.

"The lady said to leave." For good measure, he shook Clive again before setting him several feet away from Lily. "Now beat it."

Flustered, Clive straightened his coat with righteous anger. "Who the hell are you?"

"Just a neighbor."

"Then this doesn't concern you."

Given his height of six feet four, Parker had the advantage of looking down on most people, especially shorter people like Clive. "I'm a cop. I've had a shitty day." He leaned toward Clive, forcing him to back up. "I've dealt with a three-car pileup. Got knocked into a damn curb full of blackened slush by a mob of *happy* shoppers. Got jumped by a crazy woman stealing a bike for her kid. Had to break up a riot during a VCR sale. *And* wrestled with a goon robbing Santa of donations for the homeless. I am *not* in the mood to tell you twice."

Clive gulped. "I just need to explain to her . . ."

"She's not interested in your explanations."

Lily moved to stand beside Parker. "No, I'm not." She curled her arms around one of his for no reason that Parker could find. She did that a lot. If she spoke to him, she touched him—almost as if she couldn't help herself.

And it drove him nuts.

"All right." Dejected, Clive fashioned a puppy-dog face. "But you're making a mistake, Lily. I do love you. With all my heart." He turned and slunk down the stairs like a man on the way to the gallows.

When the door closed behind Clive, Parker mustered up his good sense and peeled Lily's hands off his arm. "Good night, Lily." He headed for his door.

"Good night?" She hustled after him. "But . . . what do you mean, 'good night'?"

"I'm beat. It's been a hell of a day." Parker refused to look at her. Just being near her made him twitchy in the pants. If he looked at her, he'd be a goner.

"Sounds like." She scuttled in front of him, blocking his way. "I never realized that detectives got into so many physical confrontations."

That damned admiring tone weakened his resolve. "It's the holidays." He couldn't help but look at her, and once he did, he couldn't look away. "It brings out the worst in everyone."

Gently, Lily said, "That's not true."

His day had been just bad enough to shatter his resolve. He wanted to vent. To Lily. Somehow, he knew she'd understand.

To disguise his level of emotion, Parker snorted. "The wreck I mentioned? It sent two innocent people to the hospital."

Concern clouded her beautiful eyes. "I'm so sorry to hear that."

"I got called in because the arresting officer found psilocybin mushrooms in the car of the idiot who caused the wreck. Enough to know he's a dealer."

"Hallucinogenic drugs," Lily breathed, surprising Parker. "How terrible. Will the victims be all right?"

Parker eyed her. What the hell did Lily know about mushrooms? "I don't know," he grouched. "Last I heard, the woman was in surgery." She had two kids who'd be counting on her to be there Christmas morning. Parker hoped like hell she made it.

"The dealer?"

"Escaped without a scratch."

"But you'll see to him, I'm sure."

Parker ground his teeth together, pissed off all over again. Lily sounded so confident in his ability. "I'd already arrested him once on a charge of manufacturing methamphetamine, but he failed to appear in court. At least this should cinch a conviction."

Lily inched closer, her expression sympathetic, her mood nurturing. "Your job isn't often an easy one, is it?"

Damn, she looked sweet and soft, and far too appealing. Parker cleared his throat. "Look, Lily, I'm beat. I don't want to talk about work." He didn't want to tempt himself with her. "I need to get some shut-eye."

Her hand settled over his, her fingers warm and gentle. "At least let me explain about Clive."

Cocking a brow, Parker said, "It was pretty self-explanatory."

Leaning on the wall beside his door, her gaze somber, she studied him. "I had no idea Clive harbored an infatuation. He said he wanted to talk about business, my schedule was clear . . ." She shut down on that real fast. "It was not an intimate lunch."

The nature of their business made Parker's stomach roil. "So you said."

"I guess you got an earful, huh?" She didn't sound all that embarrassed. "He lied to me, Parker, saying he wanted to help with a project of mine, telling me he wanted to be friends. Can you believe his nerve?"

"The world is full of creeps, Lily." What project? No, he didn't care. "Good night."

Lily's voice dropped. "It's barely six o'clock."

Sticking his key in the lock, Parker tried to ignore her nearness. An impossible task. "I've been up over twenty-four hours. I can't see straight anymore. Fast as I can get a shower and find some food, I'll be turning in." His door opened. He stepped inside . . .

Lily followed. "Poor baby." She touched him again, this time on his right biceps.

Even through his shirt, Parker felt the tingling jolt that shot through his system and fired up his gonads. She might as well have grabbed his crotch for the way it affected him.

Unaware of his rioting libido, Lily said, "I feel terrible that you got pulled into the middle of my mess after all you've been through today."

Before he could censor himself, Parker said, "It's getting to be a habit."

Lily tilted her head and smiled. "I can think of worse habits than drawing your attention."

Please don't go there. "Sorry." Parker ran a hand over the knotted muscles in his neck. "I didn't mean that the way it sounded."

"I understand. I . . . I do seem to have a bad track record with guys."

"Lily . . ."

"I don't blame myself, though." Rather than explain, she brightened her smile and changed the subject. "Now that Clive's gone, why don't you let me thank you with dinner?"

Parker took a step back, then stopped to curse himself. Damn it, since when did women have him retreating like a green kid in middle school?

Since Lily had moved in—smelling, looking, probably tasting like sex.

His body flinched in excitement, and he quickly steered his thoughts in a new direction. "That's all right. I'll just grab a sandwich or something."

"I have plenty of fresh leftovers. Fixing you a plate of ham and potato salad won't take any longer than making a sandwich." Coy, Lily ducked her head, and one long blonde curl fell over her breast. "Besides, today is my birthday."

Ah, shit. "Yeah?" And he heard himself say, "So are you legal yet?" The second the words left his mouth, Parker clamped his lips shut. Too late.

"Actually," Lily said, gazing up at him in adoration, "I've been legal for a while. I'm twenty-four now."

So it wasn't as bad as he'd told himself. He still felt ancient. At thirty-eight, he was old enough to be her . . . older brother.

"My folks are on vacation," Lily continued, and she took a tiny step forward, full of entreaty. "They won't get home till Christmas morning. My friends are all with their families. I don't have anyone to celebrate with—but now you're home."

Just the thought of spending the night with Lily had Parker's heart dropping to his stomach.

With anticipation.

"Really, Lily, I'm shot. I'd be lousy company."

"You don't have to entertain me."

Peculiar desperation clawed at him. If he ever had her, he wouldn't want to let her go. But the roadblocks all remained. "I need a hot shower."

Her gaze dipped over him with approval, lingering on his belt buckle, then the open collar of his shirt. Parker felt his nostrils flare at her interest, and knew he fought a losing battle.

"I think you look . . . fine."

Coming from her mouth, *fine* sounded like the greatest flattery.

"But if you want, go ahead and clean up and change out of those wet clothes. I'll get the food ready."

Seeing no help for it, Parker caved. "All right. Thanks." He made a move toward the door, hoping she'd take the hint and skedaddle so he could regroup. "Throw a plate together and I'll come over and grab it as soon as I'm done."

"Don't be silly." Lily patted his chest, then let her fingers linger. Her attention on his sternum, her voice low, she said, "Leave your door unlocked." Her gaze lifted, warm and intimate. "I'll get everything heated up and bring it to you."

He'd just bet Lily could heat things up . . . No. Hell no. "I don't want to put you to any trouble."

"I insist." She traipsed out, giving one flirtatious smile over her shoulder as if she hadn't just manipulated him. "It's the least I can do since you played White Knight for me again."

Damn. Parker shut the door behind her. Now what? Hands on his hips, he looked around at his apartment, seeing the newspapers everywhere, the layers of dust, the dishes in the sink. His neck stiffened.

So what? He worked so damn many hours this time of year, he didn't have time for fussing around the apartment.

Stalking into his bedroom, mumbling under his breath, Parker rummaged around in his dresser until he found clean clothes. In the bathroom, he stripped down to his skin and stepped under the steamy, relaxing spray. Tension eased, and his thoughts drifted—to Lily being only twenty-four, young and ripe, and so sexy.

To Lily smiling at him, touching him. Understanding him, admiring him.

To Lily naked, stretched out over his kitchen table while he—

With a groan, Parker stuck his head under the water and tried to clear his brain, but the past ten months flashed by with highlights of Lily. He saw her in her shorts, her shapely legs lightly tanned. He saw her speckled in yellow paint when she'd redecorated her kitchen. He saw her fussing over him when he got stitches in his head from a car chase that went bad, and laughing at him when he came home covered in mud for the same reason.

When with her, he felt younger and happier—and that made him vulnerable.

Dealing with the dregs of society had taught him that good

didn't always prevail over evil. Right didn't overcome might. Crimes went unpunished, while good people sometimes paid with their lives.

But Lily gave balance to the futility of his job. Her enthusiasm for life made him less pessimistic. Time and time again, she told him what a difference he made—and when she said it, he almost believed it.

Almost.

His trained ears detected the sound of his door opening. He straightened abruptly, straining to hear Lily, his heart suddenly galloping a wild beat. If he didn't greet her, would she join him in the shower?

Liking that thought far too much, Parker washed with a vengeance, rinsed, and turned off the water.

He could hear Lily singing . . . to Christmas music.

Damn. Dredging up his bad attitude, his disgust with the holiday, he scowled toward his closed bathroom door.

He didn't have any Christmas music. None. Was it on the radio? Probably. Lately, that's all they played.

She had a nice voice.

He groaned.

Parker quickly dried and dressed in loose sweatpants and a T-shirt. He finger-combed his wet hair, peered in the mirror, saw the dark whiskers on his face, the circles of exhaustion under his red-rimmed eyes, and disgusted, left the bathroom.

Before he saw Lily, he noticed the portable CD player, blaring Elvis's holiday tunes. Then he noticed the red, cinnamon-scented candle, its smell potent enough to assault his nose. He saw that the dishes, placed just so on his beat-up table, were all red and green.

And he saw Lily, standing at his counter, pouring a big glass of milk. She sang along with Elvis while rocking her hips to the beat of the music. An air of happiness surrounded her, and Parker simply stood there, watching her, his heart thumping and his mind in turmoil.

She must have felt the intensity of his gaze, because she glanced over her shoulder and gave him a quick once over, her expression warming. "I figured you must like milk, since you have a gallon of it. I couldn't see beer with dinner, and there's nothing else." She turned to face him. "Unless you want me to run back to my place and grab some eggnog?"

The thought of eggnog nearly made him gag. "Milk is fine." He gestured at the table presentation. "What the hell is all this?"

She laughed. Of course. Lily was forever laughing, because Lily was always happy.

"You sound like the Grinch, Parker."

"Who?"

"You remember. That green nasty guy who wanted to do away with Christmas in Whoville."

He grunted, thinking the similarity apt. All but the green part.

"Don't be like that. It's the holiday season. A time for good cheer." She pulled out a chair and waited for him to sit.

Determined to get the festive meal over with, Parker strode forward and took the chair. "Ladies don't hold chairs for men."

"Now you sound like a sexist grinch."

To his surprise, she pulled out a chair for herself and joined him at the table. When Parker just looked at her, she grinned. "Go on. Dig in. I want to see if you like it."

"I haven't eaten since . . . well, I forget what time it was, but somewhere around six in the A.M." And then he'd only had a hardened biscuit with a congealed hunk of sausage and cold egg. "Believe me, I'll like it."

He forked up a big bite of ham . . . and wanted to moan in sublime pleasure. Honey and brown sugar and some vague spices exploded on his tongue in a taste mamba. His eyes closed. He swallowed. *Heavenly.*

"Good, huh?" Delight sounded in her voice. "I love these caterers. They always do a fabulous job."

Parker gathered himself and opened his eyes back up. "Caterers?" That made sense. He glanced at Lily's heavy breasts beneath the soft sweater and called himself a fool. A woman like her had no use for cooking skills. Still, he asked, "Why does a single woman need a caterer?"

Her head tilted in that familiar but curious way. "To help feed the homeless. Why else?"

2

Parker choked on his food. “Homeless?” he rasped, and started wheezing.

Leaving her seat, Lily approached him and pounded on his back until he caught his breath. “You okay now?”

Jesus, he was in bad shape if getting a fist between his shoulder blades turned him on. But it was Lily’s fist, and she stood close, and he could smell her. More than enough reasons for arousal.

He nodded, took a large drink of milk, and managed an almost normal breath. “Thanks.”

Smiling, trailing one finger across the table, Lily headed back to her seat. Parker stared at her ass in the snug jeans, knew he stared, but couldn’t seem to pull his gaze away.

After reseating herself, Lily put her right elbow on the table and propped her head on a palm. The position left her breasts resting on the edge of the table. His table. Right in front of him.

“Parker . . .” She fidgeted with her hair. “May I ask you something?”

Mesmerized, he watched her delicate fingers as she teased

that long, loose curl hanging over her shoulder, twining it around and around. He asked, "What?" and was appalled at how hoarse he sounded.

"It's kind of personal."

His gaze shot back to her face. She looked far too serious, and alarm bells went off in his beleaguered brain. "This might not be the best time . . ."

"Why don't you like me?"

Damn it. Her blurted words hung in the air. She looked anxious and young, and Parker wanted to reassure her—then ravage her for about a day and a half.

"Don't be ridiculous." Unable to meet her gaze, he stared down at his plate of food. "Of course I like you."

"But you've never asked me out."

Trying to appear blasé instead of edgy, Parker forked up another big bite of ham. "We're neighbors, Lily. Friends."

She folded both arms on the table and leaned toward him, giving him a clear shot of her cleavage. His tongue stuck to the roof of his mouth. Lust churned in his belly. Heat rose.

"I'd like us to be more."

A man didn't get to be his age without meeting plenty of women. He'd liked some, he'd lusted after others. A few he'd really cared about.

But none of them had ever looked at him the way Lily did. None of them had ever sent a jolt to his system that obliterated all thought. More times than he cared to admit, he'd gone to sleep thinking of her and had awakened in the middle of an explicit dream.

"I've tried," she pointed out, as if he might not have noticed all the ways she deliberately provoked him. "But you don't even see me as a woman."

Parker did a double take, and sputtered. "That's just plain stupid."

"Is it?"

Gaze dipping to her breasts, then darting away, Parker

snorted. "Trust me, Lily. Your . . . *femaleness* is not something I'd miss."

"Then you must find me unattractive."

He rolled his eyes. She deliberately put him on the spot, but Parker couldn't stop himself from reassuring her. "You have mirrors. You know what you look like." When she remained quiet, just waiting, he huffed out a long breath. "You're beautiful. Okay?"

Pleasure brought color to her cheeks. "Thank you."

"You're welcome."

"So if you like me and find me attractive, why haven't you asked me out?"

A full frontal attack. And at a time when his defenses were down. Stalling for time, he took another bite of ham. Hell, he was too hungry *not* to eat. He swallowed, then eyed her with cynicism. "What's this all about?"

Lily pushed out of her seat and began to pace.

Parker again noted her bare feet. She really did have cute, sexy toes.

Turning to face him, she folded her arms under her breasts and drew a deep breath. "I want you."

His heart did a somersault. Every muscle in his body clenched. His neck already had more kinks than a porn star, and now he winced.

Easing back in his seat, his watchful gaze locked on her, Parker rubbed at his neck. He decided being straight with her would be his best strategy. "Look, Lily, you're a little sexpot, okay? Very sweet on the eyes. No one can deny that."

Her arms dropped and she gaped at him. "A . . . a sexpot?"

Did she have to sound so startled? Parker rolled one shoulder, trying to ease the rising tension. "That's right. But the thing is—"

An odd, unidentifiable look came over her face, alarming Parker for a heartbeat. Jesus, he hated it when women turned to tears. He opened his mouth, more than ready to apologize, to do whatever necessary to fend off the excess of emotional upset—and she threw back her head, roaring with hilarity.

He went rigid. "What's so damn funny?"

"Oh God, Parker." For several moments, she laughed too hard to answer. Her blonde curls bounced—and so did her boobs. Tears of mirth filled her eyes. She pressed a hand to her belly.

Finally, wiping her eyes and still grinning big enough to blind him with her pearly whites, Lily said, "I know you're older than me. But using a word like that makes you sound like a grandpa."

Grandpa his ass! Never mind that he'd always considered her too damn young. Now he felt challenged. "I'm thirty-eight."

Lily bit her lip, trying to stifle her laughter. "Ah. I see."

Parker's teeth ground together. He'd sounded frigging defensive even to his own ears.

"Come on, Parker. It's not like forty is old."

"I am *not* forty." Shit. More defensiveness. Just shut the hell up, Parker.

"Right. My apologies," she teased. "Thirty-eight. A gorgeous, sexy, mature, kind, and protective thirty-eight."

Was she poking fun at him? Or indulging more of that asinine hero worship?

Or was she just plain admiring?

Her lips curled. "So, by sexpot, did you mean I'm sexy, or was that an aspersion on my character?"

Another kink formed in his neck. Christ, he hated these types of confrontations. "Both." There. Let her deal with that.

But her gaze focused on his hands and on how he rubbed at his neck, and before he knew it, Lily stood behind him, pushing his hands away and touching the naked skin of his neck and shoulders, soothing, caressing.

Parker stiffened. So did the old John Henry.

"All right, Parker. Time for us to clear the air." She leaned down to the side of his face, saw his stock-still shock, and frowned. "I mean it, Parker. Pay attention."

"Trust me." He swallowed hard. Gentle breath brushed his jaw. Slender fingers dug into tense muscles, forcing them to relax. Feminine heat, scented by Lily's curvy body, drifted around him. "You have my undivided attention."

He drank in her light womanly perfume and turned his head just enough so that his jaw brushed one plump breast.

Lily straightened. A sigh shuddered out and, voice shaking, she said, "You've got it all wrong, you know."

Did he? Her fingers slid into his hair, rubbing at his scalp, his temples, then smoothing down his neck and into his shoulders. Oh God, it felt good. Better than good. Close to orgasmic.

Real men didn't melt from a woman's touch—but he wanted to. He wanted to strip those skinny jeans right off her and pull her onto his lap.

He wanted to come and then to sleep for about a week.

"I'm independently wealthy."

Jerking hard, Parker rekinked everything she'd just relaxed. "Ow, shit." Twisting to face her, Parker demanded, "What did you say?"

"Hold still." She pressed at his shoulders until he gave up and sank back into his seat.

It was as much mind-numbing shock as anything else that had Parker staring straight ahead at nothing in particular. His brain struggled to make sense of her ridiculous statement. "You say you're independently . . ."

"Wealthy."

"I see." He didn't see a damn thing, except maybe that expanding divide between his world and hers. He'd always known she was naïve about life, blind to the ugliness in it. How else could she stay so damn happy all the time? "That explains everything."

"You don't have to be sarcastic."

He was horny, not sarcastic. Okay, maybe a little sarcastic. And *real* disbelieving.

"My grandmother doted on me. I was her only grandchild." Her warm fingertips moved to his temples. "When she passed away, I became financially set. I was nineteen when that happened. I tried to find a job, but you know, I'm just too spoiled to want to work for anyone else."

He'd never considered her spoiled. Pampered, maybe. Innocent. But also generous and kind.

Definitely not spoiled.

"I donate."

Head swimming, Parker looked at her over his shoulder. "Donate what?"

Her hands rested on his shoulders. They stared at each other. Neither of them moved.

"My time. My money." Her lashes lowered. "My optimism and good nature and happiness."

How the hell did you donate happiness?

"You know, that's why you've seen so many guys hanging around my place. Like Clive, they're looking to get rich the easy way."

Aha. Finally something he could sink his teeth into. "Reality check, Lily. If you're really rich—" Which he doubted. "—then money might be a perk, but it wouldn't be the first thing on a guy's mind."

He could tell she didn't believe him, and for some reason, that annoyed him. "When men come sniffing around you, they're looking to get laid, not rich."

His crude words brought a curl to her mouth and put a twinkle in her eyes. "How come you aren't sniffing a little?"

Sniff? He all but hyperventilated around her. "A lot of reasons—but it sure as hell isn't because of the way you look."

"Enlighten me."

"All right, fine." Parker turned to face her. "You're young, and you have a very skewed outlook on life."

Her brows lifted in surprise. "What's wrong with my outlook?"

"You run around in rose-colored glasses, seeing what you want to see." Especially where he was concerned. "And this crazy fascination you have with Christmas . . ." He shook his head. "There's nothing like the festive season to force you to face facts."

"What facts?"

"That life isn't always as joyful and triumphant as we're led to believe."

While appearing to digest his comments, Lily went back to caressing his shoulders. "I can't do anything about my age, Parker. Not that twenty-four is too young, anyway."

"It's a fourteen-year difference."

She shrugged. "So?"

What could he say to that? At the moment, her age didn't bother him a bit. "I can't say as I approve of your career choices, either."

"Why? What do you have against philanthropists?"

Being a detective came to Parker's aid. He caught Lily's wrists and lifted those small, teasing hands away from his flesh. Holding her captive, he eased her around to the side of him, turning at the same time so that they faced each other.

"I'm not buying it, Lily."

She didn't try to pull away. A little breathless, she whispered, "Why not?"

"For starters, look at where you live."

"You live here, too."

"Because I make a cop's salary. If you're as loaded as you say . . ."

Lily inched closer, edging her knees between his open legs, and Parker went mute. He still clasped both her wrists in his much bigger hands, and now he caged her in, damn near embracing her.

She didn't seem to mind at all.

Focus, Parker, focus. He cleared his throat and tried to ignore the stab of sexual awareness. "Why the hell would you live here if you could afford something better?"

Her gaze softened, and she gave him a very sultry look. "Because you do."

Parker shoved back his chair and managed to stand without touching her. "What the hell is that supposed to mean?"

"Do you remember the first day I met you?" Her breasts lifted against the soft material of her sweater in a deep sigh. "I do."

Of course, he remembered. "Some yahoo was arguing with you at your door. You told him to get lost, but he didn't want to."

Lily nodded. "Another fortune hunter. I've dealt with them since my inheritance. You were all sweaty, and you had a black eye. You didn't explain, you just moved up behind him, gave him this certain look that sent chills all over me, and said in a deep, I'm-in-command-voice, *Is there a problem?* And just like that, conflict solved." She pressed her clasped hands to her heart. "You were so powerful and gallant."

Her admiration threatened his resolve. Day in and day out, he worked his ass off trying to help people, trying to serve the public. More often than not, he got disappointment and complaints instead of gratitude.

But with Lily, she appreciated every damn thing he did for her. In her eyes, he was a hero. He was the man he'd always wanted to be.

Parker retreated, which annoyed the hell out of him. He didn't retreat from anyone. Anyone except Lily.

She strolled after him.

He stepped back again—and butted up against a wall. Shit. Trapped. "I'm a cop," he said fast. "It's second nature to interfere."

"With you, it's more than that. I bet you were always a defender of the underdog, huh?"

"No." But he was. He could never tolerate bullies, and he detested cruelty of any kind. He'd become a cop because he wanted to help, wanted to make a difference.

"So modest." She stared at his mouth. "There's something so sexy about the strong, silent type. Know what I mean?"

"No."

"I bet you always wanted to be a cop."

"Wrong." God, he was a lousy liar.

"And now I know that you're attracted to me." She stopped right in front of him, with only a thin space of air separating them. "So why fight it?"

Any second now, Parker knew he'd crumble. "You wanna know what I thought you did for a living?" He didn't give her a chance to reply. She'd left him little space to maneuver, and she looked so appealing staring up at him like that—the situation called for desperate measures. "I figured you for a hooker."

Lily blinked at him.

Neither of them moved.

Even Elvis quit singing. That stunned him, until a new CD, this one Neil Diamond, clicked into place.

"A hooker?"

Feeling dumber by the moment, Parker nodded.

Her lips twitched a little, then firmed. "As in a woman who makes her living selling sex?"

Another nod, this one more curt. He waited for her to slap his face.

Instead, she giggled. "Oh my. You're giving me more credit for my sexual experience than I deserve."

Parker drew himself up. *Just what the hell did she mean by that?*

"What a dilemma for you, Detective Ross. Here you are, the quintessential defender of evil—"

"Knock it off, Lily."

"The epitome of all that's good—"

Growling, he said, "You're asking for it."

"A regular White Knight, and you thought the damsel in distress was a soiled dove."

How dare she poke fun at him! Parker loomed over her. "You keep irregular hours. You have strange men at your door all the damn time. And you look . . ." His agile tongue tripped to a halt. Jesus, he'd backed himself into a verbal corner.

She batted her lashes at him. "I look . . . what?" Fighting a laugh, she said, "Like a . . ." The laughter won, and she barely managed to get the word out around her hilarity. *"Sexpot?"*

Furious, Parker slid away from the wall and stalked over to the table. He grabbed up another chunk of ham and tossed it into his mouth. "Listen, I'm too shit-faced to be heckled right now. Take your little party home and let me get some sleep, why don't you?"

Rather than leave, she occupied his spot on the wall, collapsing back in amusement, her dark eyes all lit up and pretty. Her laughter never failed to affect him. He felt his ill humor slipping away.

And the way her breasts jiggled . . .

Parker stormed up to her, caught her upper arm, and pulled her away from the wall. "Time to go, Lily." In about two more minutes, he'd be flat on his face, passed out.

If he lasted three minutes, she'd probably be under him.

Taking him by surprise, Lily drew up short, pulled him around, and threw herself into his arms. "You're precious, Parker, you really are."

Precious? Fighting the urge to snuggle her warm little body against his, Parker ground his teeth together. "You're laughing at me," he accused.

"Because it's funny." She chuckled again and shook her head. "Believe me, if I was a hooker, I'd starve to death."

Don't ask, Parker. Just don't ask.

Her hands came to rest on his chest, and she tipped her head back to see him. "You've fascinated me from the first day we met. And now that I know why you've kept your distance . . ."

Her reaction defied logic. "I can't believe you're not insulted."

"Plenty of men have been after my money. That's a whole lot more insulting."

Somehow, his hands ended up on her waist. He could feel the heat of her, the supple softness. "Idiots."

Her gaze warmed. "But you had no idea I was rich. You thought I was a hooker." Her fingers curled, subtly caressing him. "And still, you've always been kind and considerate. And you're attracted to me."

"I'm a man. How could I not be attracted?" The words no sooner left his mouth than Parker wanted to cut out his own tongue. He needed to dampen her pursuit, not encourage it.

Didn't he?

He started to step away, and Lily launched into explanations. "I chose this apartment because it's close to one of my favorite shelters. I spend a lot of time there helping the homeless, abused women, and kids of addicts."

So that's how she knew about mushrooms. His next thought made his guts cramp: *Maybe she wasn't so innocent and naïve after all.* As much as her rosy demeanor had always annoyed him, he detested the thought of her facing the ugliness in life.

"While my house was being built, I needed a place to stay. But then I met you, and I didn't want to move until I got things straightened out between us. Only you refused to make a move beyond being friendly. I knew I had to do something to get your attention."

She waved at the table where the candle still burned and Neil Diamond growled out an old familiar holiday tune. "So I forced dinner, and a little holiday cheer, onto you."

"The dinner was great."

Cuddling closer, she asked, "But the holiday cheer?"

"It's a myth. The holidays depress the hell out of most people."

Her brows came down in a frown. "That's nonsense. The holidays give people hope. They give them something to focus on other than their troubles."

"Like lack of funds, lack of family and friends, lack of... faith." Damn it, he sounded maudlin. "Do you have any idea how many suicide attempts get called in?"

She put a hand to his jaw. "There will always be lonely and unhappy people, Parker. Neither you nor I can reach everyone. But during the Thanksgiving-to-Christmas season, the suicide rate actually drops."

"You can't prove it by me."

Now she looked indignant. "Parker, this is what I do. I know what I'm talking about." And to prove it, she added, "The American Association of Suicidology has proven that December has the lowest suicide rate of any month of the year. And the National Center for Health Statistics has documented a suicide drop by at least twenty percent during the holidays."

Anger rippled through Parker. "Christ, I fucking hate hearing people classed as statistics."

Lily's smile wobbled, not because his temper scared her, but because she interpreted his words all wrong. "You're an incredible man, Parker. A hero." She hugged herself against him again. "You care, when a lot of other people don't." With a sigh, she added, "It's what I find most attractive about you."

She offered herself so openly. It'd be beyond nice to lose himself in her slanted perception, to take all her softness and block out the ugly truths. But as a realist, Parker faced his own demons. And it was past time Lily did the same.

Hands shaking, Parker clasped her upper arms and levered her away. "Red light, Lily." He gave her a slight shake, making her eyes widen. "Put your damn brakes on that fantasy, will you already? I'm sick of it."

Appearing genuinely confused, she asked, "What fantasy?"

"I'm a cop," he rasped, "nothing more and nothing less. What I do doesn't even put a dent in the shit going on in our world. So quit deluding yourself—about me and about everything else."

She sighed again, this time in exasperation. "You refuse to soften up even a little?"

And Parker, being too tired and too horny to think straight, stared at her mouth and said, "Honey, right now, I'm about as far from soft as a man can get."

3

Lily knew when to take advantage of a propitious moment, and after Parker's bold admission, it wouldn't get much more propitious than right this very second.

Tonight, more so than at any other time, Parker needed her. Pressing into him so that she felt the hard length of his erection against her belly, she whispered, "Please kiss me."

"Lily, damn it . . ."

She smiled—and closed her fingers around him.

Parker sucked in a startled breath. His erection pulsed, grew bigger. "Stop."

Very gently, she said, "No."

"*Lily.*" He said her name like a warning.

Loving him more by the second, Lily caressed him, squeezed him . . .

And he broke. A growl rumbled from deep in his throat. His jaw locked. All his muscles went taut. And he rasped, "*I give up.*"

Crushing her mouth under his, he moved forward, driving against her until it was her back pressed to the wall—with Parker firmly against her front.

Lord, she'd unleashed a storm. And she loved it. He tasted

good. And he knew how to kiss. Or devour. Whatever. Lily couldn't breathe and didn't care.

With one hand curved around her nape, he held her head still while his tongue delved into her mouth. With the other hand, he felt her. Everywhere.

Lily moaned.

From the moment she'd met Parker, so strong, so quiet and honorable and caring, he'd touched her heart. He was every woman's dream, a hero, a real man, exactly what the world needed, exactly what she wanted.

His fingers tightened in her hair, but she didn't flinch away. He kissed her throat, nuzzled against her ear while urgently kneading her breasts.

"Is this what you want?" The low, rough words sent a shiver down her spine.

"Yes."

His groan drowned out her gasp of pleasure. He took her mouth again, stifling her excited cries as he groped over her backside, her belly, and finally between their bodies to cup her mound.

"And this?" His fingers pressed.

The sensation was so erotic, Lily tore her mouth away and gasped.

With fierce intensity, Parker watched her. His eyes were burning and bright, his expression dark and hard. He looked wild—and he looked turned-on.

He looked determined.

Wow. Barely forming the words around her escalating need, Lily whispered, "I've never had angry sex before." She swallowed, lightly touched his jaw. "I . . . I like it."

In the blink of an eye, Parker changed, pulling back to let her breathe, his scowl lifting. He looked at her eyes, her mouth. After several deep breaths, he put his forehead to hers. "Either tell me to stop, or plan on getting fucked. Your choice."

Poor Parker. She knew which choice he'd prefer her to make. She licked her lips. "Your room or mine?"

* * *

Accepting the inevitable, Parker squeezed his eyes shut, then opened them again. He hefted Lily over his shoulder, feeling like a deranged caveman, and not caring.

She reared up. *"Parker."*

"You had your chance." He cupped her rounded backside to keep her still, and he liked that enough that he fondled her as he strode into his bedroom. He'd wanted Lily too long to dredge up any nobility now.

Lily, hanging upside down, said, "Finally."

He tossed her onto his bed, bent one knee on the mattress beside her, and tackled the fastenings to her jeans. Urgency pounded in his brain. Need clawed through him.

"Lift your hips."

She did, and he stripped off her jeans. Her panties were white with little candy canes all over them. He could see the shadowing of her pubic hair beneath. He could smell her aroused scent.

Ravenous and out of control, Parker gripped the hem of her sweater and yanked it up and over her head.

She covered herself with her arms. "No fair. You have to take something off, too."

God, she had a beautiful body. Staring at her belly, he muttered, "Right. Whatever." Nearly blind with lust, Parker shoved to his feet, stripped his T-shirt off over his head and, staring at her body, shoved out of his jogging pants and boxers.

Lily started to sit up to look at him, but he said, "No way." He tumbled her backward onto the mattress and worked her panties down her legs. A little finesse wouldn't have hurt, but he couldn't dredge up even an ounce. The fact that he wasn't yet inside her showed remarkable restraint, as much as he could muster.

Her bra nearly ripped under his fumbling hands, but within seconds he had her naked. He wanted to touch and taste her all over, and to that end, he fell on her like a marauding berserker, his mouth at her throat, her shoulder, his hands sliding over warm skin and soft curves.

Lily laughed as he touched her everywhere. For only a moment, he suckled a nipple, and enjoyed her rising sounds of excitement. But at any moment, he'd lose it, so he levered up on one stiffened arm, opened her thighs and, breathing hard, stared at her pink sex while sliding one finger deep.

"Parker." She arched up. Wet, hot.

Ready.

Breathing raggedly, he found a rubber in the nightstand, rolled it on, and then he was over her, groaning, on fire at the feel of her silky flesh, her stiffened nipples, the warmth between her thighs.

He closed his mouth over hers, stroking with his tongue while pressing into her, rocking deeper and deeper until she'd accepted all of him. Her slim arms wound around his neck, her ankles locked at the small of his back, and damn it all, he started coming.

He threw his head back, managed to growl out "*Sorry,*" while thrusting deep and hard, giving over to the draining of tension and anger and regret, and accepting the pervading numbness, the awesome calm.

Vaguely, he felt Lily's hands touch his chest, cup his jaw. He heard her gentle sigh, and when he sank onto her, wrung out, shot to hell, he noted the soft kiss to his shoulder.

The events of the day got the better of him, and Parker had only enough wits left to roll off to her side, sprawling on his back, before sleep claimed him.

Smiling like a goof, Lily lay there while her heart continued a mad gallop. She could easily guess how Parker would react to his carnal faux pas when he awoke. He was such a big, macho guy, so determined to always be strong and honorable. Leaving her would probably seem the ultimate insult to him.

She turned her head to look at him, and the smile faded to tenderness. God, he was so sexy, even now while dead to the world. And she wanted him so much. Her belly tingled and her thighs trembled and her breasts ached. But she could wait until he awoke. Even heroes needed sleep.

Carefully turning toward him and lifting to one elbow, she touched him, smoothing back his dark brown hair. To her surprise, his green eyes snapped open and stared right at her. But they looked more blank than aware, and suddenly he mumbled something unintelligible and dragged her close. Lily found herself cradled to his warm chest, one muscled arm around her back, one heavy leg over hers.

She couldn't move.

But then, she didn't want to. It was too early for her, but after a while, sleep beckoned, and she relaxed enough to drift off.

The lights were still on when Lily awakened, but she sensed a lot of time had passed. A distinct chill filled the air—and a warm, wet mouth tugged at her breast.

Her eyes widened. "Parker?"

"You betcha." A teasing tongue licked across her chest, then curled around her other nipple. "You let me fall asleep."

Her breath caught. "I don't think I could have stopped you."

"I'm a pig. Mmmm, you taste good." And he started sucking at her breast again.

Shockwaves of pleasure moved over her, reigniting her earlier arousal. She tunneled her fingers into his hair. "What time is it?"

"Who cares?" And then, "Open your legs."

Wow, he sure had awakened with a "prove-himself" attitude. "Why?"

"I want to finger you. I want to feel you and get you off, and then find another rubber and take you again. The right way. The way you deserve. The way I've been thinking about for months."

She shouldn't have asked. Heat throbbed beneath her skin—and she opened her legs.

"Nice." His hands were big and rough, and he knew what

to do and how to do it. "Poor baby," he crooned, while touching her intimately. "You fell asleep all hot and wet, didn't you?"

Lily couldn't talk, not with his fingers moving over her like that, pressing into her and retreating and teasing . . .

"I should be shot. How does this feel?" Parker pushed two fingers deep, stretching her, carefully thrusting, and then his thumb rolled over her clitoris.

Her muscles jolted in reaction, stealing her breath so that she couldn't answer.

Voice low and thick with satisfaction, he whispered, "You like that, Lily."

She arched her neck and managed a small sound of agreement.

Parker smiled against her breast. "I'll make this good for you."

And true to his word, he kept up the wonderful foreplay until her entire body burned.

"Come for me, Lily. Let me redeem myself."

Such idiocy! How could he blather on while she—*oh God.* Tension suddenly gripped her and her fingers bit into his hard, sleek shoulders while her hips lifted in rhythm. Pleasure rolled through her, and then, by small degrees, ebbed away, leaving her limp.

Before she could open her heavy eyes, Parker rose over her, kneeing her legs apart to press into her, deep and deeper still. With his warm breath coming fast, he cupped her face and kissed her gently. "Just relax," he instructed, "and I'll take care of you."

"Protection?"

"Already in place." He leisurely kissed her, long and slow and consuming, then kept on kissing her. He filled her. His heat and scent surrounded her. Yet other than his tongue, he didn't move an inch.

Lily shifted her hips, felt the sweet friction of his erection inside her, and decided moving was a good thing. But when she tried it, Parker pressed down, holding her still.

She pried her mouth away from his. "Parker . . ."

"Shhh." He kissed her throat, took a soft love bite of her shoulder. "I want you to be with me this time."

"I am."

"Not yet."

Ready to press the issue, Lily trailed her fingers over his chest—and got her hands pinned above her head.

"Behave," he admonished, then his attention caught on her breasts, and he lowered his head to tongue a stiffened nipple.

She couldn't move at all, not with his hips between her thighs, his weight holding her down, her hands restrained by his. It was frustrating. And a turn-on. And she didn't want to wait anymore.

"I'm ready, Parker." And to taunt him into action, she said, "Remember, I'm younger than you. I recover quicker."

His head shot up. "I'm the one who woke you."

"I know." She stared at his mouth, a little breathless, a lot in love. "Now show me what you can do."

He seemed to harden even more, his expression, his muscles, the erection deep inside her. One side of his mouth curled in a predatory smile. "You want to come, is that it?"

"I want you to love me."

Her deliberate wording took him off guard. But Lily held his gaze, letting him form his own conclusions. No matter how he took it, he'd be right.

Releasing her wrists, his eyes locked on hers, Parker trailed his hands down to her thighs. He hooked his elbows beneath her knees, lifted her legs high, and tilted her hips up so that he sank into her even more.

Breath catching on a gasp, Lily braced her hands on his shoulders—but she didn't look away from him.

Without a word, he began a steady rhythm that gained in strength with each thrust. Harder, deeper. Gaze burning, Parker watched her. His hair hung over his brow, his shoulders strained, every muscle delineated.

Lily came first, the release taking her by storm, forcing a high cry from her throat.

Parker muffled his answering groan against her shoulder. They went limp, arms and legs tangled, hearts beating together. Lily had to bite her lip to keep from telling Parker about her feelings. She'd been half in love with him a week after making his acquaintance. Since then, she'd fallen a little more in love every day.

Now that they'd been intimate . . . well, she just couldn't imagine any other man in her life.

When her breathing calmed enough so that she could speak, she turned her head and saw the clock. Two A.M. She smiled and whispered, "It's Christmas Eve, Parker."

He grunted, struggled up to his elbows, and stared down at her. He wanted to say something, Lily could tell, and she held her breath, waiting.

But then he shook his head, kissed the end of her nose, and rolled out of her arms and out of the bed.

"Be right back," he said, and she watched the muscles flex in his shoulders, butt, and thighs as he left for the bathroom.

Should she get up, dress, and leave? Should she ask to stay? Would he *tell* her to leave?

She heard running water and splashing, the flush of the toilet, and she got up to take her own turn in the bathroom. Parker paused to absorb the sight of her nude body as she passed him in the hall. He didn't touch her, and he didn't say anything.

When she returned to the bedroom, the lights were out, but she could see the distinct shape of his long body beneath the covers.

She'd almost figured out what to say when he lifted the blankets aside to invite her in.

"Come here," he said. "It's cold. I don't want you to get ill."

Relieved, Lily slid in beside him, felt his arms close around her, and wanted to melt in contentment. She could do this every night, for the rest of her life, and never have a moment's regret.

"Happy birthday, Lily."

She smiled. "You make a heck of a birthday present."

He grunted, already more asleep than awake. She shouldn't push her luck, but . . . "Would you do me a really huge favor?"

His hand coasted down her back to her bottom. "If it's sexual, I'm your man."

She laughed, but quickly grew serious again. "It has to do with Christmas Eve."

His arms tightened. "Thank God, I'm off for a week. I'm going to unplug the phone so my mother and sister can't nag at me, then I'm going to watch television and pretend it *isn't* a holiday guaranteed to bring about depression and desperation."

Not a very promising start, Lily thought. She toyed with his chest hair and purposely misled him. "I don't get together with my family till Christmas Day, and I don't want to be alone. Will you spend the day with me?"

The seconds ticked by with no reply, and Lily wondered if he went to sleep. Or maybe she'd angered him by pushing.

Finally, he said, "As long as it doesn't involve shopping, wrapping, singing, or celebrating, then yeah, I'd enjoy your company."

She'd already done the shopping and wrapping, the choir didn't need him, and celebrating was something done in the heart, so she'd leave that up to him to work out. "Thank you."

His rock hard shoulder moved beneath her head. "I figure I owe you, anyway."

Furious, she bolted upright. "I made love with you, Parker. I didn't do you a damn favor."

Eyes glittering in the dark, he said, "I was talking about my earlier insult."

Blast. A little sheepish, she asked, "Which one?"

"Where I accused you of being a hooker."

"Oh." Lily resettled herself against him. "Now you know how ridiculous that was."

His hand slid down the length of her spine. "I dunno. I think you'd make a heck of a living selling this sweet little body."

"Flatterer." She kissed his chest and hugged him. "Seriously, after being considered a meal ticket, it's kind of nice to be viewed as a . . ." She grinned. "Sexpot, instead."

Parker swatted her ass. "Keep it up, Lily. I'm older and wiser, and have developed innovative ways to get even." His palm smoothed over the sting on her cheek, and he added, "In the morning, after I'm rested up, I'll make you pay for those taunts."

And Lily, more content than she'd ever been in her life, whispered, "Promises, promises." But already, Parker's breath had evened into sleep.

His paybacks would have to wait, because in the morning, she planned to show him how special the holidays could be. Then she planned to steal his heart. This Christmas, she wanted it all.

She wanted Parker Ross.

4

The second Parker awoke, he knew she was gone. He sat up, saw the clock, and groaned. Noon. Jesus, she'd worn him out.

He rubbed his tired face—and smelled cookies baking.

He heard Christmas music.

He heard Lily singing again.

So she hadn't gone home. No, she'd just left his bed to bake. His heart softened.

Shit, the last thing a cop needed was a soft heart.

He felt old, damn it. What happened to the days when he could put in a long shift, make love for hours after, and still greet the morning with boundless energy?

Long gone, apparently, considering his blurry brain and gritty eyes and aching muscles.

Yet, in stark contrast, Lily was up and singing and baking.

Determined to match her, Parker threw the covers aside and stalked to the closet. But all he saw were dark suits, navy blue and brown, and they all looked too . . . dated. The differences in their lives showed even in his friggin' closet.

But . . . did he still care about that?

He sniffed the air again, smelled the cookies, and shook his head. Screw the clothes and age differences.

He wanted Lily.

Bypassing the dresser drawers that held his jeans and shorts, he walked into his kitchen—and got a very pleasant surprise.

Wearing one of his shirts and nothing more, Lily bent at the stove to remove a cookie sheet. Man. What a wake-up call.

Sneaking up behind her, his approach muffled by the music, Parker waited until she'd set the hot baking sheet aside, then slid his hands around to her belly and pulled her back against his chest. "Good morning," he rumbled.

"Hey, sleepyhead." She turned in his arms, saw his nude body, and her jaw loosened. "You're . . . naked."

"Really?" He looked down at himself and said, "Damn, I forgot pants."

She returned his teasing look. "Parker."

"Doesn't matter. You look better in my clothes than I do anyway."

Hands opening on his chest, she whispered, "Hey, I wasn't complaining," and she treated him to a killer kiss that chased away the rest of the cobwebs and gave him a lethal Jones. "Coffee?"

He shook his head and snagged her close again. *"Sex."*

Laughing, she darted out of reach. "Your hair's standing on end, you've got enough whiskers to remove a layer of my hide, and I have more cookies to bake."

Damn. Rubbing his chin, he realized she was right. He turned away, intent on one thing. "Fine. I'll be back for the coffee in ten. Finish up your cookies."

"But . . ."

"You wanted me. Well, now you've got me." He sent her a quick wink. "Wait for me in the bed."

Parker closed the bathroom door on her laughter. But he realized he was smiling, too. She made him feel lighthearted, when he hadn't thought that possible, especially during the holidays.

* * *

True to his word, Parker opened the bathroom door only ten minutes later. He spotted her sitting in the middle of the bed, and like a fantasy from a dream, he started toward her, steam billowing out around him, trailing in his wake. His stride was long and sure, his whiskers gone, his wet hair combed back.

Still naked.

Yearning curled inside her, and Lily knew it'd be so easy to stray off course, to forget her plans and wallow in the sensuality he offered.

But as much as he tempted her, as much as she wanted him at that very moment, she also wanted more. She wanted forever.

She started to tell him that they needed to talk, but Parker didn't give her a chance. He never slowed, and his steely gaze never wavered. His big hands landed on her shoulders, driving her down to the mattress, and his mouth swallowed her gasp. She found herself flat on her back, covered by hot, aroused male.

"Parker," she moaned.

"Now that I've had you," he whispered near her ear, "I want you even more."

Given his confession, there probably wouldn't be a better time to segue into a discussion on their future. Lily closed her eyes, drew a deep breath, and said, "You think you'll want me in a year? Or five? Or . . ."

He pushed back from her, but Lily kept her eyes closed, too cowardly to look at him, too afraid she'd see his discomfort, or worse, outright rejection.

His lips brushed hers, his hand cradled her face. "What are you talking about, Lily?"

Well, shoot. She'd have to open her eyes for that. She peeked, and saw he looked merely curious, a little tender, still really turned-on. Not annoyed. Not angry.

Turning her face to the side, she nodded at the large memory book on his nightstand. "I have a gift for you."

Now he frowned. "We agreed—no gifts."

"No, we agreed no singing or wrapping or . . . whatever. Besides, it's not that type of gift."

Warily, he glanced at the nightstand. "A photo album?"

"Memory book."

Both hands cupped her face. "Let's make some new memories. Starting right now." And he tried to kiss her again.

Lily pressed her head back into the pillow. "This is important to me, Parker."

"God I hate when women say that."

For that, she gave him a shove. "It could be important to you, too, if you'd stop being such a grinch and just listen."

Growling out a complaint, Parker rolled onto his back and covered his face with a forearm. "Okay, let me have it. This is about Christmas, isn't it?"

Slowly, Lily sat up. Parker looked far from receptive, but still she reached for the heavy leather-bound book and cradled it in her lap. As always, touching it, thinking about it, made her sentimental and reflective. Poignant memories brought a lump to her throat and tied her stomach in knots. "There are . . . some things about me that I think you should know. Things that might make a difference."

His arm dropped away, and his expression filled with concern. "What is it?"

Heart pounding, chest tight with nervousness because this was so important, Lily stared into his beautiful eyes. Strong, tall, protective Parker—how could he not know the difference he made to so many?

Tears welled, and Lily dabbed at her eyes, trying to laugh, trying to dredge up that carefree attitude that he seemed to dislike so much.

"Oh, Jesus, honey, no." In a rush, Parker sat up beside her.

He looked crushed as he smoothed her hair and kissed her forehead. "I can't take it. Please don't cry."

"I'm sorry." Darn it, she sounded like a strangling frog. "Ignore the tears."

"That's impossible." He tipped up her chin, his expression full of compassion and concern and heart-wrenching tenderness. "Is this about Christmas? It is, isn't it? I shouldn't have been such an ass. If you really want me to wrap presents, I will. Hell, I'll even help you with the cookies. Just don't cry anymore."

Wonderful, special Parker. "It's not about cookies or material gifts. It's about the holiday spirit, the kindness of strangers." She drew a deep breath. "Without that kindness, I wouldn't be here."

A strange stillness settled over him. "What do you mean you wouldn't be here? What the hell are you talking about?"

She could never think of the generosity of the human spirit without an excess of emotion. Even as she smiled, the tears trickled down her cheeks, shaming her for being such a sentimental sap, especially since she knew Parker didn't feel the same. "I would have died, Parker. My mother, too."

For several strained moments, Parker said nothing, he just breathed deep and fast, as if her statement had left him shaken. Then he pulled her into his lap, tucked her head under his chin, and said, "Okay, I'm listening. Tell me."

Hopeful, Lily opened the book. On the first page was the most important article, but she flipped past it. It was special, so she'd save it until the end.

"See this one?" The headline read, "Man Honored for Act of Heroism." Lily explained, "The woman had a seizure and her car struck a gas pump. Flames were everywhere. The people close by could see that her doors were stuck, trapping her inside."

Parker read aloud, "Phil Benton pulled Margery Wilson from her burning car, disregarding his own peril. Moments after freeing her, the gas tank exploded."

Lily sighed. "It was Christmas Day. Mr. Benton was on his way home to his wife and children. Their dinner was ruined because he spent several hours at the hospital."

"He was hurt?"

She shook her head and forced the words out around the lump of emotion clogging her throat. "No. He stayed with Margery because otherwise, she'd have been all alone. When the hospital released her, he took her home and she had Christmas dinner with his family."

In pensive silence, Parker smoothed his hand up and down Lily's back.

She turned the page to another headline. "High School Student Survives Gunshot Wound," she read. "In a true act of heroism, high school senior Dennis Clark came to the aid of his best friend during an armed attack on Christmas Day."

"I remember that one," Parker remarked quietly. "The kid protected his friend after two masked guys had beat him unconscious and tried to rob him. He got shot in the shoulder." He stared at the photo that accompanied the article. "It was touch and go for a while there."

Lily nodded. "He still has the bullet in his shoulder."

On a deep breath, Parker whispered, "And he still has his best friend."

Pleased that he'd see it that way, Lily smiled. "Yes." She showed Parker one article after another. Twenty pages worth—and that was only one of her albums. She had others. Maybe someday she'd be able to go through them all with him.

Finally, after working up her nerve, she turned back to the first article and trailed her fingers lightly over the page. "This one is mine."

Parker stared first at her, his eyes seeing into her soul, his expression one of dawning comprehension before he gave his attention to the faded newsprint.

In his deep, quiet voice, he read, "Detective's Heroism Saves Pregnant Woman." He paused, tightening his hold on her. "Your mother?"

More tears blurred Lily's vision. "She was a nurse on call. That Christmas, we had almost three feet of snow, then a layer of ice. A lot of streets were closed. The salt trucks couldn't keep up."

"But she was a nurse, so she braved the weather."

"Yes." Lily laid her head on his shoulder. "Mom had just parked in the upper level of the garage and taken off her seat belt when . . . one of the road crew trucks clearing the garage lost control. It started sliding in the ice and the driver couldn't stop it or steer it away from her. It happened so fast . . ."

"Damn."

"It slammed into her car. The impact of the collision ejected her head first through the windshield. But that wasn't the worst of it. She landed on the garage floor and the salt truck rolled over her, snagging her underneath it before crashing through the guardrail. It didn't go completely over the side to the level below. It sort of just hung there, keeping her trapped."

The room grew so quiet, Lily could hear her own heartbeat and sense Parker's dread.

"Mom wasn't able to breathe. She was pretty broken up, with multiple system traumas and several fractures, including a skull fracture. And at any moment, that truck could have fallen to the parking level below." In a whisper, Lily added, "She would have been crushed. We know that."

Again, Parker's arms tightened on her, and he sounded almost as pained as she felt whenever reciting the story. "But someone saved her."

Turning her face up to his, Lily smiled. "A detective . . . like you." She turned back to the article and touched it with reverent fingertips. "The crash drew a lot of attention. Hospital staff ran out, but no one knew for sure what to do. It was such a dangerous situation. Anyone who got too close would be putting his life on the line. The detective didn't hesitate though. Knowing there wouldn't be much time left before Mom suffocated, he worked his way under the truck with a bag mask. My mother says she can still remember his calm voice commanding her to take slow, easy breaths, to hang on . . ." Lily gulped on her tears. "He told her everything would be okay—and she believed him."

His face buried in her neck, Parker asked, "You weren't hurt?"

"No." Lily gave a watery laugh. "They delivered me that day by emergency C-section, almost at the same time they were patching up Mom. I was small, but healthy."

"Thank God."

"And the cop who helped her." She snuggled closer to him. "He waited, you know. To make sure she'd be all right. To be there with her in case she needed him again. Mom says when she talked to him later, he said all he could think of was his own pregnant wife at home and how Christmas wouldn't be the same without her."

The seconds ticked by, and Lily's anxiety grew. She had no idea what Parker felt, what he thought, if baring her heart had made a difference to him.

Then she felt Parker nuzzling her hair, and he asked, "Did you feel that?"

Confused, Lily pushed back to peek up at him. "What?"

With the utmost care, he cradled her face in his hand and smiled. "The way my heart just grew ten times its size?"

Lily twisted in his lap to face him. "What are you talking about?"

He smiled gently, wiped away her tears. "Don't you remember the Grinch, when the true meaning of Christmas finally hit him, and his heart all but exploded in his chest?"

Lily started breathing too fast. "I remember."

"Well, that's what it feels like to me right now. Like my heart is so full, my ribs just might break." He kissed the end of her nose. "Damn, Lily, I've been an ass."

"You have not!"

"I love you."

She stared, stunned silly, speechless.

"Hell, I've loved you for a long time but didn't want to

admit it." Parker shook his head and smiled at her. "I thought you were too young, too fanciful, and way too damn happy to suit me. All that optimism scared me, I guess because it emphasized how damn pessimistic I've become."

"You're not a pessimist. You're a hero."

He grinned at her, shook his head. "I wanted to be, but I could never tell if I made a difference."

"And now?"

"Now I'm so glad, so grateful, that you're here. That you're in my life. I make a difference to you, and that has to count for something, right?"

"You make a difference to everyone, Parker." Hope burgeoning, she bit her lip. "You really love me?"

"Yeah, I really do. It took me long enough to realize it, but I figure it has to be love. Nothing else could make me feel like this."

"And . . ." She hated to push him, but she couldn't stop herself. "You believe in the Christmas spirit?"

"You're here with me, in my bed, sharing your life. Sharing you. How could I not believe? You're my own special Christmas miracle."

Happiness bubbled inside her.

"You should be in that memory book too, because, Lily, you saved me." He turned on the bed, positioning her beneath him and getting comfortable. "It's so damn easy to get jaded, to focus on the disappointments instead of the triumphs. It's so easy to lose sight of the important things."

"Like love?"

"Like you. And sharing the holidays with friends and family."

She touched the corner of his mouth. "Speaking of friends and family . . ."

He laughed. "Maybe we should divide Christmas between my folks and yours. It'll probably send my poor mother into a faint, but I'm in a mood for her Christmas dinner. And I want to meet this remarkable mother of yours. And—"

Squealing in delight, Lily threw her arms around him and squeezed him tight. "Your heart really did grow, didn't it?"

"Enough to help you at the shelter." He kissed her. "Enough to start enjoying my job again." Another kiss, this one longer. "And enough to accept that I love you—now, tomorrow, and for the rest of our lives."

Contentment settled over her. "I love you, too."

"Let's go shopping."

Given their current position—in a bed, with her under him—Lily laughed. "You want to shop *now*?"

"Yeah. For the first time in ages, I'm in the mood to buy gifts." His gaze warmed. "For you."

"Oh, Parker." Lily turned to mush. "I have you, and that's surely the best Christmas gift ever."

Do You Hear What I Hear

1

Osbourne Decker had no sooner pulled his truck into the frozen, snow-covered parking lot to start his night shift than his pager went off. Typical SWAT team biz—a barricade with three subjects holding two hostages. He'd grabbed his gear, run into the station to change so he could respond directly to the scene, and from that point on, the night had been nonstop. Being SWAT meant when the pager went off, so did the team.

After a lot of hours in the blustery cold that stretched his patience thin, they resolved the hostage situation without a single casualty. And just in time for his shift to end. He couldn't wait to get home and grab some sleep.

He'd just changed back into his jeans, T-shirt, and flannel shirt when Lucius Ryder, a friend and sergeant with the team, strolled up to him. Osbourne saw the way Lucius eyed him, like a lamb for the slaughter, and he wanted to groan.

He fastened his duty firearm in a concealed holster, attached his pager and cell, grabbed his coat, and tried to slip away.

Lucius stopped him. "Got a minute, Ozzie?"

Shit, shit, *shit*. He already knew what was coming. Lucius would be on vacation for ten days—the longest vacation he'd ever taken. He'd be back in time for Christmas, but laying low until then, soaking up some private time with his new wife in Gatlinburg. But the wife was concerned about her loony toons twin sister.

And that's where Lucius wanted to involve him.

"Actually," Ozzie said, hoping to escape, "I was just about to—"

"This won't take long."

Ozzie thought about making a run for it, but Lucius would probably just chase him down, so he gave up. He dropped his duffel bag and propped a shoulder on the wall. "Okay. Shoot."

"You think Marci is hot?"

Ozzie did a double take. "Is that a trick question?"

"No, I'm serious."

Serious, and apparently not thinking straight. Marci and Lucius's wife, Bethany, were *identical* twins. No way in hell would Ozzie comment on her appearance. Hell, if he admitted he thought Marci was beyond hot to the point of scorching, well, that'd be like admitting that Lucius's wife was scorching, and his friend sure as hell wouldn't like that.

If he said no, it'd be a direct cut to Bethany.

"She's a replica of your wife, Lucius, all the way down to her toes." Ozzie shook his head. "You really want to know what I think of her?"

Struck by that observance, Lucius said, "*No.* Hell no." He glared at Ozzie in accusation, then slashed a hand in the air. "Forget I asked. I already know you're attracted to her because you went out with her a few times."

"No way, Lucius."

Lucius warmed to his subject. "I thought you two had something going on for a while there."

"No."

"You were chasing her pretty hot and heavy—"

Ozzie forgot discretion. "She's a fruitcake. Totally nuts. Hell, Lucius, she stops to talk to every squirrel in the trees."

"She does not." But Lucius didn't look certain.

"She even chats with birds." Ozzie nodded his head to convince Lucius of what he'd seen. "She gives greetings to dogs as if they greet her back."

"She's not that bad," Lucius denied, but without much conviction.

"Not that bad? I've heard her carry on complete conversations with your dog!"

Lucius shook his head. "It's not like that. Hero doesn't talk back to her. She just . . . She's an animal nut, okay? She's real empathetic to them, so she likes chatting with them."

"No shit. But she doesn't chat the way most of us do. She chats as if she knows exactly what they're saying, when anyone sane knows that they're not saying a damn thing."

Lucius paced away, but came right back. "It's an endearing trait, that's all."

Because Ozzie loved animals, he might have been inclined to agree. But crazy women turned into insane bitches when things didn't go their way, and he'd had enough of that to last him a lifetime. There was nothing more malicious, or more determined on destruction, than a woman who ignored logic. "No thanks."

"Okay, look, I'm not asking you to marry the girl."

"I'm not marrying anyone!" Just the sound of the "M" word struck terror in Ozzie's heart.

"That's what I said, damn it, and keep your voice down."

Ozzie glanced around and saw that the others were watching them, their ears perked with interest. Dicks. Oh, yeah, they all wanted to know more about Marci. None of them would hesitate to go chasing after her. In the three months that they'd all known her, more than one guy on the team had tried to get with her.

Course, none of them had yet discovered her whacky eccentricities. Then again, maybe none of them would mind.

In a more subdued tone, now infused with annoyance, Ozzie said, "Any one of them would be thrilled to do . . . whatever it is you want me to do."

"Bullshit. This is my sister-in-law we're talking about. Any of *them* would be working hard to get in her pants."

True. And it pissed Ozzie off big time, but rather than say so, he pointed out the obvious. "And you think I wouldn't be?"

Lucius's eyes narrowed. "Not if you know what's good for you."

Ozzie threw up his hands. "Great. Just friggin' great. So what the hell am I supposed to do with her, if not enjoy her?"

Disgruntled, Lucius growled, "You talk about her like she's a pinball machine."

"Right." Ozzie rolled his eyes. "With a few lights missing."

Lucius drew a deep breath to regain his aplomb.

Ozzie watched him. He really didn't want to get on his buddy's bad side. Lucius stood six feet four inches tall, and though he was a good friend with a sense of style that leaned toward raunchy T-shirts, he also took anything that had anything to do with his wife very seriously.

"Nice shirt," Ozzie commented, hoping to help Lucius along in his efforts to be calm. The shirt read: "World's Greatest" and beneath that sat a proud-looking rooster.

"Forget the shirt." Lucius glanced at his watch. "I need to get going. Bethany's waiting for me. So do we have a deal or what?"

He had to be kidding.

On an exhalation, Lucius barked, "I only want you to keep an eye on her. There've been a few strange things happening—"

"Like her talking to turtles or something?"

"Your sarcasm isn't helping," Lucius warned him. "I meant something more threatening. Marci feels like someone's been following her. She's not a woman given to melodrama—"

"That's a joke, right?"

"So her concerns also concern me," Lucius finished through gritted teeth. "And they concern my wife, who won't be able to enjoy our belated honeymoon unless we both know someone is keeping an eye on Marci. Someone I can trust not to hurt her."

"I don't hurt women."

"Exactly." Lucius glanced away. "But I was talking about her feelings, actually."

Seeing no way out, Ozzie crossed his arms over his chest and conceded. "So what's in it for me?"

"What do you want?"

"I very recently inherited a farmhouse from my granny. It needs some work—"

"Done." Lucius stuck out his hand.

Whoa. That was way too easy. "Understand, Lucius. This is an old house. I don't want to just slap up drywall and cheap paint. I want to maintain the original design and—"

"Shake on it, damn it, so I can go."

Ozzie shook and, he had to admit, anticipation stirred within him. So he'd be seeing Marci again. Huh. He had very mixed feelings about that, but mostly he felt challenged.

Rather than release his hand, Lucius tugged him closer to whisper, "Put on your coat. You're advertising a stiffy. And, you know, I think maybe you should be wearing my shirt." Then the bastard walked away laughing.

Ozzie glanced down at the rise in his jeans. Cursing his overactive libido, especially where it concerned Marci Churchill, he turned his back so no one else in the room would notice.

He didn't have a full boner, but rather a semiboner. Though for a man of his endowments, it showed about the same.

And just because they'd discussed Marci.

How the hell was he supposed to watch over her, be close to her, and *not* touch her?

Working night shift meant that Ozzie seldom saw daylight during the winter. It was dark when he went to bed and dark when he got up. He missed the sunlight. But at least the bitter cold of December helped him keep a clear head while he pondered the ramifications of getting close to Marci again.

Oh, he saw her often enough. Bethany dragged her around all the time, and Bethany and Lucius were nauseating in their marital ecstasy. That meant whenever the team got together after work, the twins were there.

And given what the twins looked like, no doubt more than one fantasy took place in their honor. But for Ozzie, he only fantasized over one twin: the cracked one.

He saw her at picnics, at a local bar where they all hung out, at parties, and sometimes in the station, waiting for Lucius to get off work.

Marci fit right in, laughing with the men, joking, and turning down offers. Sometimes she watched him, and sometimes she pretended he wasn't in the room.

But no matter what she did, the chemistry between them was enough to choke a bear.

As Ozzie's truck cut through the snow and sludge clogging the streets, he absently took in the multitude of lights decorating houses and businesses. He liked this time of year. It was pretty. But this would be his first Christmas without Granny Decker and he already missed her so much it was nearly unbearable.

He was thinking of warm Christmas cookies, songs on the piano, and strings of popcorn, when he spotted the confusion in front of the funeral home. Lights from a police car flashed blue and red and an elderly couple, bundled in coats over pajamas, gestured with excitement.

Ozzie pulled up behind the cruiser and parked. It took him only moments to identify himself to the officer and to find out that someone had stolen a donkey from the Nativity scene erected on the funeral home's lawn.

Marci. Somehow, he just knew she was behind this. She'd probably claim the damned donkey was shy, or that he didn't like the colored lights, or God-knew-what. But Ozzie's instincts screamed, and so with a few more words to the officer, he gave up on the idea of sleep and instead headed to Marci's apartment.

Lucius used to live in the apartment across from Marci but, thankfully, he'd recently moved out—so Ozzie didn't have to worry about Lucius finding him at Marci's door. He and Bethany had purchased a home of their own. Lucius still owned the apartment building, but he left Marci in charge of it.

Not a good idea, in Ozzie's opinion, given that Marci was a kook. But far be it for him to tell Lucius how to run his business.

When he parked out front of the building, Ozzie looked toward Marci's porch window and, sure enough, her inside lights were on. Okay, so it was seven-thirty and she was maybe getting ready for work.

Or hiding a donkey.

Ozzie slammed his truck door, trudged through the crunchy snow and ice, and went up the walk, inside, and up to Marci's door. He knocked twice.

Breathless, Marci yelled, "Just a moment!"

His body twitched. More specifically, his cock sat up and took notice of her proximity. *Damn it.*

A full minute later, Marci opened the door. A look of pleasure replaced her formal politeness. "Osbourne. What a surprise."

He stared down at her and thought, if she'd just not talk about animals, if she'd just smile at him like that, he'd be happy to ravish her for, oh . . . a few hours maybe.

When he said nothing, her smile widened, affecting him like a hot lick. She wore a soft pink chenille robe, belted tight around her tiny waist. Her small feet were bare, crossed one over the other to ward off the chill. Her baby-fine, straight brown hair had the mussed look of a woman fresh out of bed—or fresh inside from the blustery outdoors.

Shaking out of his stupor, Ozzie looked beyond her. He saw nothing out of the ordinary in her tiny apartment, but that didn't clear her.

She took a step closer to him, staring up in what seemed like provocation to him, a heated come-on, a . . .

She tilted her head and said, "Osbourne?"

Lust tied knots in his muscles. He cleared his throat. "Busy?"

Big blue eyes blinked at him, eyes so soft, and with such thick, long lashes she didn't need makeup. "I just got out of the shower, actually." She patted back a delicate yawn. "It's early. Would you like some coffee?"

He'd like her.

Flat on her back.

Buck-naked.

His nostrils flared, but not from the scent of brewing coffee. "All right." Yet he stood there. He knew that once he stepped over the threshold, he wouldn't be able to keep his hands off her. Damn Lucius for putting him in this torturous position. And damn his weakness for wanting her. He knew, absolutely knew, that off-kilter broads not based in reality were a complete and total pain in the ass.

Yet he trembled with the need to gather her near and devour her. Marci got to him in a big way and he hated it. With most women, he enjoyed himself, and he made sure they got enjoyment, too. Mutual enjoyment, yeah, that's what he liked.

Not this insane torment and out-of-control craving. Not this trembling lust and gut-twisting need.

Fuck it.

He stepped in and demanded, "Where's the donkey?"

She twittered a laugh. "Donkey?" Giving him her back, she sashayed into the tiny kitchenette and got out two mugs.

Spellbound, Ozzie stared at her ass. Through the chenille, he could see the perfect heart shape of that fine behind, the softness of it, the slightest jiggle. When Marci wasn't tormenting him or conversing with critters, she taught an aerobics class, and it showed in the graceful muscle tone, the feminine strength of her willowy . . .

"What donkey, Osbourne?"

Lost in fantasies, he stared at her, confused.

Her lips curved, and she prompted, "You asked me about a donkey?"

Oh, yeah. He took an aggressive stance. "There's a donkey missing from the funeral home's Nativity scene."

She raised her brows at him, then lowered them in thought. As she came back to him, carrying the coffee, she asked, "And you assume I stole him?"

"Did you?"

She offered him a mug, and he accepted. Their fingers touched, and it struck him like a jolt of red-hot electricity. The old John Henry jumped up with a hearty, *"Hello!"*

"Why would you think I did?"

The pounding of his heartbeat almost drowned out her question. "Did what?"

This time she laughed. As if speaking to a slow-witted fool, she repeated, "I'm curious, Osbourne. Why would you think I stole a donkey? I have no record for thievery. In fact, I have no criminal record at all."

He couldn't think while drowning in lust. He had to get a grip or run like a scared rabbit, and running had never appealed to him. He dragged his gaze from her and strode to the couch, seating himself in the middle.

Rather than look at her again—because that'd do him in—he sipped his coffee, then set the mug on the end table. "I think you took the donkey because you have some weird thing going on with animals."

"It's not weird."

He smelled her approach. Like a starving man, he inhaled the scent of woman, of sex, of pure, ripe temptation.

"It's a gift." Marci sat beside him, and the instant her hip brushed his, he bounded up as if she'd goosed him.

From several *safer* feet away, Ozzie turned on her. "Do you have the stubborn ass or not?"

Again, she seemed to ponder it. "What type of donkey are we talking about?"

"What *type?*" He frowned at her. "What the hell does that—"

Her eyes locked with his, she set aside her own coffee and rose from the sofa. As she stalked toward him, he went mute.

Horny and mute.

No one stalked like Marci Churchill, with that particular enticing gait.

"Marci," he warned, and he really, really meant it.

"Is it a miniature Mediterranean, a standard, large standard, or—"

"I have no friggin' idea. There really are different types?" He shook his head. "Who cares?" She drew nearer, and he felt himself sinking deep. "The important thing is that the donkey is missing."

"Donkeys aren't really stubborn, you know. They're just more laid-back and self-preserving in nature than many animals."

Self-preserving? Why did she always say the most peculiar things? "What does that mean?"

Her gaze drifted over his body, from his booted feet to his drawn eyebrows. "They prefer to do what is good for the donkey, which isn't always what the human thinks is best, especially when it comes to getting wet feet."

Aha. Eyes narrowing, Ozzie asked, "Wet, as in standing in snow?" Is that why she stole the donkey? She thought it wanted dry feet? Er, hooves. Whatever.

With a shrug, Marci touched his chest. "Stay awhile. Get comfortable." And with that, she began unbuttoning his coat.

Ozzie was so rigid with excitement that she'd undone the last button before he thought to move. But if she got the coat off him, she'd see he had a lethal hard-on and then she'd take advantage of his weakened state.

Survival instincts kicking in, Ozzie caught her hands. But rather than remove them, he just held them still. Near his belt.

Oh, God.

Her voice lowered and she stared at his sternum. "Donkeys are friendly, Osbourne, did you know that?"

He shook his head. Hell, at the moment, he didn't even know his own name.

"They're excellent with children, too. And they make wonderful guard animals."

A guard donkey? The absurdity of that cut through the lust and he almost laughed. "You're making that up."

She smiled and pulled her hands free to slip inside his coat. His breath caught. Okay, so he still wore a flannel shirt and a T-shirt, but he wished he didn't. He wished her hot little hands were on his bare skin.

"The right donkey will take care of an entire herd of cattle, sheep, or goats." Her fingers spread out, and she pushed the coat off his shoulders. "Their natural aversion to predators inspires them to severely discourage any canine attacks on the herd. Dogs and donkeys don't mix well, but a donkey can be trained to leave the house dog or farm dog alone."

Her hands were small and soft, and warm, and like any red-blooded male, he knew when to give up graciously. "Marci?"

"Hmmm?" She started on the buttons of his shirt.

He lowered his head and inhaled the sweetness of her silky hair. "I don't think I care about the damned donkey anymore."

"Do you care about me?"

Shit. What kind of tricky question was that? Somehow, he knew no matter what he said, she'd take it the wrong way and he'd end up—

"I didn't ask you an algebra problem, Osbourne. You don't need to do equations in your head. Just tell me, yes or no."

He locked his jaw, and almost got lost in her beautiful eyes. "If I say no, are you going to make me leave?"

She looked at his mouth, and her gaze warmed. "Do you want to stay?"

Damn it, he hated getting a question answered with another question. "I want what I've always wanted."

"Sex?" She moved closer, until her breasts brushed his chest, her thighs nudged his.

"Yeah." Hell yeah. Hot, sweaty, no-holds-barred sex. Naked, gritty sex. Wet, slippery, prolonged—

"Me, too."

Ozzie almost swallowed his tongue. He forgot the donkey.

He also forgot Lucius's instructions to merely watch over Marci, *not* enjoy her. He forgot her featherbrained relationships with animals and her propensity to make him nuts.

Before he even knew what he was doing, he had her backed up to a wall, his mouth sealed over hers, his tongue past her teeth, tasting her deeply. And he didn't want to stop this time, not until he was in her, not until she wrung him out, not until she screamed out a mind-blowing climax.

Maybe not . . . ever.

Marci clutched at him. Finally, finally he wanted her again. She'd never met a man who both infuriated her and made her frenzied with need. But Osbourne Decker did just that.

Why him? she wondered, even as she struggled to get closer to him, as close as two people could be. She sucked his tongue deeper into her mouth and lifted one leg up to wrap around his hip.

He ridiculed her psychic ability with animals.

He made his desire for an emotion-free, no-ties relationship clear.

He epitomized everything she disdained in a man: pigheadedness, macho control, an overflow of confidence.

But he looked at her, and her stomach did flip-flops. He touched her and flash fires burned everywhere. He kissed her, and she wanted to be the most flagrant hoochie imaginable.

Before Osbourne, she'd been circumspect and withdrawn, and maybe even inhibited. But with him, she wanted everything, including wild, unrestrained sex.

Bracing one hand on the wall beside her head, Osbourne levered away enough to reach the front of her robe. His mouth continued to devour hers, and Marci loved every second of it—the musky taste of him, the rasp of his beard shadow on her face, the heat and strength of his big body against hers.

If Osbourne wanted her naked, fine. Then maybe he'd get naked, too, and she could finally satisfy her hunger to touch and taste him everywhere.

But he didn't reach for her belt. Instead, his rough hand clasped the leg she had twined around his hip. His fingers slid around her bare knee, then up her thigh, and onto her bottom. He froze.

"Holy Mother of God," he breathed. "You're naked under there."

Never had a man sounded so profoundly grateful. Smiling, Marci nodded. "Yes, I am. I told you I'd just gotten out of the shower."

"Bless your heart." And then he was eating at her mouth again while his hand explored, touching every inch of her backside, squeezing, cuddling, before coming around to her belly.

Muscles bulged on his body, making him seem even bigger, stronger. His hot breath fanned her face. His teeth and tongue played with her, feeding her hunger, and further inciting it at the same time.

So many sensations overwhelmed her at once that she stalled.

"Osbourne?" She could barely breathe and her limbs were starting to tremble. His fingers angled downward on the sensitive skin of her belly.

He all but panted. "Yeah?"

"It's too much too fast."

Breathing hard, his fingertips just touching her pubic hair, he considered that. Slowly and deeply, he inhaled, then carefully withdrew his hand. He cupped her chin and turned her face up.

She thought he had the most incredible eyes. Blue like hers, but darker, a midnight blue. His black lashes were thick and, on a lesser man, they would have seemed girlish. But with blatant lust showing in his gaze, Osbourne looked all male.

And at the same time, very tender.

After a gentle kiss to her lips, he slowly licked his way to her throat. Lazily, he sucked at her skin there, maybe marking her, but who cared? Marci didn't.

She turned her head to make it easier for him. His mouth was so hot, his tongue so silky, and being this close to him let her familiarize herself again with his delicious scent. Osbourne always smelled so good. Not like cologne but like a man, earthy and a little warm and raw.

As he continued to kiss her, he nudged aside the neckline of her robe.

Against her skin, he growled low, "Better?"

"Yes." Her heartbeat thundered. "Please." And Marci herself tugged the robe open so he could get to her breasts. She shuddered, waiting impatiently.

He seemed content to look at her.

"Osbourne?"

He never wavered from his perusal of her breasts, his dark blue eyes burning and bright. "I feel like a kid in a candy store." He bent his bracing arm to bring himself closer to her. So close that she could feel his breath on her nipple when he whispered again, "Beautiful."

Twining her fingers in his silky hair, Marci tried to urge him forward. But he was a muscled lug, especially thick through the shoulders and chest, and he didn't budge an inch.

He said, "Shhh," and cupped her breast in his palm. With the side of his thumb, he taunted her nipple, gently rolling over it, around it.

Months ago, they'd gone out and indulged in fevered petting, yet never consummated their attraction. But since then she had not even been kissed by another man. She couldn't take it. She needed him, now. "Enough."

In reply, he closed his thumb and finger around her, holding her gently, tugging, applying just the right amount of pressure.

Marci knotted her hands in his hair and forced him to her while arching her back. With a rough laugh, Osbourne obliged, and his mouth closed around her.

Heaven.

He began a wet, hot sucking, and she melted.

The sensation was so acute, so wonderful, she squeezed her eyes shut and couldn't stop moaning.

After treating her other breast to the same teasing torment, he whispered, "Now?" and she again felt his hand under her robe, resting lightly on her belly.

More than ready for him, she breathed, "Yes, please." She needed his touch, was anxious for it.

He wasn't subtle. He cupped his hand over her mound, searched and, separating her labia, worked one thick finger into her.

In sheer, shocking pleasure, Marci stiffened and pressed back, but Osbourne didn't let up. He stroked his finger deep, until the heel of his hand pressed flush against her, giving her even more pleasure. Her muscles clamped down in reaction.

"Yeah," he whispered, "you're nice and wet now. You won't have any problem taking me, will you, honey?"

Unsure of his meaning, Marci moved against him. "I'm not a virgin, Osbourne."

"Virginity is overrated."

"Then, what?"

He pulled his hand away and scooped both hands under her behind to lift her. "Hold onto me."

She wrapped her arms around his neck, her legs around his waist. He lifted her, and something big and hard pressed against her. "Osbourne?"

"Hmmm?"

"Your gun is in the way. It's prodding at me."

"That's not my gun, sweets." With a wicked grin, he turned them both away from the wall.

Not his . . . Well, what then?

He started toward her bedroom, and her thoughts scattered. Uh-oh. "Osbourne?"

"Yeah, babe?"

His long legs quickly traversed the limited space of her apartment. "We're going to make love now?"

"You betcha."

She bit her lip, then offered, "The couch might work better."

"No way." He kissed her hard and fast, his eyes glittering. "I need plenty of room for what I want to do to you."

Wow, that sounded . . . *enticing*. She glanced at her closed bedroom door. "But . . ."

"Don't pull back on me now, Marci. I need you."

Her heart expanded. He *needed* her. She cupped a hand to his jaw and smiled. "Okay."

"Thank God." He reached for her bedroom door.

Marci rushed to say, "If you insist on the bed, though, we'll need to do one thing first."

"Yeah?" He opened the door. "What's that?"

He no sooner asked the question than the donkey rushed him, screaming, "*Aw-ee, aw-ee, aw-ee.*"

Shocked, Osbourne stumbled back, tripped over his own feet, and they both went down in a tangle. "What the hell!"

The donkey loomed over them.

Full of apology, Marci winced. "You'll need to help me get the donkey back to his rightful owners."

2

Slowly, his gaze ripe with accusation, Osbourne turned to stare at her. Never before had Marci seen anyone so red-faced, so enraged, or so disappointed.

"You had to take the damned donkey, didn't you?"

Because Osbourne lay over her, pinning down her legs, she had to stretch to reach the donkey. She patted his soft nose and said, "He doesn't mean it, honey. You're not damned."

"Oh, God." Groaning as if in horrible pain, Osbourne collapsed back against the wall. Still tangled with her, he scrubbed both hands over his face, then scrubbed again, this time growling like a wild beast. "I'm going to kill Lucius. It doesn't matter that he's the team leader. He got me into this—"

"Did you see the donkey's flank?"

Through his fingers, Osbourne peeked at her. Just that one eye, but it looked pretty incredulous.

"His flank?"

"Yes, you see . . ." But it was difficult to talk in that particular position. "Osbourne, could you please let me up?"

He didn't look like he wanted to. That one eye glared at her, and finally he dropped his hands and started to rise.

Her robe gaped open—all the way to her navel—and he

went deaf and dumb, but apparently not blind. His gaze burned her, leaving her scorched.

He closed his mouth. Swallowed. Licked his lips.

"Stop that, Osbourne."

"All right."

But he didn't. As hot as flames, his midnight eyes examined every inch of her until Marci flushed hot with embarrassment and shoved at his shoulder. "*Osbourne.* You're pinning down me *and* my housecoat. I can't make myself decent until you move so I can rearrange things."

"Okay." He nudged aside a mere inch.

Painfully aware of her exposed nudity, Marci groaned. "Snap out of it, Osbourne." And to help him, she covered herself with both hands, but that just made him suck in a breath and lean closer again—until the donkey took exception and began its brassy, raspy braying.

"Good God." That got Osbourne moving, and quickly, too.

He stumbled to his feet, which put his crotch at eye level for her.

She stared. No, that couldn't be, but . . .

He grabbed her arms and hauled her upward. "Shut that donkey up before the whole apartment complex knows he's here."

Distracted, Marci readjusted her robe and then stroked the donkey's long ears until it quieted. "It's okay, baby. We'll get you back where you belong."

Like a man bent on murder, Osbourne growled, "To the Nativity scene."

She didn't bother to look at him. "No, to Kentucky."

"Marci," he warned.

"Osbourne," she said right back. "Let me show you. Do you see this marking here on his flank? Well, it's a discriminating mark, so I'm sure when he was stolen, it was included in his description to help identify him."

Osbourne frowned. "I see it."

"When he was a baby, he got caught in a fence and cut himself. The wound left a scar. If you'll just go check"—she shooed him toward the living room—"with whoever lists stolen donkeys, I'm sure you'll find out who his real family is, and then we can return him."

Nodding, Osbourne went to the living room but then, realizing what he'd done, he stopped. Marci almost ran into his broad back.

He turned to glare at her. "There is no damn 'stolen donkey' list."

Ignoring that, she smiled. "The phone's right over there." Again, she shooed him.

He pushed her hands back down. "Stop doing that."

"Osbourne, be reasonable. I can't keep a donkey here. It's not like he's housebroken. We need to return him."

Teeth locked, Osbourne leaned down and said, "To the Nativity—"

Marci kissed him.

He jerked back so fast he almost fell.

"I'm sorry." She couldn't hold back her long, dreamy sigh. They'd been moments away from making love, and her body still sizzled with need, and she just knew when they did finally get around to being intimate, it'd be too wonderful for words. "When you're that close, I just can't help myself."

"Oh, no." He covered his ears and fled to the other side of the room. "No, you don't. Not again." And then, finger pointing and voice harsh with accusation, he growled, "You used me!"

Confused, Marci shook her head. "No, I didn't."

"You were going to have sex with me—"

"Oh, yes I was." She nodded. "Because you're irresistible."

"For the love of—"

"And, yes, if you had agreed to the couch instead of insisting on the bedroom, you'd have been used. For sex. For satisfaction. My satisfaction." She shrugged in apology. "Again, I'm sorry, but it's been a very long time for me, and you're a terrible temptation."

His eyes crossed. "Be quiet. I mean it, Marci. You're doing that on purpose."

"Doing what?"

"Making me hard."

Scoffing, she felt compelled to point out the obvious. "You were hard about two seconds after you got here."

He covered his face again and dropped onto her sofa with a deep groan. "No," he said without looking at her. "I was semihard. There's a difference."

"Semihard?" Intrigued by that idea, she inched toward him.

But he must have heard her approach because he snarled, "Stay. Away."

"Why?"

"Because you can't be trusted. Hell, I can't be trusted. You're like a damned lodestone. You get close and my hands are all over you."

"But I like that."

"Not. Another. Word."

She sighed. "Will you quit hiding long enough to call whoever keeps track of stolen donkeys?"

His hands fell to his sides. "Surely, even you can't really think there is such a list?"

"No?"

He shook his head.

"So . . . Donkeys are just listed with the thefts of material things? But that's terrible. He's a living, breathing, sensitive creature. Why, just look at him."

In disgust, Osbourne peered at the donkey.

Lowering his ears, his big brown eyes going soulful, the donkey peered back, and then he brayed again.

"Shhh." Marci patted him while frowning at Osbourne. "You need to reassure him."

He stared at her, blank-faced, then, very forlorn, he muttered, "If only you weren't so hot."

Joy blossomed inside her. "Why, thank you." Marci beamed

at him. "You're hot, too. And, I agree, it would be so much easier if you weren't."

His blank look continued.

In explanation, Marci said, "I don't particularly care for wanting a man who thinks I'm daft."

"I never said—"

"Oh, please. You look at me like I need to be committed." She rolled her eyes. "See, you're doing it right now."

He tried to wipe all expression from his face, but it only made him look ridiculous.

"Osbourne, would you please just call whoever you need to call, check to find out about a stolen donkey with a scar on his flank and collar buttons, and that'll prove his ownership."

"Collar buttons?"

Marci stroked the donkey's throatlatch. "Yes, these small dark spots right here. They're called collar buttons."

For a moment there, Marci thought Osbourne would refuse, and she didn't know what she would do without his help. It was difficult enough stealing the donkey from the Nativity scene. Getting him back to his home would be nearly impossible on her own.

Osbourne's eyes sort of glazed over, then he shook his head as if to clear it. "Fine. I'll call and check on it. But while I do that, will you go put on some clothes?"

"If you want."

"I don't. Not really. I'd much rather you strip down to your birthday suit and that we . . . Well, forget that. If I don't find any information on a stolen donkey, I'll have to return him to the Nativity scene. You do understand that, right?"

She licked her lips, thinking it through. What if he couldn't find what he needed to be convinced? That didn't mean the donkey was wrong about his situation, only that Osbourne hadn't uncovered the proper information.

The donkey trusted her, and she supposed she'd have to trust Osbourne. What else could she do?

"If you're sincere, and you actually do all you can, follow every lead to find out if he's been stolen, then yes, I suppose we can take him back there."

"All right, then." He chewed his upper lip and, with blatant regret, dragged his gaze off her. He went to her phone.

Marci patted the donkey. "Wait here, darling. I'll be right back."

Ozzie gripped the phone a little tighter. "Come again?" Surely he hadn't heard Sanderson right.

"It was reported a few weeks ago. Actually, the owners have hired people to find him. He was a beloved family pet or something." Sanderson added, voice low, "If you've got him, there's a reward of five grand."

Five *thousand* dollars? "Un-fucking-believable."

"Yeah, but that's what the bulletin says."

From behind him, Marci replied, "Told you so."

He whirled around, and though she had covered herself from neck to toes in a pair of skinny faded jeans, thick white socks, and an oversized hooded white sweatshirt, she still turned his crank in the most sizzling way.

Remembering the taste and texture of her nipples caused his jaw to tighten. He thought of her smooth belly, and his heart thundered. He recalled her gasp as he'd pushed his finger into her, and his palms went damp.

He had to have her, no matter what. Just once. Maybe. Or twice. But not enough to get involved. Not enough to make her think she had claims. He never, ever wanted to deal with another irrational broad bent on revenge.

First, though, before anything else, he had to deal with a pilfered donkey.

Oblivious to his suffering, Marci smiled brightly. "Your truck is full of SWAT gear, I know, but I still have the truck I rented to steal him from those unscrupulous donkey thieves."

Lord help him. Giving Marci his back, Ozzie said into the

phone, "What's the address? I'll take him back to the owners right now."

After reciting the directions, Sanderson asked, "You want me to run this through the legal channels?"

"Not yet." If it turned out to be the wrong donkey, he didn't want Marci arrested for stealing the beast. He'd rather just return it quietly, and hope no one would be the wiser. "Keep this to yourself for now, will ya?"

"You got it, Oz. No problem. But I'm curious now, so let me know how it turns out."

"Will do."

After hanging up, Ozzie turned and found Marci seated on the couch, snow boots on her feet, with her coat, mittens, and scarf beside her. "Are you ready?"

Don't ask. Don't ask. Do not—"What made you think he was stolen and that he lived in Kentucky?"

"He told me."

Eyes closing, Ozzie cursed himself. He knew better, damn it. But oh, no, he had to go and quiz her.

"I'm not bonkers, you know." Marci tipped her head, sending that long, baby-fine brown hair tumbling over her shoulder and curling around a breast. "It's just, well . . . I'm a pet psychic."

No. He'd just keep looking at her chest, the way it filled out the front of that thick sweatshirt, and he'd pretend she hadn't just said that.

"Did you hear me, Osbourne?" She stood and started toward him and Ozzie wanted to jump her, to drag her to the ground and pick up where they'd left off. Although maybe he'd be smarter to get the hell out of Dodge. But if he made a run for it, would Lucius find out and tell everyone else on the team that a slip of a woman had chased him off? Would the other guys volunteer to finish what he'd started, would—

The donkey nibbled on his butt.

"What the hell!" Leaping a foot, Ozzie jerked around. The

donkey was right *there,* not two inches from him, his ears laid back and his big brown eyes soulful.

How had the damned thing moved so silently?

"He's just being friendly." Marci shared that special smile that felt like a caress. "He likes you."

Appalled, Ozzie said, "He likes my ass." And he backed out of the donkey's reach.

"I do, too."

No, no, *no*. He wasn't about to touch that one. "It'd help if you'd just be quiet, Marci."

Unaffected by his dark mood, she laughed. "Lighten up, Osbourne. It's not my fault, or the donkey's, that you have such an irresistible bod."

"Can we talk about something else, damn it?"

"Okay." Her lips curled. "What would you like to talk about?"

Ozzie shook his head. With her again so close, he noticed that she was just the right height to tuck in close. And built just right to align all her female parts with his male parts, if he bent his knees the tiniest bit. And she smelled good enough to eat. *Whoa.* Totally bad image to get in his head. Bad. Bad.

He started to back away again, but the donkey didn't budge. Hemmed in by a donkey and a doll-face, both of them hazardous to his health.

"Tell me about this pet psychic business."

"All right." Oblivious to his internal struggle concerning sexual positions that made him sweat, Marci said, "For as long as I can remember, I've had a special ability with animals."

"An ability, huh?" Ozzie edged out from between the two of them.

"I'm sorry that it makes you uncomfortable. I'm sorrier that you think I'm a flake."

His head shot up and he looked at her face. She appeared so earnest, and so wounded, that he frowned.

Damn it, he did not want to hurt her. And he had promised Lucius that he wouldn't.

But she patted his chest as if forgiving him, then went on with her explanation. "It's okay. Most people think I'm unhinged. Back when you first asked me out, I had hoped you'd be different, but . . . you're not." Her narrow shoulders lifted. "And that's okay. I understand. I'd have a hard time believing it, too."

Maybe if she explained, it wouldn't be as bad as he thought. "What exactly is it that you do, Marci?"

"I know when animals are upset and why. I understand them. I hear their thoughts and fears and worries."

"Oh-kay."

"It's easy, really." She caught his hand and pressed it beneath her breast, over her lightly bumping heartbeat. "When you bother to listen with your heart. But few people do. They arrogantly go around as if being human makes us supreme."

Ozzie snatched his hand back, but he still felt burned.

She sighed. "What other creatures feel doesn't concern most people, or at least not enough to be bothered with it."

"So . . ." What the hell was he supposed to say to all that? "The donkey asked for your help?"

"It doesn't really work like that. Obviously, he's not a talking donkey."

Well, thank God for small favors.

"But when I passed the funeral home, I felt his unhappiness."

"His unhappiness? Huh. Imagine that."

"Yes. The other animals are content. They like the attention, if not the exposure to the cold. But the donkey was so miserable, and so lonesome, I got a lump in my throat and a pain in my chest. I felt everything he felt and it nearly broke my heart. So I stopped."

He couldn't bear to think of her that upset, so he focused on something else she'd said. "Lonesome? But didn't you just say there were other animals there with him?"

"He wasn't *alone,* Osbourne, he was *lonely*. There's a difference."

His guts cramped. Maybe that was the crux of her problems. "You're alone," he pointed out. And then softly, with caution, "Are you lonely?"

For once, she seemed evasive, waving away his question. "I stroked the donkey, petted him, and I opened myself to him—"

"Opened yourself to him?"

Propping her hands on her hips, Marci huffed. "Are you going to repeat everything I say? Because if you are, we should sit down and get comfortable. But if that's the case, I'm going to take the donkey out first so he can, uh, take his constitutional in the snow instead of on my floors."

Ozzie sighed. There'd be no help for it. He put his coat back on. "Let's talk in the truck on the way. Give me the keys. I'll drive."

She frowned in disapproval. "Didn't you just get off work?"

"Yeah, but I'm fine."

"You haven't been to bed yet. You must be tired."

Tired, no. Exasperated, yes. Confused, yes. Horny as hell, yes, yes, *yes*. But he'd manage. "The keys?"

"Fine." She lifted them off a peg on the wall and handed them over to him. "But don't make any sudden or jarring turns or anything. I don't want the donkey to fall down."

Ozzie ran his hand over his head. He pictured the donkey toppling sideways and had to roll his eyes.

But he didn't want the donkey to fall down, either.

Marci pulled on a down-filled coat, wrapped a scarf around her neck, put on her hat and mittens, and then she leashed the donkey.

"Don't be nervous, darling." She briefly pressed her cheek to the donkey's head. "I'm taking you home. You'll see. It'll be okay."

And like a contented puppy, the beast followed her out the apartment door and out the building, into the snow, to take his constitutional.

And like the bigger ass, Ozzie trailed along.

* * *

As if the foot of snow they'd already gotten wasn't enough, the sky softened with flurries. As the sun struggled to peek above the horizon, an awful glare reflected off the white landscape.

"We're in for a two-hour drive." Ozzie watched as Marci opened the back of the big truck. The bottom half of the door unfolded like a loading hatch. "Will he need water or anything along the way?"

Smiling at him over her shoulder, she said, "No, he'll be okay. Before I swiped him, I put some hay inside. It's still there. Generally, donkeys need to eat less than a horse does of the same size. Two hours will be like nothing to him. But it's very sweet of you to be concerned."

Ozzie felt like a jerk. "It's not sweet. It's just that I don't want him . . . suffering."

"Or unhappy?"

A sharp quip concerning sensitive donkey-feelings tripped to the end of Ozzie's tongue, but before he could give them voice, the donkey rushed up the ramp and into the truck.

And damn if he didn't look anxious to be on his way.

Surely, the animal didn't realize . . . No, of course he didn't. Odds were, he'd been trained to get into a truck. Ozzie couldn't let Marci's cockeyed perceptions affect him.

Disgruntled, he stepped around her and closed up the truck bed securely. "Come on." Taking Marci's arm, he led her to the passenger's side door. Their feet crunched through frozen snow, wind whistled against them, ice crystals formed on their faces—and Marci kept smiling.

He'd noticed that about her early on, the way she took whatever life threw at her and stayed happy. She had the most optimistic outlook he'd ever known. Maybe because he was such a pessimist, he liked that about her.

The smile was enticement enough, but Ozzie also noticed how it nudged a little dimple in her rosy cheek. Snowflakes clung to her thick lashes and settled on the tip of her cute little nose. Now that she'd gotten her way and the donkey was ready for its journey, she positively glowed with pleasure.

He couldn't help himself. He bent and pressed a soft, gentle kiss to her cold lips. He could feel that smile of hers, and it fed something in his soul.

And that scared him.

He drew back and frowned at her.

Puzzled, she asked, "What?"

"Nothing." Catching her around the waist, Ozzie hoisted her up into her seat, then, without thinking about it, he fastened her seatbelt. With her gaze glued to his face, Marci kept that crooked, endearing smile in place the entire time.

Their eyes met, and Ozzie couldn't look away.

Would she wear that sweet smile while coming? Or would she clench her teeth and groan and . . .

When he realized he still loomed over her for no good reason at all, he cursed and stepped away, then slammed her door. On his way to his own seat, he lectured himself on the impropriety of lusting after a woman not based in reality. He knew the consequences and he knew, if he was smart, he'd satisfy his lust with a staid, no-nonsense woman.

Problem was, he'd never wanted another woman the way he wanted Marci.

He climbed into his own seat and Marci said, "That was a nice kiss."

"Forget about it."

"I don't think so. I think I'll cherish it, and remember it always."

"Oh, for the love of—"

"You're sure you're okay to drive?"

A safer topic. He grasped it like a lifeline. "Don't worry about it. I've worked fourteen hours straight and still gotten myself home."

"Fourteen hours?"

Ignoring the sexy, totally kooky broad beside him, Ozzie

started the truck and eased it from the apartment parking lot out onto the road. "Sometimes standoffs take a hell of a long time. You don't just up and leave in the middle of it."

"I'd never be able to do that. I was up most of the night staking out the funeral home so I could sneak off with the donkey without anyone knowing."

Ozzie refused to ask, but that didn't stop her.

"I parked the rental truck in the empty grocery lot and walked down that way, then hid in the bushes. It was so cold and I got so sleepy, and my feet and behind were wet from sitting in the snow."

Do. Not. Ask.

"It wasn't until this morning that the road quieted down enough for me to slip away with the donkey. I was so cold and stiff, and tired, I could barely move. I'd planned to sleep in this morning, then you showed up. But at least by then I'd showered and thawed out all my body parts."

He couldn't think about her thawing. "What would you have done with him if I hadn't showed up?"

Marci shrugged. "I was going to try some sleuthing on my own, but I realize now that I probably wouldn't have gotten very far with that." She pulled off her hat and put it in her lap, then, staring down at her hands, said, "I'm glad you did show up. Thank you." And with that, she turned on the static-riddled radio and found a station playing Christmas music.

Ozzie was glad he'd shown up, too. What if someone in her apartment building had called about the noise, and Marci had gotten arrested? Worse, what if someone had found her on that dark, cold road and . . .

That thought was so disturbing, he cut it short. Holidays or not, there were still bums and creeps hanging on every street corner.

Out of the blue, taking Ozzie by surprise, Marci said, "I'm used to ridicule and disbelief, you know."

He did a double take. "What?"

"Everyone thinks what you think. That's why I don't let

many people know about my gift. In fact, I moved here to hide it. I don't tell anyone now, and when I help an animal, I do it anonymously, to avoid some of the mockery." She turned to look out the window. "When I was younger, I used to talk about it. But I quickly learned that it's not a good thing to admit being different. I got called names by the meanest people, and the others just kept their distance."

The way he'd kept his distance.

What kind of childhood must she have had? Hell, what kind of adulthood was she having? He knew for a fact that she didn't date much, and other than her sister, she didn't seem close to anyone.

To give himself a moment to think, Ozzie adjusted the heater and defroster. Being SWAT required that he know how to deal with all types of people and their problems. He didn't consider Marci delusional, just fanciful. She wasn't a risk, except to his sanity. But she definitely had some ideas that needed special care.

When he said nothing, she sighed. "Bethany is really protective toward me. She loves animals as much as I do, but she doesn't share my intuition. When I tell her something about animals, what they feel and need, she believes me a hundred percent, and she'll do whatever she can to help. But it's harder for her than it is for me."

Never before had Marci conversed so casually with him. Their few attempts at dating had focused on the sexual chemistry between them, not on feelings. He enjoyed seeing Marci this way: relaxed, open, trusting.

Trusting? Well, yeah.

Giving it some thought, Ozzie supposed he had to consider her actions based in trust. Hadn't she just said that she didn't tell many people about her . . . gift?

But she'd told him.

And then he'd done the expected and avoided her. Stupid ass.

Okay, so he now knew enough about women to know not

to get overly involved with the . . . unique ones. But that didn't mean he had to steer clear of Marci altogether. He didn't have to shun her.

He just wouldn't entangle himself with her romantically. He'd keep things casual. Sexual, maybe, but casual all the same.

It amazed him, but Ozzie wanted to learn more about her and her strange predilections toward animals. "Since you and Bethany look identical, it's surprising that she doesn't share your gift."

Resting her head back on the seat, Marci closed her eyes. "Lucius has always been able to tell us apart."

Oh, ho. That sounded like a challenge. "And you think I can't?"

She opened her eyes again and surveyed him. "But you just said we look identical."

"Outwardly, sure. But you smile differently. You walk differently and laugh at different things. You're usually off in your own little world, while Bethany is always on the attack."

That had her laughing. "No, she is not. Well, except maybe with Lucius, before they got things ironed out." Then, more quietly, "Or when she's defending me."

And that probably explained why Bethany didn't seem to like him. From jump, she'd been prickly with him, always watching him as if she expected him to sprout horns. Or maybe . . . hurt her sister's feelings.

Shit. He hated being predictable.

Marci touched his arm, causing him to stiffen. "I've noticed that people do different things in order to protect themselves. Bethany was afraid of her growing feelings for Lucius, so she picked arguments with him, forcing an emotional distance."

The way she said that, with ripe anticipation while watching him so closely, raised Ozzie's suspicions. He scowled. "Is that some kind of dig toward me?"

"Not a dig, but an observation. If you'll be honest, you'll admit that you use sarcasm and negativity to shield your feelings for me."

Whoa. Hold the farm. *His feelings?*

Ozzie glanced toward her, but the snow flurries were thick enough now to require that he return his attention to the road. "What the hell is that supposed to mean?"

"You like me."

Despite the cold, he broke out in a sweat. "I *want* you, Marci. It's not at all the same thing."

Taunting him, she leaned closer. "But you like me, too. Admit it."

Get a grip, Ozzie. Don't let her rile you. He clutched the steering wheel and formulated a plan of response. "Okay." Forcing himself to relax, he feigned mere curiosity. "What gives you the impression I like you?"

"You watch me all the time."

True. But easily explained. "You're hot. Great ass. Stellar legs. More than a handful up top."

Hell, he was turning himself on.

In a gruffer tone, he stated, "*All* the guys watch you."

"You also glare at the other guys watching me."

He snorted, but had to wonder . . . did he? Sure, he hated seeing any man disrespect a woman. But he had no claim on Marci. Just because he'd gone out with her a few times, and hadn't yet had her, even though he wanted her bad . . .

No claim at all, damn it.

He'd refute her. He'd tell her he didn't give a rat's ass who looked at her, then she'd understand he wasn't the one smitten.

He glanced at her. "Are you saying you like the other men eyeballing you?" Appalled at himself, Ozzie snapped his mouth shut. Had that aggressive, barked question reeking of jealousy actually come from him?

Marci's smile spread slow and easy. "Not really."

He was so lost in self-recriminations, he didn't know what she was talking about. "Not really *what?*"

"If it wasn't for you," she assured him, "I probably wouldn't have noticed anyone else looking at me. But because I'm always looking at you, I've seen when you get that murderous glint in your eyes."

So he'd just clued her in? Great. Just friggin' great. He could hardly deny the truth of her observations, so he just kept quiet.

"And your reaction has to mean something, right?"

"It means I don't want anyone else jumping your bones before me." Actually, he didn't want anyone touching her. Ever. Period.

"Because you like me?"

Ozzie had never been the type to abuse anyone, but especially not a woman. At the same time, he didn't want to give her false impressions. "Look, Marci, I like you fine. Really." How could he not? She was sweet and cheerful and . . . "But I don't *like* you, if you know what I mean."

"No, I don't."

He groaned. "You're a nice-enough woman. You seem kind. And usually smart."

"Usually?"

He would not belabor her weirdness with animals. "The thing is, I enjoy being single."

"I didn't ask to marry you."

That made *twice* he'd heard that cursed word today, and both times in relationship to Marci. Driven by desperation, he squeezed the steering wheel and scowled. "I'm not looking to get involved beyond anything sexual."

Marci tilted her head, as if trying to understand him. "Why did you come to see me this morning?"

Shew. An easy enough subject, one he could discuss without caution. "Lucius says someone's been maybe bothering you." At least that was the bona fide truth. "He wanted me to keep an eye on things."

"Oh." Disappointment had her crossing her arms. "And that's why you're helping me return the donkey? Because Lucius is your friend and he told you to babysit me?"

Not exactly, but it sounded good to him. "That's about it."

Silence reigned. He could actually feel her regret as she stared at him. For the longest time she said nothing, and Ozzie was starting to squirm. What if she cried? What if he'd just broken her little screwball heart?

"Okay then."

He tucked in his chin and spared another glimpse in her direction. "Okay, what?"

"Okay, I believe you don't like me."

But . . . "Look, Marci, I don't *dislike* you. Didn't I just say that overall you're a nice, sweet woman?"

"But you only want sex?"

The Inquisition couldn't have been this tough.

Be noble, Oz.

Be strong.

Do not pull over to the side of the road to show her the exceptions you'd make for sex.

He cleared his throat and attempted to be as blunt as possible. "I want you, but then, we've already acknowledged that. The thing is, I'm sure you don't want to get involved in a purely sexual encounter."

"I don't?"

Ozzie concentrated on not getting a Jones. Again. "No, you don't." And then, because he couldn't help himself: "Do you?"

She took her own sweet time thinking about it, probably to further torment him.

"I don't know," she finally said. "I want you an awful lot, too, and I'm not sure I want to go my whole life wondering how you would have been."

Of all the dirty, rotten . . . ! Ozzie could feel himself hardening. And she'd probably done that on purpose, just to get even with him for being surly. He shifted in his seat, trying to get comfortable, and considered apologizing for his less-than-sterling mood.

He tapped his fingers on the steering wheel, figured out

what to say, and cleared his throat again. "Look, Marci, I guess I'm just tired and in a bad mood."

"And our aborted lovemaking this morning has us both edgy."

He locked his teeth. "Right. But I shouldn't take that out on you. Just forget everything I've said, okay?"

"No, I won't do that." She looked out the window at the passing scenery. "Don't you just love this time of year? Look at the Christmas lights. I especially like the blue ones. They're so pretty."

Oh, no, he wouldn't let her switch topics on him that easily! "What do you mean, no?"

"I'm sorry, but I can't forget that sweet kiss earlier, or everything you've said. It'd be impossible. I'm used to people not liking me, but it bothers me more with you."

It bothered him that she was bothered. "Marci—"

"And you should know, there *is* someone following me. I realize Lucius doesn't believe it, he just asked you to look out for me to appease Bethany. He hates to disappoint her."

Lucius was whipped big time.

"But if you look in the rearview mirror, you'll see a van. It's been there since we got on the main road. Watch and see if it stays with us."

Startled by that, Ozzie glanced in the mirror and saw the van she meant. He grunted. "Could be anyone." But there weren't many cars out and about on that early snowy morning.

"Want to make a bet?" Marci twisted toward him as much as the confines of the seatbelt would allow. "A real bet, not just a verbal one."

Everything male in him went on the alert. "What are we wagering?"

She didn't even take a second to consider it. "In a few minutes, you can pull over for gas or a drink or something. If the van pulls over, too, that'll be proof enough, okay?"

"I suppose." He looked again in the rearview mirror, and

felt his instincts kick in. They *were* being tailed, and he hadn't even noticed. He didn't like slacking. He didn't like being so distracted by a woman that he missed something that major.

"If he is following us, I win the bet."

"Not yet, woman." He wouldn't agree to anything blindly. "What are we betting?"

"That you'll spend Christmas with me."

Huh. Had he really thought she'd ask for sex?

In his dreams.

"I just inherited a house, and I'd planned to work on it over the holidays."

"Then I'll spend Christmas with you. Either way, you'll give me some time, okay?"

That didn't sound too heinous. But it brought up a new question. "So if he's not following us, what do I get?"

The dimple showed in her cheek. "What do you want?"

Such a loaded question. Ozzie firmed his jaw, flipped on his turn signal to switch lanes, and headed for the nearest exit.

The damn van followed.

"I don't think it matters," he muttered. "The bastard is following us—and I want to know why."

3

"I haven't eaten," Osbourne said. "I'm going to pull in and get a breakfast sandwich. You want one?"

It fascinated Marci to see Osbourne go into SWAT mode. Oh, he spoke casually enough, but a new alertness straightened his spine and firmed his jaw. He looked everywhere, at everything, as he eased the truck to the right and took an exit.

The few times she'd dated him, he'd been charming at first, then wary, then finally distant. All because she'd tried to be herself with him.

When he'd shown back up today, primed and in sexual overdrive, her hope had renewed. But so far he'd been churlish and sarcastic and she didn't like it. His attitude hurt her feelings when she'd thought herself long immune to the criticism of others.

Seeing that the van had also switched lanes and taken the same exit, Marci sighed. "I'll take a donut and orange juice. Thank you."

When Osbourne got in the drive-thru lane, the van went past, but pulled into a gas station nearby. No one left the van to pump gas.

Only someone familiar with Osbourne would note the growing tension in him. Not sexual tension this time, but an angry tension that bunched his impressive muscles and put an anticipatory glint into his blue eyes. It didn't bode well for somebody.

He put in their orders without an obvious care, paid, accepted their food, and then handed her the bag.

"Get that out for me, will you?" He steered the truck out of the parking lot and onto the main road, heading for the exit that'd take them back onto the highway.

Marci unwrapped his sandwich and handed it to him. He balanced it on his knee while driving.

"Osbourne? The van is following again."

"I know. Normally I'd make a few sharp turns, but I don't want to alarm the donkey."

So considerate. So why didn't he give her the same consideration? Surely it was as she suspected—that he did care for her but wanted to protect himself.

The questions uppermost in her mind were: Why? And who had hurt him?

"In fact," he said, as much to himself as her, "I'll just let the idiot follow us all the way to the donkey's home. Once I don't have to worry about the animal, it'll be easier for me to take care of this."

After a bite of her donut, Marci licked her fingers free of glaze. "Take care of it how?"

"Don't push me, Marci."

"It was a simple question."

"Yeah, well keep your fingers out of your mouth and your tongue where I can't see it."

Oh. So that's what he meant by pushing him. Feeling a little devilish, Marci took another bite of her donut. "So . . . Do I spend Christmas with you? Will you honor the bet?"

"We never actually shook on it or anything."

She wouldn't let his reluctance bother her. One way or another, she'd wear him down. "So is it that you like being alone during the holidays?"

"Usually I wouldn't be." He bit into his breakfast sandwich with gusto.

Jealousy prickled up her spine, and Marci said, "Yes, of course. I'm sure you have your pick of women to celebrate with."

He laughed without humor, and then, in somber tones, he explained, "I've spent every Christmas since my sixth birthday with my grandmother. It's always been just the two of us. But she recently passed, so this year I'll be solo for the holidays."

Oh, God. "Osbourne, I'm so sorry. I didn't realize."

"Granny was a hoot. And she'd have loved you, because she loved animals and anyone who had anything to do with them."

"Even kooks?"

"Especially kooks, being as she was a little nutty herself. But in a loveable way. When my mom died and my dad took off, she gathered me up and said she'd finally have me to herself, as if it was something she'd always wanted."

"What do you mean he took off?"

"He was young, unwilling to be burdened with a kid. Granny said I reminded him too much of her. But I think that was bullshit, just her way of softening things."

"I bet you must have missed them a lot."

"With Granny around? Hell, no. She made growing up fun."

Fascinated, Marci smiled at him. "How so?"

"Granny didn't believe in rules. If I wanted dessert instead of dinner, we'd eat it in the yard, in the rain, while listening to coyotes howl. During my rowdier teens, when I wanted long hair, she offered to dye it blue for me."

Marci laughed. "She does sound fun."

"Yeah, but she was wily. I always thought she should have been a shrink, because she sure knew how to play mind games."

"What do you mean?"

"When I was eighteen, I wanted a tattoo. You know, something gnarly and macho around my biceps. Granny thought that sounded cool, and she wanted to go along to get one, too."

They both laughed.

Shaking his head, Osbourne added, "Hell, I was afraid that if I slipped off to get it, she'd find out where, and she'd show up there to get her ass tatted or something, and I'd never be able to live it down. For sure, she'd have told the tattoo artist she was my granny, and word would have spread like wildfire."

"Pretty ingenious on her part."

"No kidding. I failed a test once because I hadn't studied. She sat down with it, looked over the answers, and damned if she didn't know them all! Made me feel like an idiot, all the while telling me how smart I am and that obviously the test was messed up because, hell, what old lady could pass it when a sharp young man couldn't? From then on, I aced everything, and she'd beam, telling me how much smarter I was than her." His voice softened. "But I never believed that. She was the wisest, most incredible woman I've ever known."

Marci touched his thigh. "I'm glad you had her in your life."

"Yeah, me, too." His hand briefly covered hers and gave it a squeeze. "Having Christmas without her just doesn't feel right."

When he retreated again, she felt the loss, both physical and emotional, deep inside herself. "Maybe it'd be easier if you had someone around to . . . you know, maybe deflect the memories." Marci knew she lacked subtlety, but she couldn't bear the thought of him spending Christmas alone.

Osbourne grunted. "Sharing holidays with women gives them the wrong idea. It puts too personal a slant to things. Women start thinking you're committed to them, whether you are or not."

"Committed?"

He worked his jaw a minute, then shrugged one heavy shoulder, as if deciding it didn't matter what he shared. "I had one friggin' holiday with a woman, and she thought we'd get married or something. I told her nothing had changed, that I liked her but I wasn't in love with her."

"I take it she reacted badly?"

His hands tightened on the steering wheel. "I'd always known Ainsley was a little screwy, but after that, I realized she was certifiable. She did everything she could to harass me. She kept calling me at home and at work. She dropped in unannounced. She stalked me, hoping to catch me with another woman. When I told her to back off, she . . ."

"What?"

"Claimed she was pregnant."

"Oh." Dread settled in Marci's belly. "You're a father?"

"No." After a deep breath, he said, "It's a long story, and I won't go into details, but for months, she put me through hell. She was pregnant, she wasn't pregnant. She'd had an abortion, she hadn't had an abortion. It was mine, it wasn't mine. I had no idea what to think. When I considered being a father . . . I dunno. I took to the idea. And then she'd say she'd aborted the baby, just to see my reaction. And the next day she'd tell me she lied, that she was still pregnant, but not by me. She ranted and raved and drove me nuts."

"How did it finally get resolved?"

"After a few months, when she would have started showing if she was in fact pregnant, she found some new schmuck to torment." He shook his head. "She wanted to make sure I didn't ruin things for her, so she confessed that she'd made it all up."

"Dear God." Marci now understood, but she almost wished she didn't.

He thought she was another Ainsley.

"Since then, I've kept things simple. Limited dating—with very rational women."

"And no holidays?"

His frown eased away. "Most of the women I know aren't the type to enjoy a quiet Christmas at home."

Forget subtlety. "I would enjoy it."

Mouth quirking in a half-smile, he said, "Yeah, you made that clear."

Still, he didn't invite her to join him, and she slouched back in her seat, disgruntled. "But I'm a vindictive flake, right? Way too cruel to have hanging around."

His frown took the chill out of the air. "Don't put words in my mouth."

"Why not? Kooky is kooky, right? You've seen one, you've seen 'em all."

"I didn't—" Osbourne huffed, glanced in the rearview mirror, then at his directions. He switched lanes. "Look, let's start this debacle over, okay?"

Now he called their time together a debacle? Worse and worse. "Start over how?"

"Forget the past. From this second on, we'll just play it by ear. One thing at a time."

She supposed she could do that. "The donkey first?"

"Right. Hopefully this is where he belongs and we can be heroes by returning him, then we'll head home."

Marci wondered whose home he meant, but she decided not to push her luck. "Deal."

"Great." From one minute to the next, the snow turned to frozen sleet, hammering the windshield and making travel more treacherous. Osbourne eased off the highway on the next exit. "Help me look for Riley Road."

The wipers could barely keep the ice off the windshield, even with the defroster going full blast. They'd slowed to a crawl with visibility limited.

A crooked road indicator came into view. "There it is." Marci pointed, and Osbourne pulled down a narrower gravel drive.

The van stayed behind them, but held back when they drove down a dirt road leading to an old, stately farmhouse fenced in and surrounded by towering trees. Osbourne parked in front but left the truck running.

Back in SWAT mode, he ordered, "Wait here."

Orders had never gone over big with her. "Why should I?"

"I don't know these people, and I don't like taking chances with you."

Well, the order sounded much nicer put that way.

"Lock the doors and I'll be right back."

"Okay."

Her quick agreement earned her a double take. Osbourne's gaze was fraught with suspicion, but he said nothing.

Marci watched as he trod through the now ankle-deep snow, up the hidden walk to the front porch. He knocked on the door and seconds later a middle-aged woman, wearing jeans and a flannel shirt, answered. As she dried her hands on a kitchen towel, Osbourne spoke, gestured toward the truck, and the woman screamed.

Even through the thick sleet and snow, Marci could see that he jumped.

The woman shoved Osbourne aside and went slipping and sliding down the walkway to the truck. Shocked, Osbourne hurried after her. The woman was still yelling excitedly, which brought a tall, portly man charging out the doorway to join her at the truck.

Over the truck's idling engine and the blasting defroster, their words were indecipherable. But their expressions were clear enough: naked, tearful, overwhelming joy.

Grinning ear to ear, Marci opened her door and stepped shin-deep into the drifting snow and ice.

Struggling against the surging wind, she reached the back of the truck just as Osbourne lowered the hatch. There was a single moment of speechless expectation, then the donkey brayed, the man and woman gave a robust shout, and within seconds, the truck bed was filled.

The man, overcome with joy, cried, "Magnus! Finally, you're home!"

The woman threw herself around the donkey and hugged him tight.

Wide-eyed and mute with incredulity, Osbourne looked at Marci. Grinning through her tears, she mouthed the words "Thank you."

And slowly, Osbourne's smile came in return.

* * *

An hour later, Osbourne continued to smile, and said again, "I can't believe it."

Marci sipped the hot chocolate that River and Chloe Parson had insisted on fixing for them. They'd also tried to give them a hefty reward, but Osbourne and Marci had refused the money at almost the same time.

Osbourne told the Parsons that seeing their happiness, especially at Christmas, was more than enough reward.

It thrilled Marci that he looked at their efforts the same way she did: as simply the right thing to do, not something done for financial gain. After their repeated refusals, the Parson couple gave up.

After a time, she and Osbourne got on their way with warm hugs, hot chocolate, and a lot of gratitude.

"It's a wonderful feeling, isn't it?" Marci asked him.

"Yeah. That donkey is like a member of their family."

"Magnus is a fine creature. I can see why they love him so much."

Osbourne laughed. "Yeah, I figured you would feel that way."

Toying with the lid on her cup, Marci asked, "So now do you believe me?"

"That we're being followed? Damn right." They'd just reached the gravel road and there sat the van, nearly snowed in, but with the engine running. As they passed, it pulled out behind them.

Well, shoot. That wasn't what she'd meant at all, but Marci really didn't feel like having her ability with animals questioned yet again. Osbourne would either believe her or not, and she wouldn't try to convince him.

"Hang on to that cup," Osbourne told her.

"Why?"

"Because I'm going to find out what the hell he wants." And with that, Osbourne turned the truck sharply, stopping it crossways in the road, blocking both narrow lanes.

Face set and brows down, he put the truck in PARK, again ordered Marci to lock the doors after him, and got out to stalk toward the van.

Marci sighed. Releasing her seatbelt so she could climb to Osbourne's side of the truck for an unhindered view, she watched him.

The van sat idling, the driver confused. But with Osbourne's stomping, hostile approach, clear alarm showed on his face. The driver looked to be in his early thirties, average in build and appearance with straight brown hair and shifty eyes.

To hear their verbal exchange, Marci quickly rolled down the window.

With one hand braced on the roof of the van, Osbourne leaned down to the driver's door and ordered, "Open up."

The man pressed back in his seat and shook his head. "What do you want?"

Rolling his eyes, Osbourne reached inside his coat and produced a badge that he held against the window. "Open it *now.*"

The man gulped. His window lowered a mere five inches. "What's going on here? Why are you harassing me?"

"You're following me. I want to know why."

"But . . . I'm not!"

Osbourne leaned closer, and the man screeched. "Don't you dare touch me! I'm warning you, I'll call the cops!"

"I am a cop, you ass." Straightening again, Osbourne put away the badge and bundled up his coat against the whistling wind and sleet. "Stop that noise and tell me why you were following me, or we can talk at the station after I have you arrested."

The man didn't ask on what charge, which Marci thought would have been a good question, especially since Osbourne was an Ohio police officer, and they were currently in Kentucky.

The man glared toward the truck—*toward her*—and said, "I'm not following you. I'm following her."

Rather than appeasing Osbourne, that seemed to annoy him more. "*Why?*"

Gaining confidence, the man lowered his window more and offered his hand. "Vaughn Wayland."

Osbourne ignored the conciliatory gesture.

"Right." Mr. Wayland retreated. "I'm working on a story, actually. I'm a freelance reporter and she's hot news."

"What the hell are you talking about?"

"You don't know?" Wayland stared toward her with anticipation. "She's a psychic."

Huffing, Osbourne said, "Don't be an idiot."

Well, Marci thought, so much for him believing her.

"But it's true!" Wayland insisted. "I'd heard about her for a few years, but I didn't believe it any more than you do. Then my neighbor's cat went missing for months. Everyone sort of figured the mangy thing had gotten run over or eaten by a dog when, out of the blue, Miss Churchill brought it back to her."

"So she found a lost cat. Big deal."

"I located another woman who claims Miss Churchill helped cure her dog of nightmares."

This time, Osbourne turned to glare at her in clear accusation.

Marci glared right back. She remembered that poor dog. A neighborhood kid would torment it while hiding in bushes so that the dog's owner didn't know. The dog was a frazzled mess because of that rotten kid. But Marci had ratted out the boy, and not only had the dog owner given him hell but his parents also.

"I have a file folder full of pet owners she's helped. They've all been more than willing to sing her praises. All I need to finish my piece is an interview with her."

"I don't believe this."

"She's the kind of human interest story that appeals to readers, especially this time of year."

"You're fucking with me, right?"

Wayland sniffed. "No, I am not. And you have no right to interfere with my research."

"Stalking her is *not* research."

Affronted, he squared his shoulders. "I'm not stalking her. I just need her to share some of her background and history."

"Have you asked her?"

"Yes. Twice."

Marci didn't recognize the fellow at all. She yelled out the window, "He could be telling the truth, Osbourne, although I don't remember meeting him."

"I asked over the phone," the man yelled back.

"Oh." Marci thought about it, and then nodded. "I always turn down that stuff, and then I change my phone number again."

Osbourne rubbed his face. "Look, she doesn't want to be interviewed, so leave her alone."

"But . . ." the man sputtered, "I can't do that. I've already promised the story to a magazine and I'm behind on my deadline as it is."

Once again, Osbourne leaned down close, and though Marci couldn't hear what he said, she saw the driver's face, and knew that Osbourne wasn't being polite.

The man cowered back as far as he could, nodded agreement several times, but still, he looked far from resigned to failure.

Maybe Osbourne realized it, too, because he took the time to write down Vaughn Wayland's name and license plate number.

When he returned to the truck, he still looked very put out.

Marci rolled up the window, unlocked the door, and slid back to her own seat. Without a word, Osbourne got behind the wheel, turned the truck, and headed for the highway.

For several minutes, they rode in utter silence. Then Osbourne asked, "Does that happen often?"

"What?"

"Jerks following you around, pressing you for answers?"

She shrugged. "Usually it's people who don't believe me, who want to expose me as a fake. They think that I extort money from people, or that I prey on their emotions."

He shook his head. "You'd never do that."

Marci blinked at him. Aha. Maybe he didn't consider her an Ainsley after all. "No, I wouldn't. I try to keep people from finding out who I am, and what I know. But it's not always possible, not if I want to help—and I do."

"If you didn't, Magnus would still be at the funeral home instead of where he belongs."

Was that an admission of her ability? A warm glow spread inside her. "True. When an animal has a problem, I can't ignore it. It hurts me too much. But whenever possible, I help anonymously."

"How does that work?"

"I'll contact the owners—maybe by a note, or phone if I can figure out their number. Most take my advice or at least listen enough to check into what I tell them. I don't have to expose myself or leave myself open to more ridicule."

"*More* ridicule?"

She flattened her mouth and looked out the window. "Trust me, it's never been easy. From the time I was a little girl, I could sense things. And any time a kid is different . . ."

Very quietly, he said, "I'm sorry."

Marci turned toward him again, wanting to explain. "It hasn't been a picnic for Bethany, either. All through school, she got teased about having a loony sister."

He winced, probably remembering the times he'd thought similar things. The difference was that Osbourne had never been deliberately cruel. Quite a distinction.

He'd dodged her, but he hadn't ridiculed her.

As if offering another apology, he reached for her knee, settled his big hand there, and stroked her with his thumb. It was a casual touch, yet at the same time intimate enough to feel special.

And to raise her temperature a few degrees.

While deciding how much to tell him, Marci finished her hot chocolate. She didn't open herself to too many people, but right now, in the quiet and cold, with Osbourne, it felt right.

She laid her hand over his. Despite the weather, his fingers were warm. She loved touching him, and even a simple touch on the hand let her feel his strength. "For as long as I can remember, guys have tried to use Bethany to get close to me."

She waited for his disbelief, or his humor. After all, they were identical twins. Most people would wonder why one twin would be preferable to another.

Osbourne considered her statement. "It's because you come across softer, less independent."

Startled that he'd hit the nail on the head, Marci barely noticed when he turned his hand to clasp hers, then tugged her closer to him on the bench seat, as close as the seatbelts would allow. "That's it exactly. Men see me as an airhead, and maybe easy."

The corners of his mouth lifted, and he returned both hands to the wheel. "I'd say they don't know you very well."

"No, they don't." Her spine stiffened. "I'm not an airhead."

"Don't confuse me with any other idiots you've known, Marci. Hell, you're more complicated than any ten women combined. And I know firsthand that there's nothing easy about you. But you're definitely smart."

"You really believe that?"

"Hell yes. You're smart enough to figure out that a donkey is unhappy, to steal him without getting caught, and to get him back home safely."

A blush of pleasure colored her cheeks. "I couldn't have done it without you," she pointed out.

He ignored that little fact to say, "You're also kind and funny and . . . caring."

The warmth spread, melting her heart. "Thank you."

"You're welcome. Now tell me more about these idiots you've known."

It wasn't easy to admit, but she forced the words out. "With

Bethany and me being identical twins, a lot of men consider us interchangeable."

"Lucius doesn't."

She laughed. "True enough. Almost from jump, Lucius treated me like a little sister and Bethany like a sex goddess."

"That must've been a change for you." Some new inflection entered his tone. "I imagine you have men hot on your heels all the time."

"No. At least, not the way you mean." Her pleasure faded. "Too many times in the past, men have shown an interest only because of my ability. Like the clown following us, they want to interview me, or maybe expose me or use my talent in a way I'd never condone. When I turn them down, they go to Bethany, hoping that they can get closer to me through her."

"That's why you don't date much, huh?"

She could feel his heat, and his caring. "I have great intuition with animals, but I'm not that good at figuring out which men to trust." And after meeting Osbourne, she hadn't wanted any other men.

Two heartbeats of silence passed before Osbourne said, "I don't work tonight, but then I won't have another day off for a week."

She tipped her head, unsure where he was going with that disclosure, but hopeful all the same.

"What about you?"

"Like Lucius, I'm on vacation. This close to Christmas, women aren't that interested in exercise. They're too busy shopping and baking and fitting in all the holiday craziness. I have the next seven days free."

"Good." He glanced at her, then away. "Will you spend Christmas with me?"

Her heart soared, her face warmed. But suspicion niggled. "Because you want to spend time with me, or because you're worried about the guy following us?"

"Both."

At least he was honest. She looked at his mouth—and wanted to melt. "And because you want to have sex?"

"Definitely."

Her toes curled inside her shoes. She gave it quick thought, but really, the way she saw it, it was a win-win situation. She smiled, and said, "Okay."

4

They returned the rental truck first, then went back to Marci's apartment so she could throw some clothes and other things into an overnight bag. He should have been exhausted, Ozzie thought, but instead, anticipation sizzled inside him.

While he waited impatiently, his mind abuzz with what would soon happen, he called the station and explained that the donkey was now at his rightful home. Someone else would take over, to figure out how the funeral home came into possession of the donkey in the first place.

When he finished that, Ozzie roamed the living room and kitchen of Marci's tiny apartment. Everywhere he looked, he saw surprising little clues to her personality. Tidy surfaces. Organized drawers. Light, feminine touches.

Even her bathroom was devoid of the clutter typical to women. Everything had a place, and was in it.

It seemed his sentimental, whimsical little elf was a neat freak. He'd honestly expected her to be scattered and somewhat disorganized. Ainsley had been so chaotic all the time, in her emotions and in her surroundings.

But then most of what he'd learned of Marci today had

proved she was not only different from Ainsley but from most other women he'd known.

Her incredible vulnerability, combined with her compassionate tears when Magnus finally reunited with his family, had pushed Ozzie right over the edge. Marci was one of a kind.

He'd have her today, and to hell with what Lucius had said.

To hell with his own misgivings, too. Getting too involved with her might be a bad idea, but he couldn't resist the sexual lure any longer.

As he left the bathroom, he thought he heard her muffled chatter. Cocking a brow, he called out, "Marci?"

"Be right there."

Curious now, Ozzie wandered to her bedroom door and silently pressed it open. He found Marci on her knees beside the bed, looking under it.

The position elevated her sexy backside and put thoughts of sex on the fast track in his brain. "Damn, I love your ass."

Laughing, she looked over her shoulder at him. She balanced herself on one hand, and with the other she held a phone to her ear. "Sorry. I can't find my car keys. They're here somewhere. The donkey sort of bumped things around so I think they must've fallen off the nightstand—"

"Who are you talking to?"

"My sister."

"So your sister *knew* you'd stolen a donkey? Does that mean Lucius knew?"

Suddenly Marci blushed and whispered into the phone, "No, Bethany. No, that's *not* what he said."

She cast an uncomfortable look at Ozzie, but he wasn't about to budge.

In an even lower tone, her face red-hot, she said, "Not *me*, my ass."

Ozzie grinned. So, Bethany had heard his comment about Marci's backside.

"It's not at all the same thing," Marci argued while turning her back on him. "I have to go. Yes, I know. You, too." When Marci faced him again, she wouldn't meet his gaze, and that bothered Ozzie enough that he decided not to tease her.

"You don't need your keys. I'll drive."

She shook her head. "No, thanks. You'll be at work at night and I don't want to be stranded."

That made sense, so he let it go. "Then let's find the keys and get out of here before the roads get any worse."

As he started to bend down to help her look, she straightened with the keys in her hand. "Got 'em." Still flustered, she started to close her overnight bag, and Ozzie noticed the thermal pajamas she'd included.

"You won't need those."

She nudged him aside and shoved the bag shut. "Maybe not tonight, but after that . . . Um. I *am* staying more than one night, right?"

Damn, but her uncertainty got to him. Catching her shoulders, Ozzie drew her toward him and kissed her soft mouth. "Through Christmas, if you like."

"I like," she whispered back.

She tried to kiss him again, but he leaned out of reach. "If we start that, we'll never get out of here."

Her tongue came out to slick over her lips. Her big blue eyes darkened. She laid one hand lightly on his chest. "Well, my bed is right—"

"No." She'd be the death of him. From one second to the next, he got so primed he hurt. "I don't want to start anything here, because I haven't been to bed yet. Let's get to my place so I can sleep afterward." If she objected to his third-shift lifestyle, better to find out now.

Her touch went from seducing to soothing. "I bet you're pretty exhausted, huh? You've been up so long now."

He was horny, not sleepy, but he didn't say so. "If it'd been a normal day, I could just stay up and sleep tonight. But it's been nonstop since I got to work."

"How come?"

He shrugged. "We had a barricade/hostage situation with lots of gunfire. Everything worked out, but that kind of situation gets the adrenaline pumping. When it fades, so does the energy level."

"And then I dragged you into my donkey adventure." She looked up at him with apologetic eyes. "I'm sorry."

"Actually, returning Magnus to his rightful owners was nice." The highlight of the day—if he discounted the intimacy he'd shared with her.

He kissed her again, quick and hard, then hauled up her bag. "Let's go."

On their way out of the bedroom, she said, "I just need to let the others know where I'll be."

That stalled him. Telling her sister was one thing, but, damn Lucius, the apartment building overflowed with busybody women. He didn't want them all privy to his business. "You're going to advertise what we're doing?"

She looked up at him, saw his discomfort, and laughed. Catching him by the front of his shirt, she towed him along.

"I won't shout it from the rooftops, but all the tenants are close and I don't want anyone to worry when they don't see me around."

"Why would they worry?"

"We're all single women, so we look out for each other. Now, come on, quit dragging your feet."

A minute later, Ozzie stood still in the hallway, surrounded by curious female gazes. After the first knock on her next-door neighbor's door, every other door opened.

Marci said, "I'm going to spend Christmas with Osbourne," and that started a barrage of questions, accompanied by several skeptical glares in his direction.

A lesser man would have withered under such scrutiny, but Ozzie held tough. When the babbling finally calmed, he said, "Ladies," and he took Marci's arm to lead her outside.

It was like walking the gauntlet.

Women of various ages and professions watched them every step of the way, some of them whispering, some laughing, one whistling, and overall acting bawdy and suggestive.

When they were out of sight of prying eyes, he allowed himself to grin. It pleased him that Marci had such close friends. She often seemed so dreamy, that he'd worried about her. But she was obviously very well liked.

"I'll follow you," she said, breaking into his thoughts, "since I don't know where you live."

"All right, but stay close. And keep your cell phone on. The road crews might not have gotten out yet and the streets could be bad."

She put a wool-covered finger to his mouth. "I know how to drive in the snow, Osbourne. Don't worry. I'll be careful."

Snowflakes gathered on her nose and lashes again. He shook his head, opened the driver's door to her blue Dodge Neon, and set her overnight bag on the passenger seat.

Marci got behind the wheel to start the engine and turn on the heat. Ozzie went to his truck, got a windshield scraper, and came back to clean away the ice and snow so she'd have a clear view.

Rather than sit in the car as it warmed, Marci got out with her own scraper and helped. It was a good ten minutes before her car was drivable.

The roads weren't as bad as he'd feared. They made decent time, all things considered. He drove cautiously, constantly checking on her and at the same time watching for that idiotic reporter. He thought he spotted the van once, but with so much blustering wind and drifting snow, he couldn't be sure.

The house his grandma had left him sat on an isolated twelve acres, surrounded by woods and overgrown fields. Not since her early days had she done any farming, but she'd been too content with her privacy to sell the land. She hadn't been rich, except in spirit and love, but she'd never really wanted for anything, either.

When they reached the long driveway, Ozzie pulled over and instructed Marci to precede him. He wanted to make sure no one followed them. She looked at him curiously through the frosty window, but did as he asked. No other cars came into view, so after a few minutes, Ozzie joined her under the sloping carport roof.

In the gray light, the house showed its age. All along the foundation and walkway, dead, brittle weeds and wild shrubs poked up from the snow. Stark, multipaned windows were in desperate need of cleaning. Ancient patio furniture had all been moved to one side of the porch, giving the appearance of a salvage yard.

He'd have to explain to Marci, to make her understand that he'd wanted to update his grandmother's house, but she'd refused to let him spend a dime of his own money. As he stepped out of his truck, she got out, too, and she looked around with awe.

"Osbourne," she breathed, "it's incredible."

Explanations died on his tongue. He retrieved her bag, saying, "It needs some work."

"It's charming. And look at all that land. How much of it is yours?"

The temperature hung in the twenties, and Marci had her arms around herself. Yet she still stood staring out at the vast expanse of snow-covered acreage.

"All of it. In front of us, it goes all the way to the road. To the sides, it includes the woods, and some into the clearing, up to the fence line. Behind us it runs to the creek. Twelve acres in all."

"A creek." She whirled to face him. "Maybe tomorrow you can show me?"

His mouth, half-frozen, lifted into a smile. She was the charming one, so delighted with everything, so nonjudgmental. "Sure. We'll make a snowman. Come on. It'll be a lot warmer inside." He led her to a door on the other side of the carport. "I usually park in the barn, but this is closer."

She stared down at the bottom half of the door. "Is that a doggie entrance?"

"Yeah. Grimshaw uses it. He was Granny's dog, but now he's mine."

The carport opened into a heated mudroom, so that when Ozzie worked, Grimshaw could get into the warmth of the house or outside to run, as his mood led him. Another doggie door opened into the main house, and when Ozzie was home, he kept it unlatched. But for reasons of safety, he secured it whenever he was away from the house. He'd had everything from raccoons to skunks try to enter and root around.

Expecting Grimshaw to come greet him as he usually did, Ozzie unlatched the door. But there wasn't a single sign of the dog.

"He must be out playing. He does that. And with me being late, he probably got tired of waiting for me. The area is all fenced, but even if it wasn't, he knows his perimeters. He's safe enough. And I've found out that he loves the snow."

Stepping from the mudroom into the kitchen, Marci asked, "What kind of dog is he?"

"I don't know. A mixed breed. That was the only kind Granny ever had. I grew up with all kinds of animals, but now there's only Grimshaw."

Marci turned a circle to take in the spacious country kitchen with lots of wood trim. As she tugged off her boots to leave by the door, she said, "Wow."

"When I find the time, I plan to refinish all the wood trim, replace the cabinets and countertops, and install new appliances." Never taking his eyes off her, he removed his snow-covered boots, too.

"It's amazing."

At the end of his tether, Ozzie relocked the main door, set her bag on the table, and put his arms around her from behind. "My restraint has been amazing. But no more." While kissing the nape of her neck, he deftly began opening her coat.

At first, she melted, but she quickly rallied. "Osbourne, wait."

"Can't." He pushed his groin against her bottom and wanted to groan. "I need you."

"I'd like to shower first."

"I hope you're joking." He got her coat free and stripped it off her.

She turned to face him, her cheeks rosy, her eyes bright. "But . . . I smell like a donkey."

Anticipation growing in leaps and bounds, Ozzie looked her over. "Trust me, Marci, you could smell like the donkey's . . ."

"Osbourne!"

"*Foot.*" He smiled at her. "And I wouldn't care." She giggled, and that was enough to send him into a frenzy of lust. Scooping her up and over his shoulder, he said, "I'll shower with you. After."

He bounded up the winding stairway two steps at a time, his hand on her behind, caressing her. Thank God, Grimshaw was out playing somewhere, otherwise he'd need to spend a few minutes greeting the dog and he just didn't have the patience right now. Poor Grimshaw had become especially needy since Granny's passing, and Ozzie never ignored his feelings.

But right now, he had only one thing on his mind.

After moving into Granny's house, he'd taken his old bedroom, the first at the top of the landing. That's where he went now to dump Marci on the big brass bed.

She surprised him again by withholding all arguments. Instead, she began stripping away her clothes with the same frenzied need he felt.

Perfect.

Watching Marci as she twisted and turned on the bed in her efforts to get rid of her sweatshirt, Ozzie reached over his shoulder, grabbed a fistful of his shirt, and yanked it off.

With her sweatshirt bunched above her breasts, Marci paused to watch him.

"No, don't stop." Putting one knee on the bed, he hauled her into a sitting position and easily removed the roomy top, leaving her in low-slung jeans and a sexy white lace bra.

To Ozzie, she looked like an advertisement. She looked like raw temptation. She looked . . . like a fantasy about to happen.

A small, feminine smile tilted up the corners of her mouth and her eyes grew smoky as she watched him through lowered lashes. Baby-fine hair hung over her naked shoulders and her breasts quivered with her deepened breathing.

He could see her nipples, stiff and rosy, against the thin bra cups. His chest expanded, his erection grew. Blindly, his gaze glued to her breasts, he popped open the front closure of her bra and at the same time, bent to take one nipple into his mouth.

On a soft gasp, Marci arched her back. Her fingers sank into his hair and together they went down onto the mattress. He wished they were already naked, but he couldn't seem to give up this pleasure to advance his position. She tasted better than perfect, and the small sounds she made, the way she squirmed, burned him.

He switched to her other breast, then stroked one hand down her narrow rib cage, to the waistband of her jeans, then onto the denim to stroke that fine behind.

"Osbourne?"

He didn't answer. He couldn't.

"I've waited long enough," she whispered. "Let's get naked." Her hands roamed his shoulders before going to his neck and back into his hair. "I want to touch all of you."

A shock of electricity couldn't have jolted him more. In a nanosecond, Ozzie was off the bed. Their hands tangled as they both tried to attack the fastenings to her jeans. Ozzie gripped her wrists, pressed them upward to lie beside her head, and said, "Let me."

With another contented smile, she settled into the covers and let him take over. Impatience had her squirming as he opened her jeans, got them down as far as her knees, and paused to look her over again.

"Osbourne . . ."

He stripped away the jeans.

Her panties matched the now-open bra. His gaze scorched her; his hand followed in the same path. From the inside of her left knee, up her thigh, over her belly and to a plump breast. She felt silky and warm, and so damn soft.

He actually trembled.

Forcing himself to a modicum of patience, Ozzie cupped his hand over the crotch of her panties.

Hot.

His guts clenched, and he accepted the inevitable. "I'm sorry, babe, but this is going to be fast and hard."

"Good."

Her agreement nearly laid him low. "I'll make it better later." And with that, he skimmed off her panties, and knew he wouldn't last more than a minute.

Marci edged her arms out of her bra straps while he finished undressing. He placed his pager, cell, and gun on the nightstand. When he dropped his jeans and boxers he heard her sharp inhalation, but he didn't look at her. Not yet.

Women always got giddy over his size; he'd learned to take it in stride. In fact, sometimes their enthusiasm almost seemed demeaning. Dumb as it sounded, and he'd *never* admit it to another guy, he wanted to be seen as more than a well-hung stud.

Doing his best to ignore Marci's stare, he pulled out a condom from the dresser drawer and ripped open the foil packet with his teeth.

"Um . . . Osbourne?"

"Hmmm?" Please don't let her start fawning on his proportions.

"Are you sure this'll work?"

His head snapped up in surprise. Marci sounded more than

a little apprehensive, and she was staring at his cock—but not with excitement.

Well, damn.

Her gaze lifted to meet his, and he couldn't help but smile at her reservation. "Don't worry. It'll work."

"You think?"

"I guarantee it." Given her wary look, he probably should spend a little more time reassuring her. But he wanted her too much to waste time with conversation. Instead of telling her, he'd just show her how great it'd be.

She pushed up to one elbow. "I had no idea . . ." Her words trailed off into nothingness.

"You'll like it, Marci, trust me."

"Somehow I'm not as sure as you."

Moving closer to the bed, Ozzie clasped her ankle and said, "I've never hurt a woman."

"I know you wouldn't on purpose, but . . ." She raised a brow at his erection.

Half-laughing, Ozzie used his hold on her ankle to open her legs a little, then he stretched out over her. He cupped her face and looked into eyes round with uncertainty. "We'll be a perfect fit." His voice turned gruff with need. "I swear."

She nodded, but said, "It doesn't seem . . ." Rather than finish that thought, she cleared her throat.

"Seem what?"

A frown marred her brow. "Why didn't you tell me that you. . . ?"

She wasn't finishing her sentences, and Ozzie managed another laugh. "That I wear a magnum extra large condom?" Her skin was so soft, he couldn't stop stroking her cheeks. "Yeah, that'd be a conversation topic, wouldn't it?"

"Magnum extra large? That big?" She nodded. "I rest my case."

Done with the chitchat, Ozzie kissed her gently on the lips and said, "Open your legs more, Marci."

As if preparing for the unthinkable, she slowly sucked in a deep breath, and her legs parted more so that he naturally settled closer. His chest pressed her soft breasts, his erection nudged against the notch of her open legs.

It wasn't close enough.

Watching her, Ozzie reached down between them and parted her soft sex. He didn't enter her yet, he just rested against her. "Okay?"

With his weight on her, she squirmed, and said, "*Oh.*"

He pressed firmly against her little clitoris, and every movement she made stroked her along the ridge of his erection.

Softly, he asked, "Feel good?"

She licked her lips, and nodded.

"How about this?" Shifting the smallest bit, he rocked forward and back, and was rewarded with a groan and the bite of her nails on his shoulders.

"That's what I thought." Cupping her breasts in his hands, Ozzie kissed the corner of her mouth. "I'll fill you up, honey. And you'll hold me so snug. But I won't hurt you. You're almost ready for me. Can you feel how wet you're getting?" He continued to move gently, holding himself in check to keep from rushing her. "Wet enough that I'll go right in. And you'll like it."

"Osbourne . . ." Showing blatant need, she held his face and kissed him deeply.

From the very first time he'd seen Marci Churchill, Ozzie had felt drawn to her. Deep down, he'd known how perfect it'd be with her.

Now he also knew that he loved the taste of her, her scent, the feel of her skin and hair. Her openness and sexual honesty.

Marci *was* a little nuts, but not in a mean-spirited way. She'd focused on his size, but without lascivious glee. How could he keep himself distant from her, when on every level, she touched his heart?

Marci was special, and he needed their time to be special,

too. While Ozzie let her control the kiss, he teased her erect nipples with his thumbs and continued that subtle body friction, back and forth, wetter and hotter with each stroke.

It seemed he'd been denying himself for a lifetime, and if she didn't accept him soon, he'd embarrass himself. That thought no sooner entered his brain than she hooked her legs over his hips, wrapping herself around him.

Out of desperation, Ozzie took that as an invitation to proceed.

He drew back, and this time when he came forward, he sank into that wet heat.

She broke the kiss with a gasp, her eyes closed, her lips parted. Watching her, gauging her every reaction, he pressed in farther. Her nails scored his shoulders, but he didn't mind.

"Easy," he whispered, feeling her clench tight around him as he worked beyond the natural resistance of her body. He kissed her again, stifling her groan, holding her still as he squeezed in deeper and deeper. He wanted all of her. He wanted to bury himself in her.

When her legs dropped to the side of him, her heels bracing against the mattress, he raised his head to look at her. She appeared dazed and excited, and very accepting.

"A little more," he encouraged.

Her breathing turned ragged, and her slender frame went taut.

He slipped one hand beneath her hips, tilted her up, and her body welcomed the rest of him.

Marci arched into him.

Ozzie held perfectly still.

Sweat dampened his shoulders, and he felt his muscles quivering with the restraint. His cock throbbed and pulsed with the need for release.

Through clenched teeth, he whispered, "Talk to me, Marci."

Instead, she moaned, not a moan of pain, but one of acute pleasure. Her arms went around his neck, her legs wound tight around his hips. She opened smoky blue eyes, and murmured low, "*Osbourne . . .*"

He was a goner.

Sealing his mouth over hers in a voracious kiss, he began thrusting, hard and fast, just as he'd warned her it would be.

Unfortunately, she liked it enough that her internal muscles clamped around him, and she made small sounds of rising satisfaction that sent him right over the edge.

He left her mouth to growl, "Sorry, so *damn sorry . . .*" and he came in a blinding rush that wiped all coherent thought from his mind.

Marci held him, caressed him, moaned with him, and when the storm finally passed, she hugged him and put small, sweet kisses on his shoulder.

Lethargy held him for long minutes. In Marci's embrace, he basked in the afterglow of release, the complete elimination of tension and the relaxation of every muscle. It had been a long night and a frustrating morning. The day had passed into afternoon and he was suddenly so tired he couldn't see straight.

He was just about to doze off when Marci let out a shuddering, soft sigh. Ozzie returned to the here and now with startling speed.

Oh, shit. *Talk about blowing it.*

With much effort, he rolled to the side of her and tried to gather his wits. After that disappointing performance, he didn't want to look at her. And with the way his legs still trembled, he wouldn't even be able to make it up to her until he got some sleep.

But he wouldn't be a coward. He'd apologize. He'd man-up and promise to do better next time. Soon. Like in a few hours.

Raising himself on one bent arm, he looked down at her, and was surprised to see her smiling at him.

What the hell did she have to smile about?

Ozzie frowned. "You okay?"

The smile widened. "I'm terrific."

He glanced down over her naked body. Her legs were still parted, and one of her socks had fallen off, leaving a small foot bare. Her silky skin looked rosy. The light brown curls between her thighs were damp.

Hell, maybe he didn't need to sleep after all.

He reached for her, and a distant bark carried over the wind.

Groaning, he flopped back on the bed.

"What's wrong?"

"The dog must have finally seen my car. He's on his way in."

She crawled over the top of him and propped her pointy elbows on his chest. "That's a problem?"

"It's just that he likes a lot of attention when I first get home." Ozzie put both hands on her bottom and patted. Damn, but being this close to her felt nice. Talking with her was nice.

Having sex with her had blown his mind.

"You don't like to give him attention?"

"I do." Her disgruntled frown eased. "But a sexy broad has pretty much taken all my steam. I'm beat."

"Oh." Her lips curled again. "I can take care of him."

That smile was starting to get to him. "Let me up, woman, or we'll be taking part in naked wrestling with a wet dog."

She moved off the bed, stood before him beautifully nude, and stretched. Without a speck of modesty, she bent and picked up her sweatshirt, then shrugged into it. "It's chilly in here."

Ozzie still felt like a furnace, but he said, "I'll adjust the heat." He scooped up his jeans and then caught her arm. "Bathroom is this way."

Leading her out of the bedroom and a little way down the hall, he said, "Wait here. I'll be right out." He closed the bathroom door on her, rid himself of the condom, and splashed his face.

God, he wanted to sleep for a week, but it'd seem pretty crass to bring a woman in, do a wham-bam-thank-you-ma'am, and then leave her to her own devices.

He was such an ass.

He pulled on his jeans and when he stepped out, Marci was peeking into the next room down.

"That's a guestroom. Granny's room is at the end of the hall, with a sewing room in between. When I get to renovating, I plan to connect the bathroom and my bedroom, and turn the sewing room into a guest bath."

She trailed her fingers along a ragged piece of flocked wallpaper in the hall. "This place is huge."

"And run-down. Granny didn't take much to change." He gestured for her to use the bathroom. "Make yourself at home. I'll go down to greet Grimshaw. Join us when you're ready."

"Wait for me! I'll only be a second." And sure enough, she was in and out of the bathroom in a flash. Bare-assed and beautiful, she darted into his bedroom to retrieve her panties and jeans.

They were halfway down the stairs when he heard the clicking of Grimshaw's nails as he raced over the kitchen floor.

Ozzie stepped in front of Marci. "Brace yourself."

A second later, tongue hanging out one side of his mouth, eyes wild with excitement, Grimshaw skidded around the corner. He saw Ozzie, and he howled with berserk rapture before pounding up the stairs in a blur of black fur.

"Oh, Osbourne, he's beautiful."

Ozzie sat on a step so the dog couldn't knock him over and then Grimshaw was in his lap, wiggling and licking to the point that Ozzie couldn't help but chuckle. He tried to get around Ozzie to inspect the newcomer, but his paws were frosty with snow and he was slobbering, so Ozzie played defense for Marci.

He should have known it wasn't necessary. With no hesitation at all, she sat down beside him and let Grimshaw shower her with affection.

Turning her face, she avoided a doggy lick on the lips, and laughed. "You're a wild one, aren't you?"

"He's always like this," Ozzie told Marci.

"He's relieved that you came back." She stroked the dog as he moved back to Ozzie's lap. "With the way your grandmother passed so suddenly, he's never certain if you'll leave him, too."

Ozzie froze at that awful thought. He hugged Grimshaw close and frowned at Marci. "What the hell are you talking about?"

She smiled at the way Grimshaw rested his head on Ozzie's shoulder. "Losing your grandmother has been really hard on him, and adjusting to your schedule isn't easy, either. She didn't work, did she?"

"No. She didn't have to. She owned the house and had enough in the bank to live off the interest."

"So she spent most of her time here with him." With Grimshaw quieter now, Marci studied him. "She died in her sleep?"

"Yeah." How the hell had she known that?

Ozzie had the weird suspicion that she was reading the dog's mind. He shook his head at himself.

"Granny wasn't sick or anything. I spoke with her every day. One day she told me she was feeling tired, so she planned to go to bed early. She was always so full of energy, it worried me, so I told her I'd come out after work. When I got here that next morning, she was gone."

"Whenever she went into town to shop, or whenever she had an appointment, she took Grimshaw with her. He wasn't left alone very often. That's why he runs the property, to keep busy, to try to find someone to keep him company." She scooted closer and held Grimshaw's face up to hers. "Poor baby, you're lonely, aren't you?"

Fury, fueled by guilt, rushed through Ozzie. "I have to work and I have to sleep."

"Oh, I know that. But he doesn't. He's just a dog. All he knows is that his days are suddenly long and empty."

"So what the hell would you have me do?"

She put her arms around Grimshaw and hugged him tight. "You need to get him some permanent company."

Ozzie stiffened. "Uh . . . permanent company?"

Did she mean herself?

Was it such a repugnant idea?

Marci nodded. "A friend to be here when you're not." Looking up at Ozzie, she stared him in the eyes. "I could make a really good suggestion, that is, if you're interested."

And then she started smiling again.

5

Osbourne looked like he'd swallowed his tongue. Why, she didn't know. He obviously loved animals, and he had a big heart, so why would he be so stunned at her suggestion?

"I don't know about this, Marci. To be honest, after our discussion, I hadn't expected you to push like this. I mean, why would you even want to, after that less-than-perfect performance of mine?"

What in the world was he talking about? "Your performance?"

"Well . . . yeah. I pretty much molested you."

Realization dawned. "Oh." She grinned as pleasurable memories swirled through her, then she sat up away from the dog. "Your, er, performance seemed pretty perfect to me."

"Perfect?" If anything, he went more rigid. "You're kidding, right?"

"Not at all. I liked it that you were all wild and out of control and turned on. It was exciting. You're exciting." Then in a whisper, "I'm sorry if I was a little precipitous in my reactions. But there were . . . sensations I've never felt before. And I've wanted you a very long time."

Heat shot into his face and he shoved to his feet. Hands on his hips, brows down in a hot glare, he stared at her for what felt like an eternity. "Are you telling me you came?"

"Osbourne!" Marci covered the dog's ears, but then thought better of that and stood to face him. In a quiet rush, she said, "We should discuss this in *private*."

"Oh, for heaven's sake. The dog doesn't understand us, so answer me."

She tucked in her chin. "You don't know?"

He brought his nose close to hers. "I was a little preoccupied—and don't you dare start smiling again."

Puckering her lips to keep the smile at bay, Marci stared at his sternum. She absolutely, positively, could not look him in the eyes while discussing this. "Yes."

"Yes what?"

A glance at the dog proved they had his undivided attention. She went on tiptoe and breathed into Osbourne's ear, "Yes, I climaxed." And she thought to add, "You were wonderful. Thank you."

He clasped her shoulders and brought her into his chest. "You came?"

She still couldn't look at him. "Of course I did."

Then her feet left the floor and his mouth covered hers, and the dog started barking in glee. By the time Osbourne ended the kiss, she hung limp in his arms.

His now-damp mouth lifted in a cocky grin. "All right."

Marci shook her head at him, totally confused.

His tone gruff and indulgent, he said, "I suppose you can move in."

That brought her gaze to his. "*What?*"

"You can keep Grimshaw company." He lowered her feet to the floor and patted her butt. "We both welcome you."

Marci wasn't at all sure she understood him. Hoping to clarify, she asked carefully, "You want me to move in with you?"

Now he looked uncertain. "You said you wanted to."

"I did?"

"Didn't you?"

She hadn't. But she loved that idea. Surely, Osbourne wouldn't make such an offer unless he cared for her beyond the sexual.

"Marci?"

She gave a firm nod. "Okay."

He groaned in grievous confusion. "Okay *what?*"

"Okay, I'll move in." So that he couldn't change his mind, she patted his chest and then hurried down the stairs. "Show me the rest of your house, then you can go on to bed and get some sleep."

Both he and Grimshaw were hot on her heels.

"Damn it, Marci—"

"You shouldn't swear in front of the dog. You're stressing him."

"He doesn't understand me."

"Maybe not your words, but he feels your tension."

She was almost to the kitchen when Osbourne caught her elbow and spun her around. She landed in his arms, hugged up to his massive chest. "Enough, woman."

Loving the way he put things, Marci smiled.

"And no more of that sappy smiling. It confuses me even more."

That made her laugh. "I smile when I'm happy. Forgive me."

"You said you had an idea of who should keep Grimshaw company. I assumed you meant—"

"Myself? Oh, no, I would never be so presumptuous. But that is an excellent idea, and naturally I'd be thrilled to stay here and be his companion." Even more, she'd love being Osbourne's companion. However, she still wanted to fulfill her other plan. "The thing is, I also know a dog at a shelter that no one wants, but she's wonderful and she'd fit right in here. She's about Grimshaw's age, and she's very passive, so Grimshaw could remain the dominant male—much like his owner. She's used to being kept outside, so all this land will be a joy to her."

If anything, Osbourne looked more furious. She worried about that, until he demanded, "What do you mean, she's used to being outside?"

Such a wonderful man. He was already worrying for the dog when he didn't even know her. "Her previous owners kept her chained to an old car in the backyard. When they decided to move, they dropped her off at the shelter."

"Bastards."

"Yes." Remembering the dog's desolation put a very real pain in Marci's heart. She pressed a hand there and her voice lowered. "She's not the prettiest dog, Osbourne, but she has beautiful brown eyes and a gentle heart and she wants so badly to find a loving home. All she's really known before now is neglect."

Osbourne's hand covered hers. "How about you call the shelter and tell them we'll take her? If the snow doesn't get too thick, we can go pick her up tonight."

Well. If she hadn't already loved him, that would have done it. "Really?"

"Yeah." When she launched herself at him, he caught her and swung her around. Grimshaw went nuts again, barking and running circles around them.

Catering to the dog's excitement, Osbourne lifted Marci into his arms and then sat on the floor. Both she and Grimshaw shared his lap.

They ended up playing for a good fifteen minutes before Marci recalled that Osbourne really did need to get some sleep.

She put a hand to his jaw. "You're exhausted. Go on up to bed and Grimshaw will show me around."

Reluctant, Osbourne glanced at his watch and winced. "Yeah, I suppose I could use a few hours." He yawned and stretched. "You're sure you don't mind?"

She patted Grimshaw. "We'll be fine."

"Don't leave the house."

Another order? "Excuse me?"

"Your reporter buddy might still be poking around. I don't trust him. I'll feel better if I know you're safe inside."

"Oh." His concern pleased her. "Okay, then. Now go." She shooed him away.

Rather than leave, he bent to give her a sound smooch on the lips. "Make yourself at home." Then, to Grimshaw: "Keep an eye on her, boy, and as soon as we can, we'll go get you a woman friend."

Whether or not Grimshaw understood, he yapped at that promise.

Later, when Ozzie awoke from a sound sleep, he noticed several things at once.

First was the time. He'd planned to sleep only a couple of hours to refresh him, and instead he'd conked out for five hours. It was nearing Marci's bedtime now. Shit.

Next, he heard the barking, and not just Grimshaw's bark. Another dog? He sat up, wondering if she'd gone out without telling him. He didn't like that idea at all, and if they were going to make this work, they'd have to set up a few ground rules.

Then he inhaled the delicious scent that filled the air. Marci had cooked for him? His stomach rumbled, reminding him that he hadn't eaten anything since that breakfast sandwich early in the morning.

As he left the bed, he also heard the chatter and laughter. Did she have company? Had that damned reporter come back?

In his boxers, he left the bedroom and went to the top of the stairs. He could hear music playing and Marci speaking, but she didn't sound alarmed. Curious, he went to investigate.

The kitchen was empty, but a big pot of soup simmered on

the stove, filling the air with fragrant steam. His stomach rumbled again.

Stepping back into the foyer, he listened, and realized the music came from the family room. One glimpse into the room, and he froze.

There in front of the television, with music videos turned on, wearing only a T-shirt, panties, and socks, Marci was doing aerobics. While she moved to the beat of the music, she talked to the dogs. Plural.

Grimshaw paid no attention to Marci's prattle. He was too focused on a big, loose-skinned female dog sprawled on the floor. From Ozzie's quick glimpse of the animal, she appeared to be a Labrador–Beagle mix. A few scars marred her beige fur, and she was missing the tip of one drooping ear. She lay flat on the floor, her head on her front paws. Her eyes—big, beautiful eyes, just as Marci had claimed—took in everything at once: Marci, the television, and Grimshaw.

Whenever Grimshaw got near her face, the dog half-cowered, and licked him.

Ozzie's heart turned over.

He started to speak, and Marci bent from the waist, causing the words to strangle in his throat.

"Don't worry, Grimshaw. I'll explain to Osbourne when he awakens, and we'll see what we can do. I'm sure he'll agree, and it might even be a comfort to him, too. But I have to be careful. He thinks I'm a kook and I don't want to do anything to encourage those sentiments."

Guilt roiled inside him. She was a kook, but now he considered it cute. And sweet. She used her kookiness to help animals, even when it earned her disdain from others.

"It's a miracle I'm here in the first place. Most guys are really freaked out by me. Do you know one young man I dated was so certain I'd flipped my lid that he went to Bethany and offered to help her get me committed!"

Torn between the luxury of watching Marci's sensual, fluid

movements in a state of undress, and hearing the painful reminder of how hurt she'd been, Ozzie didn't know if he should speak up or slip away unannounced.

"Deep down," she continued, "I think he cares as much about me as I do him. From the beginning I've felt connected to him."

He'd felt that connection, too. And sometimes it spooked him, because Marci was so unlike other women. Not just unique but gifted in a way that defied all reason.

"It didn't matter that I scared off other men, but I don't want to scare off Ozzie. I want to try to make this work. It's just that with him—I suppose because I trust him and care for him—I sometimes blurt things out, and then everything is ruined."

Because he couldn't tear himself away, Ozzie cleared his throat and asked, "So this is my new dog?"

Screeching, Marci straightened upright and pushed sweaty hair away from her face. Eyes watchful, she tried an uncertain smile and said, "How long have you been there?"

"Not long." He eyed her up and down. "You look great, by the way."

Both animals had jumped at the intrusion. As usual, Grimshaw went berserk, more so now that he had something to show Ozzie, meaning a new friend. Running between Ozzie and the other dog, he barked and pranced and acted much like an excited puppy.

The new dog stood, but she tucked in her tail and lowered her head, and basically tried to make herself as small as possible.

Then she peed on his hardwood floor.

Marci said, "Oops. Sorry about that. She's still nervous. I'll clean it up."

"No. It's okay. I'll get it in a minute." Doing his best to ignore Marci's exposed legs and the way he could see her nipples through the tee, Ozzie went to one knee and held his hand out to the dog. "It's okay, girl. Don't be afraid." Then to Marci, "Does she have a name?"

"Lakeisha."

He smiled. "Did you name her that?"

She shrugged. "Her previous owners just called her dog, but Lakeisha suits her, and it goes well with Grimshaw."

"I agree." The dog watched him, then crept forward with hope bright in her big eyes. "You're a beauty, aren't you? It's okay. I won't bite, even if you do. C'mon. That's it."

She finally inched close enough for Ozzie to stroke under her chin.

Relying on Marci's talent, he asked, "Am I winning her over?"

Marci eased over to sit beside him. "Yes. She's more worried than afraid. This is all so new to her."

Grimshaw plopped down by Marci and tipped his head at Lakeisha.

"Is he jealous?"

Laughing softly, Marci said, "No. He's just trying to figure her out. He really wants to get to know her, but she's shying away from him. Grimshaw is a very gentle dog. He doesn't want to spook her, either."

Lakeisha got near enough to sit by Ozzie. She kept her head low, her ears down, but the more he petted her, the closer she got.

"She likes you, Osbourne. Isn't that wonderful?"

"Yeah." He rested his right hand on Lakeisha's neck, and gave Grimshaw a few pats with his left. "How'd she get here?"

"When I called the owner of the shelter to say we'd take her, he offered to drop her off. He's a friend and I think he was afraid we'd change our minds."

Ozzie acknowledged that with a nod. "What is it you want to tell me?"

She pokered up and stared at him. "You said you hadn't been there long."

"I wasn't. Just long enough to hear you tell the dogs that you'd talk to me about something. I'm starving and that soup smells awesome, but I want to hear what you have to say first."

It wasn't easy for Ozzie, because she sat beside him cross-legged, smelling of warm woman and wearing very little. But he sensed this was important and, like her, he didn't want to blow things.

"Your grandmother always decorated for the holidays."

Of all the things she might have said, he hadn't expected that. "Yeah, so?"

"Grimshaw misses it. He wants to see the decorated tree and the lights, and he wants to hear the music. Did you know your grandmother always had a real tree and Grimshaw had a terrible time resisting the urge to mark it?"

Ozzie stared at her. "How do you know that?"

Her expression went blank.

"Did you see photos of the house during the holidays?" He didn't know of any photos left lying around, but he wanted to be sure.

"No."

Lakeisha rolled to her back, and Ozzie absently scratched her belly. "So, tell me, Marci. How did you know?"

Staring down at her twined hands, she whispered, "Grimshaw has those memories."

"And you're a pet psychic."

Her shoulders sank. "I won't apologize for who I am."

"Of course not."

She frowned at him. "I know you don't believe me, but it's true. Grimshaw knew your grandmother as well as you did. He knows that she was very proud of you, and that she made special cookies for you at Christmas."

"She always sent a batch home with me."

"He has memories of playing in the snow with you. You've always been good to him and—"

Ozzie bent and took her mouth in a gentle kiss that sufficiently hushed her. "I like who you are, Marci Churchill."

"You do?"

"Yeah." Rather than belabor that point, he added, "And you're sexy as hell when you're sweaty."

"Sweaty?" Her brows pinched together, then shot upward. "Oh, I forgot!" She jumped to her feet and plucked the damp shirt away from her breasts. Fidgeting, she said, "I think I'll go shower while you eat."

He pushed to his feet, too, then stared down at her. "Tomorrow we can put up the lights. Maybe not all of them, since it's so close to Christmas already, but enough to make Grimshaw happy. And we can go find a tree. Granny always took one from the property. Not the best, you know. But a scraggly one that looked like it wouldn't have made it anyway. With the right decorations, even a half-dead tree looks nice."

Her smile lit up the room. "I'd love that."

"I'll clean up Lakeisha's mess. Go get your shower."

"You don't mind?"

"She's my dog now, right? I know she needs time to adjust. It's not a big deal."

She looked at him with naked adoration, then touched her fingers to his chest. Shyly, she asked, "What about you? Do you want to shower?"

An invitation? "Will the soup keep for another hour or so?"

Her eyes darkened. "I'll turn it on low."

Marci knew she should feel a little timid. After all, her sexual experiences were limited, and she'd never been with a man like Osbourne. But all she felt at that moment was anticipation. She wanted them both naked, now. She wanted his body against hers, she wanted to taste him—she wanted to feel him inside her.

He wore only snug boxers, and she loved looking at his broad chest, his strong shoulders. And his abdomen. The man had an impressive six-pack that begged to be stroked.

Locking her fingers together, Marci cautioned herself not to rush him. Earlier, when they'd made love, she'd been such a twit. First, his size had startled her, but Lord have mercy, she'd known only average men, and there was nothing average about Osbourne.

Then, within minutes of him touching her, she'd forgotten her worries and had been ready to climax. She'd tried to hold back, without much success. Luckily, he'd been just as aroused, and in his own release he hadn't even realized how uncontrolled she'd become.

She wasn't a wild woman. Sex for her had been pleasant, but not overwhelming. With Osbourne it was . . . explosive. Mind-blowing. So very, very special.

"You're okay?" Osbourne asked.

She nodded, cleared her throat, and said the first thing that came to her mind. "That tub doesn't look big enough for both of us."

He smiled. "We'll have to stay close, won't we?" He bent to turn on the shower, and the small room began to fill with steam.

Old-fashioned black and pink ceramic tiles surrounded the narrow tub. Osbourne parted the clear shower curtain, and when he straightened and faced her, his expression was hard and dark with desire. A quick glimpse down proved he was already hard, and it was all she could do not to reach for him.

He stood within inches of her. She'd pinned up her hair to keep it from getting wet, and Osbourne smoothed back a wayward curl. "The dogs are outside playing, so we shouldn't be interrupted."

Marci cleared her throat. "Do you have a condom in here?"

He shook his head. "We'll start here, but finish up in the bedroom. I'm not going to be rushed this time."

"Oh. Okay."

"You're not still nervous?"

"Nervous?" She wanted to jump him.

"You know, most women who comment on my . . . proportions, do so with excitement. I wasn't expecting it to worry you."

Marci licked her lips and gave him a dose of honesty. "I was startled, that's all."

His big hand cupped her face. "But now you like it?"

Her smile came easily. "Don't be silly. I want *you,* Osbourne Decker. It doesn't matter if you're big or small, or somewhere in between. You're still you."

For the longest time, Osbourne just stared at her. He had an odd, arrested look on his face. Then he gave a wry smile. "Well, I prefer big, but thank you for the sentiment."

Without her realizing it, he'd caught the hem of her T-shirt, and before she could think to say anything he whisked it off over her head. For only a moment, he admired her breasts, saying, "You are so beautiful." Then he bent to tug down her panties.

While on his knees, he cuddled her bare behind, drew her forward for a sizzling kiss to her navel and a slow lick down . . .

"*Osbourne.*" Stumbling, Marci stepped out of reach and climbed into the shower. The warm water trickled down her body, doing little to help compose her. From the inside out, she trembled.

Wearing a sexy half-smile, Osbourne stood again. "Shy?"

She shook her head. "Sweaty. From my workout. Perhaps we should shower first—"

He laughed. "You taste good, Marci." After shoving down his boxers, he joined her in the shower. "But I want a better taste."

She'd never survive this. "Okay." Marci put her arms

around him and kissed his mouth. But Osbourne allowed that for only so long. The man seemed intent on devastating her.

Using the fragrant bar of soap, he lathered his hands and washed her all over, taking his time on her breasts, her belly, her behind. The soap made his fingers slippery, adding to the sensations.

This time when he knelt, Marci braced her back against the cool tile wall and planted her feet apart. Anticipation built, but Osbourne only looked at her, stroked her belly with the backs of his knuckles, trailed his fingertips through her pubic hair.

Her heart threatened to punch through her ribs. She couldn't take much more of this. She was about to encourage him to hurry things along when, after gently parting her, he leaned forward and closed his mouth over her.

"Oh, God."

There was no prelude, no easing into things. His hot tongue moved over her, in her, and his teeth nibbled on her most delicate flesh. Marci squeezed her eyes shut and moaned.

To keep her close and still, Osbourne opened one hand over her backside. With the other, he touched her and teased her. It was enough. It was too much.

Slowly, with infinite care, Osbourne concentrated his efforts on her clitoris while working his fingers deep inside her.

Somehow, he kept her upright through the orgasm, even though her legs felt useless and her bones were like noodles. When the sensations began to fade, Osbourne stood with her and cradled her close.

Marci had no idea what to say. "Thank you" didn't seem appropriate. "Wow" would be an understatement. "Your turn" was a given.

"Let's dry off and head to the bed."

Marci nodded, but she couldn't quite stand on her own.

Chuckling, Osbourne reached for the towel and did all the work for her. By the time he finished, she'd recovered enough to walk to the bedroom under her own steam. As they went down the hall, they heard the dogs back in the kitchen, and it sounded like they were playing.

Marci felt good. Really good. Things were coming together nicely.

And when Osbourne put on his condom and stretched out over her, it was even better. Now, she thought, if only it lasts.

6

It was nearing midnight, and Ozzie couldn't keep his thoughts—or his hands—off her. Marci curled into his side, her naked thigh over his, her head in the crook of his shoulder. Cuddling with her left him with a deep sense of inner peace, and a physical sense of desperate need.

She was quiet, but she wasn't asleep, not with her hot breath brushing his skin and her inquisitive fingers busy on his chest.

He kissed the top of her head and said, "I feel like a horny high school kid."

With a purr, Marci trailed her hands down to his abdomen, perilously close to his groin. "You feel like a very sexy man to me."

After making love, they'd eaten soup, talked quietly, and then played with the dogs for a while before getting them settled in the hallway.

Ozzie should have been sated, but already he wanted her again.

Given the way she toyed with him, she felt the same.

His second effort at making love to her had been an improvement, but it hadn't abated the urgency he felt. He was starting to worry that he'd always feel that way with Marci—on edge, anxious, soft and hard at the same time.

She left him so confused, he didn't know what he wanted, or for how long, or when. Sex, definitely. Time with her, sure. A future? He'd never thought so, not with lessons learned from Ainsley.

But were there any real similarities between the two women? It nettled him to think he'd allowed Ainsley's machinations to affect him so deeply. So she'd lied, and tormented, and—

Marci slid atop him and put her mouth to his chin in a gentle kiss, then his brow, each cheekbone—and Ozzie was a goner. Her touch obliterated all thoughts of other women. Concerns drifted away, replaced by arousal.

He cupped her face, kissed her hungrily, and Marci kept pace with him every step of the way.

Very early the next morning, bright sunshine, reflecting off the snow-covered landscape, flowed in through the windows and stirred Ozzie awake. Automatically, he reached for Marci but found her side of the bed empty. He opened one eye. Huh. He'd need to talk to her about sneaking out on him, and he knew she had sneaked, because he was a light sleeper. She should have awakened him.

He glanced at the clock. Seven-thirty. Still early enough to put in a full day. He stretched, and grinned.

Today they would put up lights and a tree . . . things he hadn't considered doing because the loss of his grandmother had taken him out of the holiday mood.

Marci had gotten him right back into it, in a big way.

He wanted to make her happy. He wanted to make Grimshaw and Lakeisha happy.

And he knew that pleasing them would have pleased his grandmother also. She had no patience for melancholy and she'd loved him enough that she never wanted to see him in a funk.

He couldn't wait to go pick out a few gifts for Marci, and

maybe a few things for the dogs. Because he often took walks with Grimshaw around the property, he already knew the perfect tree to cut. He could envision the house lit up with twinkle lights after he cleared the walkways and porch. This Christmas would be a special one, a tribute to his grandmother, and a chance to get closer to Marci.

Sudden, furious barking brought him out of his revelry and upright in the bed. Grimshaw sounded outraged. The dog was so friendly that Ozzie wasn't accustomed to hearing that particular sound.

Seconds later, as he was leaving the bed and searching for his jeans, Grimshaw's paws hit the closed door and he demanded immediate entrance. Forgoing the jeans, Ozzie opened the door and Grimshaw, overly anxious, immediately turned to go back downstairs.

Ozzie didn't need to be a pet psychic to know that Grimshaw wanted him to follow. Something was wrong.

Buck-naked, Ozzie raced down the steps. He could hear Lakeisha snarling and his heart shot into his throat. He rounded the corner of the kitchen—and came to a stunned stop.

Marci had her hands full holding Lakeisha back. Lakeisha fought her, but with good reason.

That damned annoying reporter, Vaughn Wayland, had wedged himself in the doggy door, apparently trying to break in. From all appearances, he was stuck. Grimshaw joined Lakeisha with a lot of threatening bluster and a growl that sounded feral and deadly.

Vaughn whimpered and choked in fear.

Marci spoke to the dogs, saying, "It's okay, guys. He's an idiot, but we don't want him to be a mangled idiot. Now, please calm down. Osbourne will take care of him. You don't have to do a thing."

Neither dog appeared to be listening to her.

Ozzie shouted, "*Just what the hell is going on here?*"

Silence dropped like a lead weight.

Everyone turned to look at him—Vaughn and Grimshaw

with relief, Lakeisha with uncertainty, and Marci with wide-eyed shock.

"Osbourne!" Her face went red-hot. "You're *naked.*"

He slashed a hand in the air over that. "How long has he been there?"

"Not long," she choked, then she ran to get a dishcloth to try to cover him. He took it from her and tossed it aside. The dogs sat back to watch.

"Vaughn, you've got some explaining to do."

The idiot started whimpering again. He had his head, right shoulder, and arm through the opening. But the rest of him remained in the mudroom.

Ozzie took two steps to stand over him.

Marci covered her eyes, but Vaughn stared up at him in fear.

Crossing his arms over his chest, Ozzie said, "You know I'm going to have your sorry ass arrested, don't you?"

In a pathetic whine, Vaughn cried, "I just needed an interview, that's all."

"There'll be an interview, all right. With the authorities. You can explain to them why you broke into my house."

Vaughn turned pleading eyes on Marci. "Just a few confirmations, that's all I need."

She joined Ozzie's side. "You're lucky I didn't turn the dogs loose on you. Lakeisha really doesn't like you at all, and that makes Grimshaw, who's usually such a friendly fellow, despise you as well."

Vaughn's head dropped and nearly hit the floor. "I'll do the article anyway."

Shaking her head, Marci said, "Go ahead. It won't be the first time. But people will call you a fool. Trust me, Mr. Wayland, no one will believe you."

His head lifted again. "But it's true, isn't it?"

Marci sniffed. "I have no idea what you're talking about." She turned on her heel and strode away.

"Where are you going?" Ozzie asked.

Over her shoulder, she called back, "To get you some pants. If you're going to call your police friends, I don't want them to see you like this."

He grinned—until he looked back at Vaughn Wayland. The bastard looked utterly defeated. How must Marci feel? She'd said it wasn't the first time someone had done an article on her. She also said no one ever believed in her ability.

Yet that didn't stop her from helping animals. Her heart was too big for her to stop.

Damn it, he was falling in love with her.

To the dogs, he said, "Watch him while I go make a call."

Grimshaw perked up his ears and plopped down right in front of Vaughn. His lips rolled back to show sharp teeth and a growl poured out of his throat.

Looking love struck, Lakeisha sat behind Grimshaw.

As Ozzie strode over to the phone, he thought, *What a way to start the day.*

Then a pair of jeans hit him in the stomach and he looked up to see Marci eyeing him. Or, more precisely, she eyed a certain part of his anatomy.

"Does my nakedness bother you, Marci?" he teased.

She muttered, "You're shameless," but her gaze remained below his navel.

He couldn't help it—he smiled. Marci Churchill was in his house. She eyed him with lust.

It really was a hell of a way to start any day.

He was beginning to think it'd be a good way to start most of his days, from now until the end of eternity.

Now that he didn't have to worry about the reporter bothering them, Ozzie looked forward to Christmas morning with a lot of anticipation.

Since Marci had come to stay with him, everything had changed. For the better. In too many ways to count, she enhanced his life. The dogs loved her, and he loved the dogs.

Dining with her was always a unique experience, because Marci never indulged in ordinary conversation. She could still make him nuts on occasion, but now he was starting to like it.

She kissed him good-bye and welcomed him home with a hug, but she didn't smother him. She was independent, but not prickly about it. She had her own interests, and he was one of them.

Making love with her was the stuff of fantasies, but sleeping with her, listening to her even breathing, holding her close, was pretty damn sweet, too. Because of his third-shift job, though, he didn't get to sleep with her as often as he'd have liked.

When it came to his house, Marci had wonderful ideas about how to remodel. When their ideas clashed, she didn't push the issue. Unlike other women he'd known, she didn't insist that her view was the right or better one. For that reason more than any other, he found himself agreeing with her more often than not.

Little by little, Marci taught him how to read various signals from the dogs. A certain look or gesture, a sudden show of excitement. When he paid attention, it wasn't so hard to figure out what the dogs felt and why.

They knew when he started to get ready for work, and they reacted to it. Lakeisha would get antsy and Grimshaw would mope. Now that Ozzie was keyed in to their moods, he took the time to reassure them each and every night, and he felt better about leaving them with Marci there to keep them happy.

He couldn't decipher their thoughts the way she did, and when it came to other animals, he was hopeless. She loved to chat with the birds and squirrels that came each day for the seed she put out. She even conversed with white-tailed deer and the occasional fox. It amused Ozzie, but he no longer felt so clueless about her talent.

He no longer doubted her.

After the holidays, she'd probably need to return to her aerobics job. That thought didn't set well with him. He'd gotten used to having her around. The dogs needed her. They all meshed.

He considered cementing their relationship in some way, but he was still cautious enough that he held back. Marci's uniqueness made her special, but it also made her unpredictable. When he used his brain, instead of his gonads, he knew it'd be wise not to rush things.

For that reason, he refrained from any and all declarations and just tried to enjoy his time with her.

The night before Christmas Eve, while Ozzie was at the station working, another storm dumped seven inches of snow, topping it with sleet. He imagined the house would look beautiful all frosted in white, glowing with the lights they'd strung up from every window and door, every bush and tree.

In another hour, his shift would end. Marci would be up waiting for him. She and the dogs would greet him at the door. After breakfast, he'd take the dogs out to play, then he and Marci would indulge in some alone time. A wonderful routine.

He could hardly wait.

Ozzie had just pulled out of the parking lot when his pager went off. A rape-and-kidnapping suspect had barricaded himself in a woman's home. Neighbors said they heard the woman's screams.

With everything he'd need for a call out already on his person or in his truck, Ozzie turned around and headed to the location. He figured it'd take him less than fifteen minutes to get there, but fifteen minutes could mean life or death to a hostage.

As SWAT, he was used to being on call and didn't even think to resent the intrusion. It was his job, and he was damn good at it. Marci faded from his mind and he went into SWAT mode.

As soon as Ozzie and the other team members arrived, a detective filled them in. Ozzie learned that the suspect had a violent past and an extensive criminal history.

"Everything I've got right now is really vague," the detective explained. "I know that we've got an adult female being held against her will. Her mouth and hands are duct taped."

Ozzie nodded as, by rote, he prepared himself.

"We believe the victim is an old girlfriend of his, but we haven't been able to confirm that yet."

In rapid order, the SWAT team evacuated all the neighbors. Some joined a television crew outside a blockade down the street, while others made use of an enclosed unit brought in to offer a place of warmth for the residents. Even though uniformed officers kept the reporters and camera crews too far away to interfere, Ozzie detested having them around during a time of crisis. He could do nothing about it, so he ignored them.

The SWAT team concentrated on establishing contact with the suspect. The man was antagonistic, desperate, and probably pumped up on drugs. After a couple of hours, when he still refused to come out peacefully, the team formulated a new plan.

They couldn't wait any longer, not with a female hostage inside.

Most of the SWAT team spread out, taking sniper positions that gave them the cleanest shots. Then, a couple of them deliberately broke the front windows of the home, drawing the suspect's attention while Ozzie slipped in through the back. On silent feet, he crept forward. He could hear the suspect cursing, outraged over the broken windows.

And he could hear the woman crying.

Keeping his H&K .40 caliber at the ready, he edged around a wall—and came face to face with the suspect. The panicked bastard fired a shot at him, but Ozzie was already moving.

Without a single second's hesitation, Ozzie brought his forearm up and slammed it into the man's face.

The man's nose shattered and he dropped his gun while staggering backward. In a heartbeat, Ozzie had him contained.

He called in the rest of the team, and the crisis was over, with no innocents injured.

All in all, a job well done.

Once the scene had been cleared, the suspect arrested, and the hostage transported to the hospital via ambulance, Ozzie started for home. Reporters tried to interview him, but he dodged them.

As usual, the adrenaline began to fade, making him bone tired. But today, he wouldn't be heading home to an empty house. He thought of Marci waiting for him, and contentment seeped in.

The snow was thick on the ground and it crunched beneath his tires as he pulled down the long drive. He parked, trod through the white stuff to the door, and stomped to clear his boots.

To his bemusement, no one stood at the door waiting.

He walked in, heard an awful racket, and located Marci seated on the family room floor with both dogs, in front of the television. Tears tracked her cheeks and the dogs were howling, which probably explained why she hadn't heard him arrive.

"What's going on?"

They all looked up at once. For two seconds, time stood still—then they rushed him. The dogs reached him first, jumping and barking and circling. Sniffling, Marci threw herself against him.

Getting worried, Ozzie caught her close. "What is it, honey? What's wrong?"

She hiccupped, and burrowed closer. "I'm sorry," she said, and her voice sounded strained and unsteady. "I know you don't want a woman who frets. I tried not to."

Her hands knotted in his coat and she pushed back to glare at him. "But let me tell you, Osbourne, it's unreasonable of you to make such demands."

He had no idea what she was talking about. As usual.

When he said nothing, she tried to shake him. "We saw

that awful situation on the news!" New tears welled up. "The reporters said what you did, and that you got shot at, but they didn't know anything beyond that."

"Damned reporters," he grumbled. "I'm fine."

"I see that. *Now.* But you could have been killed."

His mood lightened and he had to fight a smile. "So you were worried about me?"

"Worried, and . . ." She gulped, hugging him close again. "And so proud. You saved that woman."

Still amused at her, and touched by her concern, Ozzie ran his hands up and down her back. "It's my job, honey."

"And, thank God, you're very good at it."

She wasn't going to complain about the danger? She wouldn't ask him to quit? Ozzie had never felt so loved—until Lakeisha peed on his foot in excitement.

"Oh, hell." He jumped out of the way and poor Lakeisha lowered her head in shame.

Marci switched alliances in an instant. "Osbourne, she's sorry. It was just an accident. She's been as worried as me."

"Is that so?" More than likely, the dogs were reacting to Marci being upset, but he didn't want to correct her.

"It's okay, Lakeisha," she said to the dog. "He understands. Osbourne, tell her you understand."

"I understand." He scratched the dog's ears and she relaxed again.

Marci nudged Ozzie, saying as an aside, "Don't forget Grimshaw. We don't want him to get jealous."

Ozzie wasn't sure if it was Marci's emotional upheaval, her instruction, her understanding, or the way she catered to the animals, but in that instant, everything became crystal clear to him.

Marci wasn't like other women. She sure as hell wasn't like Ainsley. Marci didn't have a mean or manipulative bone in her entire body. She was so open with him that she showed him a side of her he'd once scorned.

Her heart was big enough to care for everyone and everything, even when it earned her derision from others. And most of all, she trusted him.

Ozzie realized that he not only trusted her, too, he loved her. Everything about her.

Before he could think to censor his thoughts, he said, "I'm proud of you, too, Marci."

"You are? But why?"

"You're gifted, and caring, and strong. Strong enough to keep helping animals despite the grief people give you."

Her eyes welled with more tears. "Thank you."

"I love you, Marci."

She froze. Dashing away the tears, she blinked at him, then nodded. "I love you, too. I have almost from the first time we met. I knew you'd be different." And to the dogs, she said, "Didn't I tell you he was different?"

Ozzie touched her chin to bring her attention back to him. "Will you move in with me for good?"

"Yes."

Her quick answer had him grinning so big, his cheeks hurt. "Will you help me remodel the house so that we both like it?"

"I'd love to."

He went for broke. Dropping to one knee and taking her hand, he asked, "Will you marry me?"

Her smile trembled, then broke into a grin that rivaled his own. "The dogs think it's a wonderful idea."

"They're obviously smart dogs." He kissed her hand. "So what do you think?"

Laughing, she straddled him, then laughed some more when the dogs started jumping on them. "I think I'm getting everything I ever wanted this Christmas."

And he was getting everything he hadn't even realized he wanted. Thank God Lucius had insisted he keep an eye on Marci, otherwise he'd still be a lonely, miserable fool.

Now all he had to do was explain to Lucius why he'd disregarded his order not to touch Marci. Maybe when he got a ring on her finger, that'd do the trick.

"You want to go shopping?"

She pressed back to look at him. "Now?"

"Yeah." He kissed her. "I have one more gift to buy you, but I'd like your input."

"What is it?"

"An engagement ring." Ozzie stood with her still wrapped around him and started for the stairs. "I want every available male to know you're mine."

She laughed. "I knew you watched them watching me."

Of course she had. There was a lot Marci knew, because she was a very special, intuitive person. And now she knew they belonged together.

What had started out as the loneliest Christmas of his life was now the very best. He hugged her tightly and said, "Thank you, Marci."

"You're very, very welcome." She kissed him, and whispered, "Merry Christmas."

The Christmas Present

1

Why, oh why, couldn't this be a normal storm? Instead of soft, pretty snowflakes dotting her windshield, wet snow clumps froze as soon as they hit, rendering the wipers inadequate to keep the windshield clear. Even with the defroster on high, blasting hot air that threatened to choke her, the snow accumulated.

Refusing to stop and refusing to acknowledge the headlights behind her, Beth Monroe kept her hands tight on the wheel. Let him freeze to death. Let him follow her all the way to Gillespe, Kentucky.

She'd still ignore him.

She'd ignore everything that had happened between them, and everything she felt, everything he'd made her feel.

Oh God, she was so embarrassed. If only she could have a do-over, an opportunity to change the past, to correct mistakes and undo bad plans. That'd be the most perfect Christmas present ever.

A simple do-over.

But of course, there was no such thing, not even with the magic of Christmas. And there was nothing simple about the current mess of her life, or the complicated way that Levi Masterson made her feel.

Finally, after hours that seemed an eternity, her stepbrother's hotel came into view. Beth breathed a sigh of relief. Now if she could just park and get inside before Levi shanghaied her. Ben knew of her imminent arrival. She could count on him to send Levi packing.

Not that she wanted Levi hurt . . . or Ben for that matter.

Fool, fool, fool.

Tires sliding on the frozen parking lot, Beth maneuvered her Ford into an empty spot. After shutting off the engine, she grabbed her purse, a tote bag loaded with presents, and her overnight bag. Arms laden, she charged from the vehicle.

Three steps in, her feet slipped out from under her. The stuffed overnight bag threw her off balance and she went flying in the air to land flat on her back. Her bag spilled. Wind rushed from her lungs. Icy cold seeped into her spine and tush.

For only a moment, Beth lay there, aching from head to toe, stunned and bemused. Then she heard Levi's hasty approach.

"Beth, damn it—"

Determination got her back on her feet. She gathered her belongings with haste and then, slipping and sliding, wincing with each step, she shouted into the wind, "*Go away, Levi.*"

Harsh with determination, he yelled back, "You know I won't."

Daring a quick glance over her shoulder, Beth saw him ten feet behind her. He hadn't even parked! His truck sat crossways in the middle of the lot to block hers in, idling, the exhaust sending plumes of heated air to mingle in the frozen wind.

Good God, he looked furious!

Beth lunged forward and reached the door of the diner attached to Ben's hotel. She yanked it open and sped into the warm interior. The tote bag of presents fell out of her hands, scattering small gifts across the floor. Her overnight bag dropped from her numb fingers.

Several people looked up—all of them family.

Oh hell.

Why couldn't there have been crowds of nonfilial faces? An unbiased crowd, that's what she sought. Instead she found Noah and Ben in close conversation at a table. Their wives, Grace and Sierra, sat at a booth wrapping gifts. And her father and stepmother paused in their efforts to festoon a large fir tree situated in the corner.

Upon seeing her, her father's face lit up. He started to greet her—and then Levi shoved through the door, radiating fury, crowding in behind Beth so that she jolted forward with a startled yelp to keep from touching him.

In a voice deep and resolute, vibrating with command, he ordered, "Not another step, Beth. I mean it."

She winced, and peeked open one eye to view her audience.

Not good.

Levi obviously had no idea of the challenge he'd just issued, or the uproar he'd cause by using that tone with her in front of her family.

And now it was too late.

She hadn't wanted this. She wanted only time to think, to hide from her mortifying and aberrant behavior, to . . . She didn't know what she wanted, damn it, and it wasn't fair that Levi refused to give her a chance to figure it out.

Muttering to herself, she dropped to her knees to gather the now damp and disheveled gifts one more time. As she did so, she said, "Hello, Dad. Hello . . . everyone else." She tried to sound jovial rather than frustrated and anxious and at the end of her rope.

She failed miserably.

With a protectiveness that still amazed Beth, her stepbrothers moved as one. Noah's expression didn't bode well, and Ben appeared equally ready to declare war. Even her calm, reasonable father stalked forward with blood in his eyes.

Plopping her belongings on a nearby booth, Beth held up both hands. "Wait!"

No one did. From one second to the next, Levi had her behind him . . . as if to *protect* her? From her *family?*

Unfortunately, even that simple touch from him, in no way affectionate or seductive, had Beth's tummy fluttering and her skin warming.

She quickly shrugged off her coat.

Levi took it from her, then asked, "Did you hurt yourself when you fell?"

"No. You can leave with a clear conscience. I'm fine." She reached for her coat.

He held it out of her reach. "I'm not going anywhere, so you can quit trying to get rid of me."

The men drew up short. Her father barked, "Who the hell are you?"

Levi turned to face their audience. Positive that she didn't want him to answer that himself, Beth yelled from behind him, "He's a friend." And she tried to ease backward away from him.

"A whole lot more than a friend," Levi corrected, and he stepped back to close the distance she'd just gained.

"Where's her fiancé?" Noah asked.

"Busy," Beth said.

"Gone," Levi answered in a bark. He reached back and caught Beth's wrist. His thumb moved over her skin, a gentle contrast to the iron in his tone. "For good."

Confused, Ben asked, "You mean dead?"

"Far as Beth is concerned, yes."

Oh, for crying out loud. Knowing she couldn't let this continue, Beth yanked her wrist free and, without quite touching any part of Levi's big, hard body, went on tiptoe to see beyond him.

The masculine expressions facing her didn't bode well.

She summoned a smile that felt sickly. "Hello, Dad. Brandon is fine, but we're not engaged anymore."

Kent Monroe brought his brows down. "Since when?"

"Since she's with me now instead," Levi told them.

"No," Beth corrected sweetly, "I'm not."

Levi half turned to face her. "Wanna bet?"

His challenge got everyone moving again.

Oh God, she had to do something. "Dad," Beth begged, "I don't want him hurt."

Her father stopped in his tracks. Noah and Ben did not.

But her lovely sisters-in-law took control.

"Noah," Grace called from across the room. "You heard her."

Frowning, Noah paused about three feet from Levi. "I also heard him."

Sierra, a little more outgoing than Grace, raced up to Ben's side and thumped his shoulder. "Knock off the King Kong impersonation, Ben. You're embarrassing me."

"You'll survive." Keeping his eyes on Levi, Ben crossed his arms over his chest and waited.

For reasons that Beth couldn't begin to fathom, Levi stood there as if he'd take all three of them on at once. Idiot.

Determined to gain control, she chanced touching him long enough to give him a good pinch. "They're my *family*, Levi."

He nodded, but didn't relax.

Fed up, Beth moved around him. "I'm sorry for the dramatic entrance everyone. Levi is a friend—"

"Damn it, Beth, we left friendship behind days ago."

Beth let her eyes sink shut. She'd kill him. She'd never speak to him again. She'd—

His hand caught her shoulder and he turned her to face him. As if they stood alone, as if he had no concept of privacy or manners, Levi lowered his nose to almost touch hers.

In a voice that carried to every ear in the room, he ground out, "I've had enough, Beth. I mean it. We're both adults, both healthy, and finally we're both single. It's ridiculous for you to be embarrassed just because—"

"Don't!"

But her warning came too late, and Levi had already said too much. Silence reigned as everyone absorbed his meaning.

Then she felt it, the smiles, the amusement, the awful comprehension.

It took three breaths before Beth could speak.

Eyes narrowed, she nodded at Levi, turned to face her family, and announced, "I've changed my mind. Hurt him all you want."

And with that, she literally ran away.

Noah and Ben kept Levi from following.

In rapid succession, a dozen different emotions zinged through Levi's mind. Damn it, he'd loved her forever, he'd finally had her, and the reality far outshone the fantasy.

But she was ashamed—of him, and of what they'd done. It didn't matter that he'd given her a dozen mind-blowing orgasms. It didn't matter that she'd taken everything he'd offered and begged for more.

Some ridiculous prudish streak now had her denying her own feelings.

One way or another, he'd get her to accept him, and to trust him and her own basic nature. Because one way or another, he planned to have her—for the rest of his life.

But when Levi started to go after her, two large muscled bodies got in his way. Why hadn't Beth told him that her brothers were enormous? Well, at least one was enormous. Noah was a big brick wall of a guy. But Ben, no slouch, stood on a par with Levi.

Together, they looked pretty invincible.

Removing his coat, too, Levi told them, "This is none of your business," and he knew that somehow, if necessary, he'd walk right through them. He would not let Beth keep dodging him.

Noah grinned—which only made him look more imposing. "It's our business now."

Levi glanced beyond the hulks, but the more reasonable women were nowhere to be seen. Damn.

"Forget it," Ben told him, knowing the direction of his thoughts. "They went after Beth to find out what the hell you did to upset her so much."

"She's not upset," Levi argued. "She's embarrassed when she has no reason to be."

"Says you," Ben remarked right back. "She thinks differently."

"She's in denial," Levi explained. "She's uncertain, and she's surprised. That's all."

First, he'd strip Beth naked and get her in bed, and then he'd hash out the future with her. He'd found that the more he touched Beth, the more reasonable she became.

Noah's grin widened. "I wonder why she's embarrassed. I don't suppose you plan to tell us?"

"No."

"Doesn't matter," Noah said. "I already have an idea what's going on."

"Me, too," Ben said. "But given Beth's reaction, you must not have handled it right. If you had, she wouldn't have come back to us."

Levi stiffened. "I'll straighten out everything. I just need her to listen to me."

Another voice, thankfully less provoking, intruded. "Quit crowding him, boys. He doesn't look like he's about to back down, and regardless of what Beth said, I don't think she wants him mangled."

Levi didn't think so either, but it surprised him that her father might be an ally. "Thanks."

The older man nudged Noah out of the way. "Let's all take a seat."

Levi shook his head. "I need to go after her."

"Not just yet," he was told. "Ben, could we get some coffee, do you think?"

Ben grumbled, but agreed and took himself off. Noah stepped farther to the side, giving Levi room to move and the opportunity to address Beth's father.

Pulling himself together, Levi eyed the man before him. He had Beth's blond hair and piercing blue eyes, but where Beth was delicate in the most delicious ways, this man looked solid and hard.

On the best of days, Levi hated meeting dads—not that he'd often been serious enough about a female to warrant the need of parental approval. In fact, since meeting Beth, no other woman had held his attention long.

Now, under these conditions, it really sucked to await judgment by Beth's father. The man knew she'd been engaged to a doctor. By comparison, Levi had to be one hell of a letdown. Brandon could have set Beth up in style. Lots of luxury. Guaranteed security.

All Levi had to offer was fidelity, devotion, and a job that barely paid middle-class wages.

Seeing no help for it now, Levi stuck out a hand. "You're Beth's father."

Accepting Levi's hand in a strong, calloused grip, he said, "Kent Monroe."

"Levi Masterson. And as Beth said, I apologize for the theatrics."

"That's my girl. She got that dramatic streak from her mother." Kent gestured him toward a table. "How about you tell me what's going on without all the drama?"

Because Kent was being reasonable, Levi hated to disappoint him. But much of the story would be Beth's alone to tell. The second they were seated and Ben had returned with mugs and a coffeepot, the three men stared at Levi in expectation.

To appease them, Levi gave the shortened, censored version of the past week. "Brandon is out of the picture. I'm in, whether Beth admits it or not. I love her, and I'm pretty sure she cares the same about me." He shrugged. "Either way, I plan to marry her."

Everyone waited.

Levi poured himself a mug of coffee.

"That's it?" Noah asked.

"Afraid so."

"What happened to Brandon?" Ben asked.

"You should ask Beth."

In disbelief, Ben fell back in his seat. "You really think that's all you're going to tell us?"

Levi sipped his coffee. "Yeah."

Kent laughed. "Did you propose to her yet?"

"I've tried, but she hasn't exactly given me a chance when she's avoiding me like the plague."

"And?"

"I'm working on it." Levi set the mug down. "That's why I'm here."

Noah propped an elbow on the table. "So you followed her here to propose to her?"

"I followed her here because she's been trying to hide from me. I have to get her to accept all the sudden changes before I can ask her to marry me."

"Yeah," Ben said, "she sounds real smitten."

"She is." Levi *had* to believe that. Beth wasn't a woman who would go wild with a man that she didn't love. "It's just that she'd gotten really comfortable with her plans for the future, and now those plans are gone. Beth's having a hard time accepting it all. That's why I can't let her out of my sight for long. She'll convince herself she doesn't care, or that we don't belong together if she gets a chance to think about all this too much."

"Think about all what?" Noah asked.

Wild sex. Unrestrained passion. Fantasies come true, and imaginations gone wild. Levi cleared his throat. "You'll have to ask—"

"Beth," Noah finished. "Got it."

"So," Kent said, sounding cordial and almost amused, "you're stalking my daughter?"

"Sort of." But he didn't want Kent getting the wrong impression. "If she'll just admit it, she wants me to."

Ben tapped his fingers on the tabletop. "Did you know she was coming home when you followed her?"

"Yeah, I figured that's where she was headed." Levi shrugged. "It's the holidays. She's emotional and confused. Being with family made sense." He eyed each of the men in turn. "Maybe you can help me."

It was Noah's turn to drop back in his seat. "Help you?"

"That's right." Levi leaned forward. "For starters, I'd appreciate it if you'd keep her from running off again."

"For starters?" Kent asked. "I gather there's more?"

"Yeah. I wouldn't mind being alone in a room with her for a while, too." And before any of them could start grumbling about that, Levi added, "To talk. To work through things."

"The changes?"

"That's right." It wasn't every day a woman found her fiancé cheating, broke an engagement, and realized she loved someone else anyway.

Kent nodded slowly. "You know, I believe you."

"Thank you. I give you my word that Beth has nothing to fear from me. I love her. I would never do anything to hurt her."

"That's good," Ben told him. "Because if you do anything—"

"Yeah, I've got it. You don't need to finish that thought."

"Good."

"If one of you would go park my truck, I'd really appreciate it. I left it idling in the lot, blocking Beth's car."

All three of them looked toward the diner door, but none of them made a move toward it.

Levi settled back in the booth and lifted his mug of coffee. "Or someone can steal the damn thing. I don't give a shit. I just want to talk to Beth without being interrupted and without her sneaking away."

The gazes all transferred to him.

Levi felt his shoulders go rigid. If they thought to stop him, they'd be sorely disappointed. "So where is she? I don't think it's a good idea for her to have this much time away from me."

Kent tapped his fingertips together. "You could be right."

Taking their clues from him, Ben and Noah made sounds of reluctant agreement.

"But I won't send you off to a room alone with her, unless Beth decides that's what she wants. I remember being young and in love."

Ben snorted. "You're old and in love and no better now than you probably were then."

Kent just smiled. "Ben, can you tell Levi of someplace he can talk to Beth without interruption? Someplace that's not too private, though?"

"Someplace," Noah interjected with a narrow-eyed look at Levi, "where we can hear her if she calls out."

Ben thought about it a moment. "Sure, I know just the place. *If* Beth presents herself. Because right now, I have no idea where the women are. Sierra knows every hiding place in this joint. If Beth doesn't want you to talk to her tonight, then you won't be talking to her."

"We'll talk," Levi assured him with confidence. "She won't trust me alone with the three of you for too long. I'll give her fifteen minutes, tops. Then she'll be out here again, giving me the perfect opportunity I need."

Her head in her hands and her shoulders slumped, Beth sat on a stool between her sisters-in-law with her stepmother pacing in front of her. So far, they'd tried to make her eat, encouraged her to drink, smothered her with hugs, and very impatiently waited for explanations.

She had to tell them something.

The truth seemed her only option.

Forcing herself to straighten, Beth faced her family. "Brandon cheated on me with a female colleague of his."

"That bastard," was followed by a heated, "Miserable jerk," and finally, "Oh honey, I'm so sorry."

Beth nodded in acknowledgment of each sentiment. "He claimed it was a mistake, that it just happened. He said he was sorry and that he still loved me." She gulped back her humiliation. "He said he'd make it up to me in our marriage."

All three women made sounds of disgust and disbelief.

"All I really wanted," Beth confided, "was to get even, to maybe make him as miserable as he'd made me. I wanted him to know what he'd thrown away and to regret what he'd done."

Sierra asked, "So you ended the engagement?"

"Yes."

"I hope you threw the ring at him," Grace said.

"I did."

"And?" Brooke asked.

Drawing a deep breath, Beth whispered, "I gave him tit for tat by sleeping with his best friend."

Mouths dropped open in shock, only to snap shut in realization. Beth could almost hear the blinking of their wide eyes and feel the burn of their condemnation.

Brooke recovered first. She looked back at the closed kitchen door, and for some reason, she spoke in a whisper. "That young man out there?"

"Yes." Hiding her face in her hands again, Beth wailed, "That's him."

Grace cleared her throat. "I take it he wants a repeat performance?"

"But I don't." She lifted her shoulders. "Only now he won't go away."

No one had any suggestions.

"Do you really want him to go away?" Brooke finally asked.

"I . . . I think so." Beth gulped, and wondered where to start. "It had seemed like such a simple plan in the beginning." She looked at Sierra and Grace and almost laughed at their identical expressions of disbelief. "It did, really."

"What was the plan?"

Saying it aloud made it sound even dumber, but Beth forced

herself to honesty. "Brandon had cheated, so I would cheat. It was just supposed to be sex, and it was just supposed to be one time."

Sierra scooted closer. "It was more than once?"

Boy, was it ever. Beth nodded miserably, and her voice dipped to a mere whisper. "I went to his place on a Friday after work. I figured I'd be there an hour and be back home before dinner so I could call Brandon and tell him what I did. He'd be heartbroken and full of regret, I'd be avenged, and that'd be that."

"How long were you there?" Grace wanted to know.

"The entire weekend." To Beth's amazement, no one looked shocked. They didn't even look surprised. They just . . . looked curious to hear more. "Actually," Beth added, so they'd be sure to understand, "we both missed work on Monday, too."

Grace scooted in closer. "You're saying that you lost track of time?"

"I lost track of *everything*. The plan. Propriety. I lost track of *me*." And that was the hardest part of all. "I don't know what happened. I was a . . . a . . ."

"A what?" Sierra asked.

"A deviant," Beth blurted. "A sex freak. A . . . I don't know. Inexhaustible, I guess."

Brooke cleared her throat. "And that concerns you?"

"Well, of course it does." How could Brooke look so cavalier over her confession?

Grace grinned. "Nothing wrong with a little deviation now and then, as long as you're both willing."

"Yeah," Sierra agreed. Then she leaned closer. "So what exactly did you do that was so freaky?"

Brooke said, "Now Sierra. I don't know that we should be discussing this."

"Oh, come on," Sierra said. "Everyone sees how you look at Kent. And everyone sees Kent, so they all know why you look at him like that. You're not fooling anyone."

Pretending affront, Brooke said, "Young lady, that's entirely . . ." her stern expression broke into a grin, ". . . accurate."

Sierra and Grace chuckled. "We know."

"And that's probably something else that we shouldn't talk about."

Leaning in close again, Grace whispered, "You should see how Brooke watches your dad when he's working on landscaping."

"Now stop," Brooke insisted, but everyone could see that she didn't mean it.

Suffering a different kind of uneasiness now, Beth looked at Brooke.

"All right, it's true," Brooke admitted. "Kent looks incredible when he gets all sweaty and he takes off his shirt and his muscles are bulging." She shivered. "He's such a hunk. I'm so glad I met him."

Beth blinked. Her father was a *hunk?*

"Noah is very inventive," Grace confided without a single ounce of discomfort. "I can always trust him to keep things interesting."

"Ben's a nut." Sierra looked at her mother-in-law. "Don't listen to this part, Brooke."

After rolling her eyes, Brooke put her hands over her ears and paced to the other side of the room.

Sierra smiled. "Since Brooke is Ben's mother, she doesn't really like to hear about how sexy he is. She just wants him to be happy."

"And he is," Grace noted.

"So am I. But when I first met him, I thought he was a complete perv. And that he made me into a perv, too. It was really unnerving. I wasn't me anymore."

Because that was exactly how she felt, Beth nodded. "What did you do?"

"Well, whatever else Ben might be, he's incredible. And considerate. And I love him more every day. So naturally, I just gave in and enjoyed it." She gave Beth a certain look. "Trust me, I've never regretted that decision."

Brooke looked back at them, lowered her hands, and asked, "All clear?"

"Yes." Sierra stood. "So Beth, if you had a good time, there's no reason to be so upset."

"But . . ." Beth didn't know what to think. "It's like I went into this fog and I didn't want anything to stop, ever." Desperate to make them understand, Beth turned to Brooke as she rejoined their little circle. "It was never like that with Brandon. I mean, it wasn't bad, but it wasn't . . ."

"Overwhelming?" Grace asked.

"Mind-blowing?" Sierra added.

"Stupendous?" Brooke offered.

"All that." Beth slumped in her seat.

"I'd say it's a good thing you didn't marry Brandon."

Sierra agreed with Grace. "For sure." She patted Beth's hand. "You did the right thing."

"I don't know." In for a penny, in for a pound, Beth decided. "For those few days, I was shameless—and I loved every second. But now that I'm myself again, my behavior seems horrifying."

"You were a virgin when you met Brandon, weren't you?"

There were times, Beth thought, when Grace proved very astute. "Yes."

"When I met Noah, I was, too. But I just thought it was all really exciting."

Sierra gave Beth a sympathetic look. "Did you think it was exciting with Brandon?"

Beth started to say yes, but she hesitated. "I don't know. Cementing our relationship was exciting. And the sex was pleasant—"

Grace made a face. "*Pleasant?*"

Agreeing with her, Sierra said, "Brandon must've been a putz."

Brooke sympathized. "I'm so sorry, honey. Before Levi, you probably didn't even realize that sex could and should be more."

Beth decided that the conversation had veered too far off course. "The problem is that now I can barely look at Levi, but he won't give me any space. To hear him talk, you'd think we were engaged or something."

"Ah." Brooke pulled up a chair. "How so?"

Relieved to finally have someone to talk to, Beth blurted, "He says he always wanted me."

Brooke's eyebrows shot up. "Really?"

"He claims that he never said anything because he and Brandon have been friends since grade school. He didn't want to interfere between us."

"Wow." Grace let out a long sigh. "He put your feelings before his own. That's so romantic."

"Levi sounds like a great guy," Sierra agreed.

It struck Beth that he did sort of sound terrific—in an infuriating, devastating kind of way.

Sierra tilted her head. "So I'm dying to know—how did Brandon take it when you told him about Levi? Did you get your revenge?"

"I never told him." Beth winced with that admission. "I *couldn't* tell him. Not because I care about Brandon still. I really don't. And isn't that weird? I mean, obviously I wouldn't marry a cheater, but shouldn't I still be a little brokenhearted or something?" She didn't give anyone a chance to reply. "I'm not. I'm too busy dealing with this new situation to barely give Brandon a thought. And what happened with Levi . . . well, it feels very private now. I don't want anyone to know, not even Brandon."

Brooke smiled and took her hand. "Are Levi and Brandon still friends?"

"I don't know." That was another worry keeping her awake at night. "Since I've been trying to avoid Levi, and I haven't answered Brandon's calls, I don't know what's happening between the two of them."

"So," Grace said, "Levi might have lost a longtime friend for you."

"Maybe." Guilt nudged at her. Had Levi been motivated by caring, and not just lust?

Sierra stood. "You know, I think you just need to face up to things."

"Things?"

"How you feel about Levi. You have to decide that first, and then you can consider everything else."

"I almost lost your father," Brooke said, "because I didn't want to own up to my feelings for him."

"Same here," Sierra admitted. "I fought the idea of falling for Ben."

Grace looked at them both and shrugged. "Not me. I wanted Noah, and that was that."

Brooke grinned. "Beth should take a lesson from you, then."

"It did work out in the most awesome ways," Grace told her. "I say if you want Levi, then go for it."

"But . . . what about Brandon?" What about her reputation and her life and her sanity?

Sierra snorted. "Forget Brandon. He had his chance and he blew it."

And the rest? How did she forget the person she'd always thought herself to be, and just accept this new overly-sensual woman who threw caution to the wind?

Brooke squeezed her hand. "You said you didn't want anyone to know about you and Levi."

"No, I don't." And that was part of the problem. She could just imagine the gossip when everyone found out she'd jumped between best friends.

After glancing at the other women, Brooke gave her an apologetic smile that Beth didn't quite understand. "But you just told us."

"That's because it was eating me up inside. And Levi did follow me here, so I had to explain somehow."

Sierra caught on to Brooke's meaning. "You know, Levi

could feel as conflicted as you do. Maybe he didn't mean for the one time to turn into a weekend marathon, either."

Grace followed their insinuations. "Yeah, and he's sitting out there with Noah and Ben and Kent. And like you said, his appearance and behavior need to be explained somehow."

Brooke nodded. "The same way that you told us, he could be telling them—"

"Oh my God." Beth shot out of her seat. "He wouldn't." She looked at the other women in a desperate bid for reassurance. "Please tell me he wouldn't."

Brooke lifted her shoulders. "I'm sorry, honey, but your father loves you an awful lot. He'll want to know what has you upset. I'm not sure he'd let Levi get by without an explanation."

"And," Grace pointed out, "you did tell them to hurt him. He might not have a choice but to explain."

"Oh. My. God." Beth spun around and raced from the kitchen. Surely, the men wouldn't hurt Levi. They had to know sarcasm when they heard it. They had to have some concepts of the working of the female mind. After all, her sisters-in-law and stepmother had just confessed to being very, very happy women.

With her heart in her throat, Beth plunged through the double dining doors, charged into the dining room—and slid to a frozen halt at the sight of the men in close, amicable conversation.

They were drinking coffee.

They were smiling.

Sierra, Grace, and Brooke almost plowed into Beth, and still she couldn't unglue her feet.

Had Levi told them everything? Had he blurted out about her awful, wanton behavior to her *family*?

Heat flooded into Beth's face so quickly, it made her lightheaded.

She'd pay the men to beat him up.

She'd beat him up herself.

She'd—

Levi looked up and saw her. "Finally." Walking away from the male conversation, he strode toward her. As if he'd had his hands in it multiple times, his brown hair looked disheveled. Determination glowed in his green eyes. And that sensual mouth of his was set in a firm line.

When he reached her, Beth prepared to blast him with her ire.

But because he didn't stop before her, he didn't give her a chance. No, he just caught her wrist and kept right on going, towing her along with him.

"Levi!" She tried digging in her heels. "What are you doing?"

Without pausing in his exodus, he glanced over his shoulder and said, "Come along, Beth. Your brothers and father are curious enough without us putting on another show."

If they were still curious, then did that mean . . . In a squeaky whisper, she asked, "You didn't tell them anything?"

He stopped, turned to stare down at her in what looked like anger, then leaned close so she'd hear his whisper. "Of course I didn't."

Beth glanced around, saw they had the undivided attention of one and all, but she didn't think anyone could hear them. "Well, how was I to know? You're always trying to talk to me about it."

"There's nothing that you and I can't talk about. But what's between us is just that—*between us*. It's private." His eyes narrowed. "You should know better than to think I'd do anything to deliberately embarrass you."

"I . . ." Beth closed her mouth and swallowed. Face up to things, Brooke had said. She nodded. "You're right. I should have realized that. I'm sorry."

His eyes darkened even more, as if he didn't quite know what to make of any giving on her end.

"So." Beth took another quick glance at their rapt audience, and smiled an apology to them. She'd put on more spectacles tonight than anyone should share in a lifetime. Hoping to make amends for doubting him, she asked Levi, "If you didn't tell my dad the truth, what did you say to him?"

"Only that I'm going to marry you."

Only *what*? New heat radiated through her. The world tilted. On a thin breath, she gasped out, "You didn't."

"I did." He smiled. "Because I am."

"But . . ."

Done talking, Levi lifted her into his arms. "No buts." He put a soft, fast smooch on her mouth. "Now come along quietly so we don't incite a riot with what I plan to say and do to you."

Her body tightened. "Do to me?"

"That's right." He glanced down at her. "And it's all best handled in private. Don't you agree?"

It took no more than that simple, sensual suggestion from Levi to have Beth melting in a dozen delicious ways. She might want to forget what transpired between them, but her body was in no hurry to give up the memory.

She gulped, thought again of Brooke's advice, and finally found her voice. "Yes, I suppose so."

2

With each step he took, Levi pondered what to say to Beth. She needed to understand that she'd disappointed him.

Infuriated him.

Befuddled him and inflamed him.

In order to get a handle on things, he had to get a handle on her. He had to convince Beth to admit to her feelings.

He needed time and space to accomplish that.

Thanks to Ben's directions, Levi carried her through the kitchen toward the back storage unit, where interruptions were less likely to occur.

The moment he reached the dark, private area, Levi paused. Time to give Beth a piece of his mind. Time to be firm, to insist that she stop denying the truth.

Time to set her straight.

But then he looked at her, and he forgot about his important intentions. He forgot everything but his need for this one particular woman.

God, she took him apart without even trying.

Among the shelves of pots and pans, canned goods and bags of foodstuff, Levi slowly lowered Beth to her feet.

He couldn't seem to do more than stare at her.

Worse, she stared back, all big dark eyes, damp lips, and barely banked desire. Denial might come from her mouth, but the truth was there in her expression.

When she let out a shuddering little breath, Levi lost the battle, the war . . . he lost his heart all over again.

Crushing her close, he freed all the restraints he'd imposed while she was his best friend's fiancée. He gave free reign to his need to consume her. Physically. Emotionally. Forever and always.

Moving his hands over her, absorbing the feel of her, he tucked her closer still and took her mouth. How could he have forgotten how perfect she tasted? How delicious she smelled and how indescribable it felt to hold her?

Even after their long weekend together, he hadn't been sated. He'd never be sated.

Levi knew if he lived to be a hundred and ten, he'd still be madly in love with Beth Monroe.

The Fates had done him in the moment he'd first met her. She smiled and his world lit up. She laughed and he felt like Zeus, mythical and powerful. She talked about marrying Brandon and the pain was more than anything he'd ever experienced in his twenty-nine years.

Helpless, that's what he'd been.

So helpless that it ate at him day and night.

Then, by being unfaithful, Brandon had proved that he didn't really love Beth after all—and all bets were off.

When Beth came to him that night, hurt and angry, and looking to him for help, Levi threw caution to the wind and gave her all she requested, and all she didn't know to ask for.

He gave her everything he could, and prayed she'd recognize it for the deep unshakable love he offered, not just a sexual fling meant for retaliation.

But . . . she hadn't.

She'd been too shaken by her own free response, a response she gave every time he touched her.

A response she gave right now.

They thumped into the wall, and Levi recovered from his tortured memories, brought back to the here and now.

He had Beth.

She wanted him.

Until she grasped the enormity of their connection, he'd continue pursuing her.

Lured by the sensuality of the moment, Levi levered himself against her, and loved it. As busy as his hands might be, Beth's were more so. Small, cool palms coasted over his nape, into his hair, then down to his shoulders. Burning him through the layers of his flannel shirt and tee, her touch taunted him and spurred his lust.

Wanting her, right here and right now, Levi pressed his erection against her belly and then cradled her body as she shuddered in reaction, doing her best to crawl into him.

His mouth against hers, he whispered, "I need you, Beth."

Beyond any real verbal response, Beth moaned and clutched at him.

And that gave him pause, because Levi knew she was with him—and he knew that she'd hate herself for it later.

Damn it.

Why did his conscience have to snap to life now? Why couldn't he have stayed in the sensual fog a little bit longer?

But he knew why; he loved Beth and he wanted her happy, not more humiliated. Until she admitted that it was love they shared, her embarrassment would continue. He had to remember that. He had to keep the ultimate goal—Beth as his wife—at the forefront of his every intention.

Lifting his mouth from hers, Levi whispered, "Beth, wait."

Her mouth followed, seeking his again. She licked his bottom lip, pressed her breasts against him.

Holding her shoulders, Levi managed to put a small distance between them. "Honey, no, wait."

Big sleepy eyes opened, heavy with lust, dark with desire. "I don't understand how you always make me feel this way."

"I know." He put his right hand to the back of her head

and urged it to his shoulder. "But that's why we're here. So I can explain it to you."

Both rigid and soft, anxious and needy, Beth willingly leaned into him, giving him the weight of her worry. His left hand on the center of her back registered each broken breath, just as his heart understood her confusion. He put his cheek to her crown and inhaled the scent of her silky blond hair.

Muscles prepared for her reaction, Levi said, "I want to marry you, Beth."

As he expected, she almost lurched away.

"Shhh. I know that's something of a shock. You thought for so long that we were just friends. But it doesn't change anything—I want to marry you."

Her silence felt like condemnation. Like the ultimate rejection. "There's something going on between us." Something called love, but Levi didn't want to spook her. "You go wild when I touch you."

"I know." Her whole body trembled. "That's why you can't touch me."

Her panic struck Levi like a low blow. "Wrong. It's why I *have* to touch you. It's the only time you're honest with me and with yourself."

"No." She shook her head.

"Now that we've been together, the feelings aren't going to go away. You may as well accept that."

"There's nothing to accept."

As if she hadn't spoken, Levi continued with his well-rehearsed speech. "You have to accept that Brandon doesn't love you." The last thing Levi wanted was to see her hurt, but denying the truth would only spare her for so long. "If he did, he wouldn't have cheated."

"I *know* that. I'm not an idiot."

Relief closed Levi's eyes.

"But this . . ." Flattening her hands over Levi's chest, Beth tried to shove away.

Irritation brought his eyes open again, and he kept her secure.

". . . has nothing to do with Brandon."

"Of course it does." Taking her shoulders in his hands, Levi stepped away so that he could see her face. "You're condemning yourself because Brandon fooled you. He had you believing that you were in love with him, and that he loved you, too. He convinced you that you'd share this picture-perfect life together."

"And that was all a sham."

"Because he misled you."

"It's easy to fool a fool, apparently."

Levi wanted to shake her, so instead he released her and turned his back. It took two deep breaths to steady himself and tamp down on his anger. "You are not a fool, Beth."

"Then I'm a tramp."

He whirled around and stared at her in furious disbelief. "What did you say?"

With one arm crossed over her middle, the other raised so she could rub her brow, Beth laughed without humor. "You said it yourself. I thought I was in love with Brandon. I slept with him, made plans with him. But even I have to admit I wasn't really in love with him, or I'd be more hurt by his betrayal."

So she wasn't hurt. Levi considered that a very good thing.

Her gaze lifted to his, and she looked so lost and so ashamed, that Levi almost couldn't bear it. "Instead, all I can think about is the situation with you."

"It's not a *situation*, damn it. It's a relationship."

"A friendly relationship, or so I thought. But now . . ." She ducked her head and groaned. "I've known you for two years, Levi. And not once did I ever think of sleeping with you."

"Liar."

She drew back in affront. "I beg your pardon?"

Stalking closer, Levi said, "You've thought about it, honey.

At least admit to that much." Whether she'd ever planned to act on it or not, they'd been too close for her natural sensuality not to take over. "You've seen me at my worst, and at my best. We've swam together, danced together, laughed and complained together."

"Always with Brandon there!"

"So?" As Levi advanced, Beth sidled away from the wall and backed up. Levi kept going—and so did she. "It didn't stop me from fantasizing about you."

Her eyes widened.

"A lot. I never would have sabotaged your relationship with Brandon by acting on my fantasies, but you can bet your sweet little ass that you factored into my dreams on a regular basis."

She shook her head, and continued backing away.

"It's human nature, Beth. Men find it impossible to block a sexy woman from their thoughts." His gaze dipped to her heaving breasts, proof of her agitation. "And vice versa."

"You think you're sexy?" she taunted, hoping to distract him.

Levi grinned. "I'm the opposite of Brandon. Rough instead of polished. Open where he's reserved. Daring when he's cautious."

Beth had nothing to say to that.

"Most importantly," he added, watching for her reaction, "I would never cheat on you. I would never shame you." He stared at her hard. "I would never do anything that I knew would hurt you."

She bit her lip.

"Do you understand me, Beth? *Never.*"

In a small voice, she said, "I believe you."

Those words thrilled Levi. At least she knew him well enough to trust in his honor. That had to count for something.

He waited until she looked up at him, then added, "And whether *you* think I'm sexy or not, you've thought about me."

Temper sparked in her eyes. "Where Brandon's modest,

you're obviously vain." Done retreating, Beth took a stance and lifted her chin. "Add that one to the list, why don't you."

Levi laughed. God, he adored her. "If I am conceited, then honey, you made me that way the night you came to me."

She inhaled so fast, she nearly strangled herself.

Levi grinned at her. "Don't get me wrong, honey. I loved it. A lot."

In a display of belligerence, Beth crossed both arms under her breasts. "So now you're blaming me for your character flaws?"

He stepped close enough to touch her, and then paused. "Think about it, Beth. When shit fell apart with Brandon who did you go running to?"

Her mouth tightened, but she refused to reply.

Levi touched a thumb to his chest. "Me."

"I thought you were a friend."

"Uh huh." Levi nodded. "That's why the first plan to come to your mind was having sex with me, right?"

A rush of color stained her smooth cheeks. "I wanted to get even with Brandon."

Slowly, so he wouldn't send her packing, Levi reached out and smoothed her hair behind her ear, then cupped her jaw. He could feel that flush of embarrassment, so warm and honest and sweet. "Sure you did." And already knowing the answer, he asked, "So tell me, honey, what did old Brandon say when you told him?"

Her brows came down, her eyes closed and her mouth pinched in denial of the obvious truth.

Using both hands now to hold her face, Levi repeated, "Beth?"

"I didn't."

He tilted his head in deep satisfaction. "What's that?"

Braced by irritation, Beth slapped his hands away. "I didn't tell him, all right? I couldn't. After that weekend . . . after we . . ." She shook her head hard. "I didn't tell him."

Of course, she hadn't. "I haven't said anything to him, either."

On a low growl, she stormed away, but only to put a little space between them.

Staring at her stiff back, Levi said, "It doesn't feel right to use something that was so wonderful as revenge, does it?"

She whirled on him in a blaze of anger. "Wonderful? Is that what you think?" Three big strides brought her within touching distance of him again. She leaned into him, her eyes bright with fury, and used one finger to poke at his chest. "It was carnal and extravagant and totally inappropriate."

"It was incredible. And hot. And *honest*," Levi countered.

"Honest?"

"That's right." He was hard again, damn it. "You were everything I'd ever imagined and more. No one else will ever measure up for me now, not with the memory of how it is with you."

Beth's expression went from rage to awareness in a heartbeat. "Levi, don't."

"I lost count of how many times you came."

She groaned, and covered her face.

"I loved every one of them though." He eased himself into her space, then eased her into his arms—where she belonged. "The small sounds you made, and how they became throaty, rough sounds right before you climaxed."

"Stop."

That single word sounded weak and uncertain, so Levi disregarded it. "I have scratches on my shoulders, a bite bruise on my thigh."

"Oh God." Her forehead dropped to his chest and her groan became a moan.

Levi stroked her back, tangled his hand in her hair and kissed her ear. "When I close my eyes at night, I can still taste you, Beth."

Her hands curled into small fists. Her breathing deepened.

"I can still feel you around me, squeezing me tight, and I

can still smell you with each breath I take. It makes me hard every time." Using the edge of his hand, Levi tipped up her face. "I'm hard now."

Her lips parted and he kissed her, soft and easy, long and deep. Without conscious thought, his hand sought her breast, cuddling her through the layers of her clothes and still able to feel her tautened nipple. Using his thumb, he circled her, rubbed over the tip, and gently applied pressure.

"Levi . . ."

"Yeah," he murmured in approval, "that's what I like to hear, you saying my name, your voice rough with lust." He kissed her temple, her cheekbone—and all the while, he toyed with her breast.

Beth leaned into him, nearly panting, heat pouring off her.

Once again, her physical need helped her to forget her grievances, her embarrassment.

It ate Levi up to know she'd also been with Brandon, and only one fact made it easier to take.

Brandon had never really satisfied her.

The night Beth came to him had started out awkward enough. She'd angrily stammered out what she wanted. He'd been floored, excited, and relieved.

Hearing of Brandon's infidelity had thrilled him, and that made him feel like the biggest jerk alive.

But he didn't turn her down on her offer. No way.

Seducing an enraged woman wasn't easy, especially when she'd asked him to "just get on with it." But Levi gave it his all.

Beth had wanted sex.

He wanted lovemaking.

Beth wanted revenge.

He wanted an opportunity.

At first, she'd been stiff and distant, guided by her hurt feelings—until she succumbed to her first climax with sheer astonishment. Levi would never forget her blurted words after he'd left her replete and lax, her skin damp with sweat, her hair tangled, her skin rosy.

Levi, she'd whispered. *I had no idea.*

Her shock had left him so pleased and proud he wanted to shout. Then she'd reached for him with enthusiasm, and the next few days had been an orgy of exploration and, as Beth claimed, carnality.

For Levi, they'd also been days filled with love.

Everything he did to and with Beth had left her wide-eyed with wonder and excitement. She reveled in each new experience and glowed with sexual satiation. There'd been no denials, only anticipation.

Just as there was now.

"Levi," she said again, and he knew what she wanted, what she needed.

"Let me help you, honey." He put one leg between hers, cupped her bottom, and snuggled her in close. She shivered as she dropped her head back in wanton acceptance.

Levi guided her, one hand helping her keep a rhythm against his thigh, the other dipping into her shirt so he could touch the bare skin of her breast, really get to her nipples and—

A shrill whistle pierced the thickening air of the storage area.

Levi straightened in shock. Well, shit.

Knowing they were about to be interrupted, he looked at Beth's face. She looked relaxed in the way of rising release. Panting breaths puffed from between her parted lips. Her unfocused gaze and heavy eyelids, her warming skin, proved she wouldn't have needed but a few minutes more.

What to do?

The whistle sounded again, and Beth blinked into reality. "Levi?"

Damn, damn, damn. "I'm sorry, honey." His hands remained on her, but still now. "We're about to have company."

Confusion gave way to horror, and in a flash, she jerked free. *"Ohmigod."*

"Easy, honey. It's just your brother. I think." Keeping Beth shielded by his body, Levi half turned. He saw no one. "Ben?"

"Sorry to interrupt, kids."

The voice came from near the door—out of sight, but audible. Levi wanted to clout him. "What is it?"

"We're all ready to head to bed, so unless you two want to sleep in your vehicles, I need to know if I should put your coats and bags in two rooms . . . or just one? I have vacancies, so they're on the house, but I wasn't sure of your plans."

Levi said, "One room," at the same time Beth snapped, "Two."

"That's clear enough," Ben remarked, and he sounded amused.

Levi quickly cupped Beth's face. "I'll promise not to touch you, if that's what you want."

"Ha!" she said loudly, and then slapped a hand over her mouth. In a lowered voice, she whispered, "You know what I want, and you keep using it against me."

That almost made Levi grin—because it was partially true, although there were times when he just plain lost control. "You have my word, Beth. Unless you beg me, I won't touch you. But please, we do need to talk. I'm staying the night whether you hear me out or not. Tomorrow your family will cluster around you again and it'll be impossible to get any privacy without making an issue of it. Is that what you want?"

Ben rattled a pan, the bastard.

"Give us a minute," Levi snarled.

Beth hesitated, but Levi could see her weakening.

"I'll stay ten feet away from you," he cajoled, "if that'll help."

All morose, Beth admitted, "It probably wouldn't."

"You see," Levi teased in a whisper, "that's why I'm getting conceited."

Finally, she relented. "Ben, we'll take one room, please. But with two beds."

Levi let out a long breath.

"You got it," Ben said around a laugh. "You can have the same suite you always use when you visit, Beth."

Levi raised a brow. "A suite?"

"Ben saves it for family."

Proving he'd been able to hear their every word, Ben said, "Actually, I give it to family to use because most of my guests are only interested in a one or two-night stay in an economy room, which makes the suite available more often than not. But don't expect anything fancy. Being a suite just means you get a couch, microwave, and tiny fridge."

"It'll do," Levi told him. "Thanks."

"I'll get your bags to your room, but you'll need to come to the front desk for your keys."

Beth twisted her hands together. "Would you mind getting the keys from Ben?"

Levi raised a brow. Did she plan to slip out on him? "Ben parked my truck, honey. He has your coat and your purse. And your father and brothers have agreed to let me know if you try running out on me again."

"Traitors."

"I convinced them that I wanted only the best for you."

She made a face. "Great. If only I knew what the best might be. And no, Levi, don't say it." She scowled at him in reproach. "You've shown enough conceit to last a month at least."

She ignored his laughter.

"I'll have you know that I wasn't planning to sneak off anyway. I intend to be with my family for the holidays."

"So why the delay, then?"

"I want to talk to the women before we . . . retire."

That made Levi a little suspicious. "Talk to them about what?"

Beth looked frazzled and on the verge of losing her temper. "None of your damn business. Now go get the keys. I'll meet you at the room in a few minutes."

Rather than push his luck, Levi agreed. "Don't be too long, okay? After chasing you across the state, I'm a little on the skittish side. I'd hate to call out the National Guard if you're just sitting in the kitchen lamenting the Fates with family."

"Ha-ha." Beth flipped a quick wave in his direction and went in search of reinforcements.

Feeling success on the rise, Levi watched her go with a smile. He'd have the night with her. Surely, that'd aid him in making headway.

He could hardly wait.

3

When Beth entered the dining room, only her father and Noah were there, and Noah had already donned his coat, ready to leave. Undecided on what to do, she stalled. It wasn't that she really wanted more time with the women; she just needed more time to prepare herself for the night with Levi.

It was herself and her own lack of restraint that scared her.

As Noah went out the door to the parking lot, her father said, "Come on in, honey."

He hadn't even looked up to see her. It seemed no matter how old she got, her dad always stayed one step ahead.

"We've got a few minutes," he assured Beth. "Grace is in the car waiting for Noah, Sierra has already turned in, and Brooke is just saying good-bye to Ben. Come sit with me."

Dragging her feet, Beth did just that.

"So," Kent said, "you and Levi, huh?"

There'd be no point lying to him, but that didn't mean she wanted to make confessions, either. "What exactly did Levi tell you?"

"That Brandon is out of the picture, that he's now in the picture, and that if you'll stand still long enough, he intends to marry you."

"Oh." Beth put her elbows on the top of the booth and propped up her chin. "I caught Brandon cheating, so he's definitely out of the picture."

"How do you feel about that?"

Beth smiled. Leave it to her dad to hold off on the sympathy until he knew where she stood on the matter. "It's a little confusing, but in a way, I'm relieved." She thought about that, and felt compelled to add, "Humiliated and majorly peeved, too."

"Peeved I understand. You have every right. But why are you relieved?"

That one was easy enough to explain. "I keep thinking how close I was to tying myself to him. But what if I'd married him, and then found out he was a cheater? Everything would be so much more complicated."

"True."

"Obviously we weren't meant to be together, and this forced the issue sooner rather than later, when our lives might have been more entangled."

"Divorce, joint property, kids?"

"Exactly." Beth shuddered at the thought of so many legal and emotional ties.

"So it's a good thing then?"

Beth snorted. "It would be, except I really am too humiliated for words." And Levi refused to let her deal with that, blast him.

"I don't see why," Kent said. "Brandon is the one who shamed himself with his behavior. He's the one who cheated, not you."

Her father definitely didn't know about her wild weekend with Levi, or he wouldn't be able to say that. "I suppose."

"How did you find out? Did Levi tell you?"

"No. Levi didn't know any more about it than I did." If he had known, Beth knew in her heart that he'd have found a way to tell her—after he gave Brandon hell for being a jerk.

"He was shocked when I told him." And even more shocked when she shared her plan for getting even.

"You're blushing, Beth. Want to tell me why?"

No, never. "It's a curse of my fair skin, Dad. You know that."

"If you say so." But Beth could tell he didn't believe her.

She quickly distracted him. "Brandon and I were invited to a party with some of his colleagues. I had to work that night, so I told him to go on without me."

"And he did?"

She shrugged. "It didn't make any sense for us both to miss it." A dull throb started behind her eyes. "But then I got off earlier than expected."

"Let me guess. You decided to drop in and surprise him."

"It seemed like a good idea at the time."

Getting a mental picture of the ensuing fiasco, Kent made a face. "Ouch."

"Yeah. Ouch is right." Beth trailed her finger along the edge of the booth tabletop. "There were so many people there, and at first, I couldn't find Brandon. People kept looking at me funny, especially when I asked if they knew where he was. I suppose that should have been my first clue."

Retelling the story brought back the burn of embarrassment. "Finally one woman told me to check the hot tub. That didn't make any sense. It's winter and freezing cold, and Brandon was never that interested in anything to do with water. Whenever we went to a lake or the river, Levi and I would swim and Brandon would sit on the shore and read."

Kent's interest sharpened. "You three hung out together a lot?"

"Well, yeah." Why did her father look so funny about that? "Levi and Brandon were best friends."

"Did Levi bring a date to these little excursions?"

"Maybe a couple of times, but not usually." Frowning a little, Beth asked, "Why?"

"Hmmm." Kent reached for his empty coffee cup, tipped it

up to get the last sip, then said, "No reason. Go on with your story. What happened at the party?"

He definitely had a reason for asking, but the hour grew late and she didn't want to hold him up, so Beth finished her tale. "I went around to the back of the house in the direction the woman had pointed. There was an enclosed porch and a fancy hot tub, and sure enough, I found Brandon there."

Kent plunked the coffee cup back down. "With company, I take it."

"He was making out with a woman I'd met several times, but didn't know well."

"One of his colleagues?"

"Another doctor. They might have had their underwear on, but with the churning water, it was hard to tell. They sure weren't wearing much more than that." Beth flopped back in her seat. "I saw them, they saw me, and the woman screeched."

"Screeched?"

"Loudly." Beth snorted. "Then she started scrambling out of the tub. I don't know if she thought I'd cause a scene or attack her or what, but she was wrapped in a towel and running away before I could blink."

Her father coughed, probably to hide a laugh. "I reckon Brandon was surprised, all right."

Beth smirked, too. "No kidding. You should have seen his face."

"Comical?"

"Oh yeah. I've never seen him look like that because he's usually so self-assured. But then, I guess my face looked pretty ridiculous, too. And I had to go back through that whole room full of people so that I could leave. It was like walking the gauntlet. I could feel everyone watching me."

As the memory of it scoured through her, Beth squeezed her eyes shut.

"That was the worst part of it, the fact that everyone there saw me as this sad victim. Most of them were mutual friends."

"Were?"

"I don't think I could ever face any of them again."

"Then they must have been more his friends than yours." Kent put his muscled forearms on the table and gave her a direct look. "Just think about the fact that the other woman went through there first, wet and in a towel."

"Believe me, I've thought of it. It helps only a little."

Kent reached for her hand. "Want me to sic Noah and Ben on Brandon? You know they'd be happy to show him the error of his ways."

Beth shook her head at his teasing. Whenever possible, her father had always allowed her to fight her own battles. This time wouldn't be any different. "No. Brandon's not worth the trouble, especially during the holidays."

He nodded acceptance of that. "So where's Levi fit into this?"

Looking away at nothing in particular, Beth said, "I don't know yet."

Kent squeezed her hand. "I hope you'll give him a chance to help you figure out that one."

Beth didn't want her father to know she'd be spending the night with Levi, so she hedged a bit saying, "Levi and I will talk more when it's not so crazy."

"Tell me a little about Levi. Other than playing third wheel with you and Brandon, what does he do? What do you know about him?"

"I know . . . everything." As soon as Beth said it, she realized it was true. She knew Levi as well, and in some ways better, than she knew Brandon. "What do you want to know?"

"Start with what Levi does for a living."

Finally, a neutral subject that Beth could discuss with enthusiasm. "He's a physical education teacher at a middle school, and he coaches the soccer team."

"How about that?" Kent nodded in approval. "Teaching's a tough job. He has my respect."

Easier, happier memories filtered into Beth's discontent, helping her to relax. "You should see him with kids, Dad. He loves them, and they love him. He has this easy camaraderie that really reaches out to people of all ages."

"I must've missed the camaraderie when he chased you in the door."

Beth could tell by his wry smile that he only teased. "That really didn't make the best first impression, did it?"

Kent shrugged. "They say you can tell the character of a man by the way he interacts with kids and pets."

"He loves animals," Beth rushed to say in Levi's defense. "He doesn't have any of his own right now. He says it wouldn't be fair when he works so much. But if he ever settles down and gets married . . ." That thought petered off because, really, the person Levi mentioned marrying was her.

Her new discontent made Kent grin. "So you've seen him at work, huh?"

"Brandon and I used to go to the soccer matches. I enjoyed it more than Brandon did, so I volunteered to help Levi on field day. It was fun."

"I see." Kent rubbed his chin. "You always did like kids, too."

"They're great."

"Brandon doesn't like kids?"

"I guess he does. But he always had to work, so he couldn't help out with other stuff. You know how it is in the medical field."

"He sounds like a good man, honey."

"Brandon?"

Kent laughed. "I used to think so, but now I'd just say he's an ass." His voice softened. "I meant Levi."

"Oh. Yes, I guess he is." Beth didn't want to speculate on just how good Levi could be. Brooke saved her by walking in just then.

When Kent looked at his wife, something a little primitive gleamed in his eyes.

Beth saw it, and was amazed.

Own up to your feelings, the women had told her. It had sure worked out for Grace, Sierra, and Brooke.

Before Brooke reached them, Kent was on his feet. He greeted her with a gentle, short, but somehow intimate kiss that left Brooke flushed.

Clearing her throat, Beth pushed to her feet and said, "I'll let you two get out of here. It's getting late and I've kept you long enough."

Brooke leaned against Kent. "We were planning Christmas dinner when you arrived."

"It's at our house this year." Kent looped his arm around Brooke as if he'd been cuddling her all his life. "I know Christmas is a few days away, but we hope you can stay for an extended visit."

"I'd like that, thanks."

Nonchalant, Brooke said, "And Levi? Will he be staying, too?"

Beth had no idea. "He's on a break right now, but," she warned them, "even during the holidays and summer he has things for the school that he works on. Sometimes he takes additional classes, and he often works with the soccer team."

"Just let us know when you can," Kent told her.

"I will. Now go." Beth shooed them toward the door where their coats hung. "That snow's piling up, and the temperature is dropping more by the minute. I'd hate to see you get stuck in this storm."

"Beth," Brooke said, "you know if you want to talk to either of us at any time, we're only a phone call away."

Her heart softened. It was so nice to see her father happily settled with such a wonderful woman. "Thank you. I'm fine, I promise."

"Either way," Kent said, "give me a call tomorrow, okay?"

"Will do."

Kent gave her a quick kiss on the cheek. "Try to get some rest tonight."

Alone in a room with Levi? Not likely. But Beth smiled in an attempt to look agreeable.

As soon as her father and Brooke left, Beth girded herself, locked her trembling hands together, and went to find her room with Levi.

With every step she took, her anxiety grew. Would Levi keep his word and his physical distance, or would he finish what he started in the kitchen?

It was a toss-up on which one Beth would prefer the most.

When the tentative knock sounded on the door, Levi practically leaped off the bed. He swung the door open and there stood Beth. She looked a little uneasy, and a little turned on.

Damn.

This had to be the worst idea he'd ever had. But he wanted her so much, all the time, that sound thinking no longer factored in for him.

Beth smiled, and then looked beyond him. "Ben brought everything here?"

Levi glanced behind him at the stack of her once-gaily wrapped gifts. "Yeah. I can help you repair those tomorrow if you want."

"Why?"

He turned back to her. "Because you dropped them on account of me. Running away from me."

Her smile slipped. "I wasn't running."

Looked like running to him, but he didn't want to antagonize her. "Okay." Levi soaked in the sight of her, then caught himself. "Sorry." He held the door wider. "Come on in."

She did. Cautiously.

"We've got two beds, like you requested." The suite came with a queen-sized bed, but Ben had also delivered a rollaway. "I'll use the crappy one."

Beth frowned at the lumpy, bent-in-the-middle cot. "You'd barely fit. I'll use it."

"No, I—"

"Don't be noble, Levi, okay? I really don't mind, and I really will fit better." She eyed him head to toe and back again. "You're what? Over six feet, right?"

That look put him back on his heels. In a low voice, he said, "Six-two."

"There, you see?" She nodded. "A good eight inches taller than me. And heavier."

Why this conversation made him hot, Levi didn't know. But maybe just the comparison of her small female frame to his larger, stronger body was enough to remind him how well they fit together. "By at least seventy pounds."

As if that proved her point beyond argument, Beth said, "So I'll use the rollaway and you can have the queen, and we'll both be comfortable."

Baloney. He'd be miserable all night and he knew it.

Beth waited for his agreement. "Okay?"

"Fine." Since they wouldn't be sharing one, he didn't want to argue about the beds. "Are you hungry? Ben was nice enough to bring us up some stuff from the kitchen. I put it in the little fridge."

"Ben is my hero. I'm starved." She headed for the kitchenette. "What do we have?"

"I'm not sure. It was all in containers." And he'd been too anxious to see her to worry about food. Levi followed her. "It smelled good."

"Well whatever it is, it's sure to be good. Ben's cook is the best." In short order, Beth emptied the fridge of the containers and opened them all on the minuscule counter. "Mmmm," she purred, peeking into the first container. "Chicken salad, my favorite." She also found croissants, pickles, fruit, and slabs of chocolate cake smothered in icing. "*Manna* from heaven."

Watching her made Levi hungry—just not for food. Beth wasn't a big woman by any stretch, but he'd never seen her fuss about her weight or struggle with a diet as most women seemed prone to do. "I have some paper plates here. Do we have anything to drink?"

"There's a cola machine around the corner." Assuming he'd go, she said, "I'll take a Coke."

"You'll owe me fifty cents."

Busy loading the croissants with the chicken salad, Beth laughed. "I'd rather owe you than cheat you out of it." She winked at him. "While you're gone, I'll put on coffee to drink with our cake."

Fifteen minutes later, Beth slumped back in her seat with a hearty sigh. "Delicious. I'm stuffed."

"You were right." Levi finished off his coffee. "Ben's cook is incredible."

"I'll tell Horace you said so."

Levi studied her relaxed pose. "It's nice seeing you like this for a change."

She immediately stiffened. "What do you mean?"

"Ever since last weekend, you've been so guarded around me, it's like being with a stranger. I missed the old Beth."

After pushing out of her chair, she put her arms around her middle and paced across the small room. She kept her back to him. "I was trying to bring the old Beth back by pretending it hadn't happened, and there you go, bringing it up again."

Levi's temper went up a notch. "I won't let you pretend, so forget that."

"Right." Taking Levi by surprise, Beth spun around and blasted him. "You won't let me have any space. You won't let me deal with the changes." She punctuated each word with another stomp closer. "And now I'm not allowed to pretend, either? Well, newsflash Masterson. You don't control me. I'll pretend all I want to!" She ended that challenge on a high note.

Levi, too, left his seat. In a metered pace, he finished closing the distance between them. "You've got one hell of an imagination, Beth. I know because I benefited from it for a whole weekend and a day."

She gasped.

"But even your imagination isn't good enough to pretend nothing has ever happened between us. It's there, and we both remember it."

"*You . . .*" She seethed, but apparently she couldn't think of anything to say. With visible effort, she gathered herself. One deep breath, then another.

Fascinated, Levi watched her. Her behavior even sparked a memory, one that amused him and left him a little more controlled, too.

He and Beth had a history; he could build on that.

Little by little, Beth's tensed muscles relaxed and she even smiled. Sarcastically. "I'm done talking to you, Levi."

Even her acerbic smiles looked beautiful to him. "Is that right?"

"Yes. I'm going to take my shower and go to bed." With that, she grabbed up her overnight case and stormed toward the bathroom. "I'd prefer it if you did the same."

"With you?"

She almost tripped. "*No.*" Spine stiff, she took a few more breaths. "You may use the shower when I'm done."

"Thanks. I showered right before I found out that you'd skipped town. I'll just clean up our mess and go to bed." Maybe in bed he'd have power over his libido. Because right now, he could feel himself getting hard again.

Maybe it was the thought of Beth naked, under the water.

Maybe it was just being with her.

Whatever the case might be, he needed to be a calm, rational man with her, not a lust-craved maniac with a perpetual boner.

"Suit yourself," Beth said, right before she closed the bathroom door.

Right. If he did that, they'd both be on the bed, naked and entwined right now. Better that he go with a plan.

By the time Beth came out of the bathroom, Levi was in the bed, under the covers, and ready to tackle her stubbornness.

* * *

Other than the bathroom light slanting across the darkened floor, Beth couldn't see a thing. "Levi?"

"Careful, honey. Your bed is all ready for you. Do you need me to turn on a lamp?"

"No." Feeling like a prude, she'd put on her heavy flannel pajamas, the ones that were too big but comfy, the ones that hid every speck of skin and any curves she might possess. "I'm fine, thank you."

"Do you feel better now after your *long* shower."

Levi's emphasis couldn't be missed. But then, she *had* lingered in the shower for a good hour, thinking over everything the other women had said. Though they'd reassured her on many levels, it was still unsettling how Levi affected her so easily. It seemed that whenever she was alone with him, she wanted to rape him, harangue him, or flee him.

Why couldn't she just be herself?

For a little while there, after she'd first come into the room, the old familiar companionship returned. Talking with Levi had always been easy. Enjoyable. Somehow . . . comforting.

That insight was a little too profound, because it made Beth consider the possibility that she'd always had hidden feelings for him.

And the possibility that she'd been oblivious to *his* feelings.

"I'm fine," Beth finally told him. "The hot water felt so good after this nasty frigid weather that I just hung in there for a while. I hope you didn't really mind?"

"Course not."

Beth could hear him shifting on the bed. She cleared her throat. "I'm pretty tired tonight. Do you think we could just talk more in the morning?"

"Sure."

She found the edge of the little cot and eased down. "Thanks for clearing up our food mess."

"I stacked everything. Tomorrow morning the maid can grab it."

"That works." The new awkwardness was crushing. A little chilled now that she'd left the steam of the bathroom, Beth tucked under the covers. "Good night, Levi."

At first, she didn't think he would respond. Then he asked, "Remember that time you were upset and we talked for hours?"

By necessity, Levi had opened her cot at the end of the queen-sized bed. The dimensions of the room didn't allow for any other positioning, not if they hoped to be able to move around without bumping their shins.

Beth turned her head and stared toward Levi's voice in the darkness. "Yes."

"You were thinking of buying a new car because a few of Brandon's associates had teased you about driving an older model sedan with primer on the fender."

"My old faithful transportation. That car got me through college." She averted her gaze toward the ceiling. "Brandon agreed with them. He said as his fiancée, he wanted me to look classier."

The bed springs squeaked as Levi sat up. "I didn't know that."

A reluctant smile tugged at her lips. "You were already lecturing me for caring about what others thought, so I saw no reason to tell you that I cared what Brandon thought, too."

"As I remember it, you got mad at me for lecturing you." And then: "Brandon actually agreed with those idiots?"

Shadows shifted with the wind outside the window. Beth went back in time, to the first and, other than recent events, only conflict she'd ever had with Levi. "I wasn't really mad at you."

"No?"

"It's just that I knew you were right. What they thought didn't matter, not even a little. I was too old to give in to peer pressure or to start feeling inadequate about anything as superficial as the appearance of my car." She shifted onto her side. "And yes, Brandon agreed with them."

"You stayed for three and a half hours that night." Levi's voice was low and even, and she could hear the smile in his tone. "We ordered Chinese takeout and watched a back-to-back *Jeopardy!* marathon."

Beth remembered every second of that night, but it surprised her that Levi recalled so much.

"I suppose if you weren't mad at me," Levi questioned aloud, "then you must have been mad at yourself?"

"Yup. For letting those judgmental snobs get to me."

Levi laughed.

"That was almost a year ago, wasn't it?" The winter storm stirred the air outside, sending sleet to peck gently against the window. The wind moaned and a chill pervaded the room.

But in the dark, talking with Levi, Beth felt warm and cozy and strangely at peace. "What made you think of it?"

"Earlier, when I made you mad. You acted the same way you did that night. You deliberately reined in your anger. It's amazing to see. And cute." Before she could get too riled over that, Levi said, "I'm sorry that I upset you."

He was such a macho guy, yet he didn't hesitate to apologize when he felt the need. For Beth, that made him more macho than any other man she knew. "Thank you, but an apology isn't necessary. Once again, I'm more angry at myself than you."

"I wish you wouldn't be. There's no reason." He sat up again in the bed. "I never told Brandon about that night. Did you?"

"No. He wouldn't have understood."

Two heartbeats of silence passed before Levi asked softly, "Understood what?"

In the dark and quiet, alone and relaxed with Levi, it never crossed Beth's mind to give anything less than the truth. "That talking to you was easy."

The bed squeaked as Levi shifted around. He moved toward the foot of the bed—closer to her. Even without seeing him clearly, Beth knew he rested on his stomach with his fists beneath his chin.

"Ever wonder why, honey?"

His close proximity did crazy things to Beth's libido. "No."

He tsked. "Your nose is going to grow with all that fibbing."

Beth didn't confirm or deny that charge, but she did smile to herself.

With the casual comfort of long acquaintance, Levi rolled to his back. Their heads were close together, but their positioning felt more easy than intimate.

"I remember that time you got sick with a nasty chest cold. Your nose was bright red and you sneezed in the middle of every sentence."

Beth remembered it well, too. "Brandon had an extra long shift at the hospital, so you brought me soup."

"And a video."

"One of my favorites." Because she'd seen him in that position many times, Beth could almost picture Levi with his arms folded behind his head, biceps bulging, chest muscles defined. As a phys-ed teacher, he stayed active and in shape, and it showed. "Brandon always refused to see it with me."

"I know."

The way he said that twisted Beth's heart. "It surprised me that you liked it."

"Liked it?" Levi gave a short laugh. "I hated it. It sucked. It was too sappy and over the top emotional. Give me a good old-fashioned action flick any day."

"But you rented it!"

"Yeah." His tone softened and became every bit as sweet as the movie. "Because like the soup, I knew it was your favorite."

Beth held silent for several moments. Brandon hadn't known about her favorite soup, or her favorite video.

Was Levi that much more observant?

"You watched it with me," she accused.

"I watched you watching it," he corrected. "There's a difference."

When Levi turned back onto his stomach again, Beth could not only see the glow of his eyes in the darkness, she could actually feel his gaze touching on her.

"Back then," he whispered, "I guess I was into masochism, because being there with you, so close when you were so untouchable, was pretty torturous."

In the same whisper, Beth asked, "So why did you do it?"

"Because not being with you was worse."

Oh God. An invisible fist squeezed her heart, and Beth couldn't bear it. She came to her knees on the lumpy cot mattress. "Levi?"

He sat up to face her, only inches away. "I'm right here."

Beth laced her fingers together to keep from reaching for him. "Why do you want me?"

"You're smart."

That ultra-quick answer surprised a laugh out of Beth, and helped to put her need in check. "And brains turn you on?"

"Your brains do." He said that with a lot of gravity. "Especially when they're mixed with a great sense of humor, and sensitivity, and a big heart."

Beth inhaled his scent, somehow warmer now, more potent. "So it's not how I look?"

Sounding darker and deeper, he asked, "How do you look, Beth?"

"Female."

He fell silent for a moment. "Very female."

She sensed his restraint and it turned her on, making her feel powerful, seductive, and sexy.

In near confusion, he whispered, "I always thought I preferred dark women. Rich, dark hair, chocolate brown eyes. I always thought long legs were the sexiest. And big boobs."

"Gee, that's a surprise."

He paid no attention to her mocking interruption. "And lots of confidence."

"I'm confident."

"Maybe. Sometimes. But you're also petite and fair skinned, and you have beautiful legs, but honey, they're not super long."

Quickly passing the point of no return, Beth sighed. "I

guess I'm not really overly endowed in the chest department, either."

Somehow, even without the aid of light, his hands found her face. They were big and warm, and oh so gentle as they touched her. "You are perfect."

"I am?"

His thumbs brushed her cheekbones. "And very sexy."

Beth thought about that. "If you could change one thing about me, Levi, what would it be?"

"Your worries."

Her heart melted. So he wouldn't make her better endowed, sweeter, less headstrong?

"Levi," she chastised, because he hadn't taken any time to think about it, to consider all the possibilities. Still, his answer touched her. "I meant physically."

"Weren't you listening when I said you're perfect? You are. You're the most beautiful woman I've ever met."

Beth figured she could pass for pretty, but beautiful wasn't a word to describe her. She hesitated to speak her mind, but fair was fair—and fair was easier now, in the dark and in the quiet. "I think you look pretty perfect, too."

Levi said nothing.

"And . . . I have thought about you."

A sexual charge broke the stillness of the room, splintering it like static electricity. Then Levi's hands fell away from her. "I would love to hear more about what you thought, but I made a promise to you, and that means I need to go take a cold shower. Right now."

Thinking that he joked, Beth started to laugh, until she heard him leave the bed and she felt him move past her. "Levi!"

"Stay put, honey. I'll be back out in two minutes. Five if I decide I have to take care of business first, in order to keep my word."

Beth almost fell off the cot. She did stumble to her feet. *Take care of business?* Surely, Levi didn't mean what she thought he might mean.

Or did he? "*Levi.*"

His only answer was the closing of the bathroom door. A light came from beneath the door, and then the lock clicked into place with a quiet snick.

Staring through the dark and mostly empty room toward the bathroom, Beth stood there utterly mute.

Seconds later, she heard the shower come on.

In disbelief and pounding disappointment, she crawled face down onto the cot and pulled the pillow down over her head.

She would have screamed in frustration, but she was so turned on she couldn't draw a single deep breath. Her sisters-in-law and stepmother were right. She had to face the facts that her feelings for Levi were physical, but they were more than that, too.

She wanted him, yes indeed.

But because she admired him and appreciated him, and had always respected him; talking with Levi only made the physical need more acute.

Brooke, Grace, and Sierra knew what she hadn't wanted to accept: Levi was the guy for her. For too many years she'd missed the obvious. She'd been so blind that she'd almost married the wrong man. Brandon's unfaithfulness had given her an opportunity to set things straight.

Now she had to decide what to do about it.

4

Levi stood beneath the spray of the icy water and called himself ten times a fool. He couldn't touch her. He *couldn't.*

God, had he really made such an asinine promise?

Idiot.

Moron.

He pictured Beth on the cot, heard again her quiet confession, and knew he'd never survive his stupid promise without taking care of business first.

Letting his imagination go, he wrapped a hand around himself and slowly stroked. His teeth locked.

He saw Beth's eyes, dark with excitement. His muscles twitched.

He remembered the bite of her nails on his shoulders when he'd given her a third climax. Tension coiled inside him.

He felt again the way her teeth closed on his shoulder in an attempt to muffle her own shouts of pleasure. Close, so close.

He remembered when he took her from behind doggy-style, how he'd touched her belly, and lower. He visualized the mix of pleasure and uncertainty when he'd put her legs over his shoulders and entered her so deeply that she couldn't have taken any more of him.

He recalled the taste of her when he'd knelt on the floor and opened her thighs wide . . .

With a low groan, icy water streaming over his body and visions of Beth spurring him on, Levi came. It wasn't the same. It sure as hell wasn't enough.

But for now, it'd have to do.

With the edge of tension removed, Levi slumped against the hard-tile wall and tried to even his breathing as the cold water washed away the evidence of his release.

What was Beth thinking?

Would she be as ashamed for his behavior now as she'd been of her own during their long weekend? Would she even be waiting for him when he returned?

That thought got him moving and he dried off in record time. Without bothering to dress, he switched off the light and jerked the door open. "Beth?"

Like nails on a chalkboard, she gritted, "What?"

Uh-oh.

She didn't sound embarrassed. Nope, she sounded pissed.

Oddly enough, that relieved Levi. He'd take anger over her humiliation any day. "Just making sure you didn't skip out on me." He refrained from saying *again*.

"Where would I go, Levi? What would I say to Ben if I up and left?"

There was a punching sound as if she mauled her pillow, then she heaved an angry, frustrated sigh.

Poor baby. He doubted a cold shower would have the same effect on her. She was too new to satisfaction to take half measures.

"You know, Beth, you could say that you're so irresistible I couldn't take it anymore, but that I made you a promise I didn't want to break, so I had to excuse myself to—"

"Argh! It was a rhetorical question, you jerk. I do *not* want a blow-by-blow report of your . . . shower activities."

Levi stepped into his boxers. "No?" And just to tease her, he asked, "Are you sure?"

A pillow hit him square in the face.

Levi stumbled back into the wall, nearly falling. Good shot, especially in the dark. She impressed him, but he wouldn't tell her so. "Damn it, woman. Don't throw things at me."

Another pillow barely missed him, but knocked a lamp off the dresser. It crashed to the floor.

They both went silent.

"Now see what you made me do." Beth flipped on a light, turned to Levi, and froze.

Dressed only in black boxers, he straightened. "Sorry. I left the shower in a hurry when it occurred to me that you might flee."

She stared.

He nudged the fallen lamp with a bare toe. "It isn't broken, luckily."

She blinked, swallowed audibly.

Taking a relaxed stance, Levi let her look. "You've seen me before, Beth."

Without shifting her gaze to above his neck or below his knees, she said, "Shut up about that."

Exasperated, Levi put his hands on his hips. "I meant even before last weekend, actually. We've swam together so you've seen me in trunks plenty of times. And you've helped with practices, so you've seen me play in shirts and skins in soccer. You've even seen me—"

"Yeah, yeah. But this is different."

Because now she knew what was under the boxers, and she knew how good they were together? Levi wanted to hear her say it. "Why?"

"Because now I know you . . . intimately."

"And that makes it different?"

She nodded.

"Beth?"

"Hmm?"

"Do you think you could look at my face?" At his leisure, Levi leaned against the wall. "I mean, I did just come, I won't deny that. But I'm not sure how helpful that'll be if you keep looking at me like you want to eat me alive."

Her gaze clashed into his. Her hands fisted. Lips stiff and voice low, she growled, "You are such a jerk, Masterson."

"Maybe on occasion. I'm human. But you want me anyway," he taunted. "Don't you?"

Her teeth sawed together. Her eyes sparked. Then . . . on a sigh, she said, "Yes."

That knocked the humor right out of him. Levi straightened. "I wish you'd have admitted that before I made my promise."

"Forget your promise."

If only he could. "You might feel differently in the morning, honey. You might be mad at yourself again, and you'll take it out on me."

She bit her lip. "What if I swear not to?"

Heart hammering, Levi lifted the lamp off the floor and plunked it back onto the dresser. As he gathered his thoughts, he approached Beth's narrow cot. Though he didn't like himself for trying it, her need right now could be a bargaining chip toward their future.

Anticipation burned through him. "What if you swear to me that tonight won't be the only night? What if you marry me and—"

She blanched.

Damn it. "I take it that appalled look on your face is a no?" Propping his hands on his hips, Levi shook his head. "You think I'm asking for too much, don't you?"

Pleading, Beth whispered, "It's too much for so soon, yes."

For her, maybe. But not for him. Levi knew how he felt, how he'd always felt. He'd never acted on his feelings because Beth was as off-limits as a woman could be.

Was.

Not anymore.

"Sorry," he muttered, unwilling to torture himself further tonight. "Let's just go to bed and forget about it." Ignoring her stunned and disappointed expression, he stepped past Beth, stretched out on the bed, and pulled the covers over his body.

Beth kept her back to him. "No."

Levi eyed her militant stance. Her disheveled hair tumbled down her back. Pajamas a size too large swallowed her petite body. And still he could see the rigid way she held herself. "What did you say?"

She turned and began marching toward his bed. "I said no."

She looked so resolute that Levi hurried to sit up. But she'd already reached him and before he could stop her, before he even realized her intent, she grabbed the covers and ripped them right off the bed.

Wow.

Forget the shower; Levi was hard in a nanosecond. His heartbeat thundered, but he said calmly enough, "Now Beth . . ."

Flattening both hands on his bare chest, she shoved him onto his back. "You started this, Levi, and you can damn well finish it, whether we have a lifetime together, a year together, or even just tomorrow together."

As Beth threw a leg over his waist to straddle him, Levi gave up. He was only human. And male. And madly in love.

He cupped her face. "At least give me tomorrow, Beth."

She bit his chin, his bottom lip. "Tomorrow," she agreed. And then her mouth was on his, her kiss grinding and brutal and devouring him. Her tongue slicked over his lips, and then past them to tangle with his.

When she switched to his throat, he said, "Beth," meaning to slow her down.

"No more talking," she commanded. She nipped his earlobe, his collarbone.

"But honey . . ." Levi fought to remember his promise. "Beth, my willpower is dwindling fast."

"Good."

But his love for Beth was too important to give up to a flash of sexual satisfaction. "I promised you that I wouldn't—"

"Wouldn't touch me unless I begged." She sat up on his abdomen, looked down at him, and said, "Please, Levi." She spread her fingers over his bare chest and purred, "I'm begging."

His control evaporated. "Come here."

Full of enthusiasm and need, Beth fell on him. Trying to slow her down, to dredge up a bit of much-needed finesse Levi gentled her with a deep kiss.

When she went soft and warm against him, he coasted his hands over her narrow back to her waist, where he encountered the baggy pajama bottoms. With no more than a tug, they slid easily to her knees. Hooking his toes in the material, Levi kicked them away from her body and then off the side of the bed.

Beth raised herself above him. Her eyes were glazed with need, her lips parted. One by one, Levi opened the buttons of her pajama top and parted the material, leaving her breasts exposed. He wasted no time lifting himself up for a leisurely tasting of each swollen nipple.

Beth dropped to her elbows with a groan. Her thighs tightened around him, her eyes closed.

Carefully, without releasing her nipple, Levi turned her to a more submissive position under him. Giving her all his weight, he pinned her down and took his time licking a puckered nipple. He loved the texture of her, the scent that clung to her body, the broken sound of her breathing as he went from licking to sucking gently, then not so gently.

Her hips lifted against him in a frantic rhythm.

"*Levi . . .*" she begged again.

Never would he tire of hearing her say his name, especially in such a pleading way. "Patience, honey." He went back to kissing her breasts.

She tangled her fingers in his hair and forced his gaze up to hers. "Now, please."

Doing his best to hide a smile, Levi nodded. "You've got it."

She tried to pull him up to her then, but Levi had an alternate plan. Kissing a lazy, damp path down her rib cage to her belly, he let her know his intent. She groaned again, this time in eagerness for what he would do.

Voice hoarse and rough, he murmured, "Let's get rid of these panties."

Beth lifted her hips to accommodate his request, and Levi skimmed the slinky scrap of material down her legs. On his elbows, he looked up the length of her.

So beautiful. And all his, whether she accepted that yet or not.

Except for the pink-flowered flannel shirt framing her shoulders, she was completely naked.

Levi wanted to tell her that he loved her, but she wasn't ready to hear that, not yet. Hell, he'd barely gotten her to commit to tomorrow, when what he really wanted was a lifetime. If he rushed things, he could scare her off. Again.

For now, for right this moment, Beth only needed the relief he could give her.

He laid a heavy hand on her belly. She kept her eyes closed, her bottom lip caught in her teeth. Her breasts shimmered with each anxious breath she took.

Tonight she admitted to wanting him again. That was more than he'd had yesterday.

He'd drown her in pleasure, and maybe tomorrow she'd acknowledge that what they shared was more than sexual, and more than temporary.

Then she'd ask for a repeat. Tonight, tomorrow, the day after, and the day after that . . . until finally she realized that their friendship had grown from a mutual belief in life and love, a bone-deep compatibility enhanced by sexual chemistry and a shared view of the future.

She'd understand that love made it so special between them, and then she'd agree to a lifetime with him.

Keeping his hand on her belly, Levi said, "Open your legs, Beth."

Her muscles twitched—and she complied. But not enough to suit him.

"A little more, honey. Bend your knees, don't be shy . . . that's it." And just to tease her, he added, "I want to taste you."

Her breath shuddered out. Her belly sucked in.

"You're going to come for me, Beth. And you're going to love it, just not as much as I will."

Her neck arched, and her body bowed as she lifted herself toward him. "I want you to come, too."

With his mouth touching her heated skin, he groaned. Yeah, he'd come. No doubt about that. She was so soft that Levi loved touching and kissing her. And she had a unique scent that affected him more than a potent drug. He got near Beth, and his head swam, his heart raced, and heat suffused him.

Even before he could make a move on her, he'd known she was the woman meant to be his mate, just by the primal reactions of his body.

There was so much pleasure in being near her that Levi could have spent the rest of the night just nibbling on various erogenous parts of her body and enjoying her response to each flick of his tongue or warm suckle.

On her inner thighs, he left hickeys that no one would see except him. But Beth would go through her day tomorrow knowing they were there, and remembering him.

Though it wasn't necessary, he held her legs open as he teased his tongue along her pelvic bones, dipped into her navel, and trailed downward.

Finally, when he knew she couldn't take much more, Levi glided his fingertips over her and found her damp and swollen. In a gentle back and forth motion, he insinuated two fingers into her, all the while watching her face and seeing how even that simple touch nearly put her over the edge. Between her expression and the feel of her slick, hot, and tight around his fingers, he nearly lost control.

"You're squeezing me, Beth. I like that." He pressed a little deeper, slow but firm, until she gasped. New moisture bathed him, and he bent to nuzzle his lips around his fingers, tasting her and exciting himself more.

Trying to find relief, Beth moved her hips against him. Her inner muscles rhythmically clasped and released him in a building torrent of sensation.

Levi inhaled the spicy, pungent scent of her arousal, licked his tongue over her, around her, and gently drew her throbbing clitoris into his mouth.

Her reaction was instant and explosive.

With a throaty groan she came, her entire body rigid, pulsing, suspended with pleasure. Once again, her nails stung his shoulders as she struggled to ground herself and keep him as close as he could be.

The rush of it almost had Levi spiraling away, too. He eased the pressure as her body slowly sank back to the mattress and only little aftershocks rocked her. He took one last lick over super-sensitive flesh, felt her flinch, and retreated. Her ragged breathing filled the air. The mattress shivered with her pounding heartbeat.

Levi didn't want to leave her, didn't want to give up the heady taste of her, but he forced himself to move up beside her.

To his surprise, she immediately turned into his arms, tucking her head under his chin as she squeezed him tight.

"Hey?" he murmured, still a little unsteady himself from her release. "You okay?"

In answer, she took a gentle bite of his pectoral muscle.

"Ouch." Okay, so a bite wasn't tears. Or regret. It was sort of . . . playful.

He felt her smile against his heated skin. "Thank you, Levi."

Confused, he considered her actions and her sentiment before cautiously replying. "You're welcome."

"Now it's your turn."

He squeezed his eyes shut. "I don't know if that's a good idea."

But Beth wasn't listening. Lazily, given her recent climax, she sat up beside him. "Off with the boxers."

Levi weighed his options, knew he wasn't strong enough to resist, and decided he'd better ensure protection first. "Give me just a second." Sitting up, he stretched his arm to the chair beside the bed and snagged his jeans. From his back pocket he withdrew several connected condom packets.

"How many did you bring?"

"I don't know. When I realized you'd left, I just grabbed some." He separated one packet and, after shucking off his shorts, opened it.

Beth said, "Let me."

Just the thought of that had him shaking. "Not this time. If you start handling me, I'll be a goner."

She trailed her fingertips along his naked thigh. "Really?"

In a rush, Levi rolled on the condom. "Sorry, babe, but I've wanted too much for too long to show much restraint. Maybe in a decade you'll be able to tease me some. But not yet. Definitely not tonight." And with that, he put Beth on her back again. On the ragged edge, he growled, "Now open up and let me in."

Wearing a big, sexy smile, Beth did just that.

As he sank into her, Levi closed his eyes. Being joined to Beth made him feel like an idiotic poet. It was profound. It exceeded anything he'd ever known or felt.

He pressed in harder, deeper. "I'm not going to last." He pulled out, and then, watching her, thrust in again.

Her smile disappeared on a gasp. "Okay." Wrapping her fingers around his biceps, she held onto him. "Anytime you're ready." Her legs twined around him until she locked her ankles at the small of his back.

Levi straightened his arms so he could watch her breasts, and began thrusting in a steady rhythm. With each glide and retreat, Beth got wetter, hotter, and she clenched tighter. He locked his teeth. *Not yet,* he told himself, but he knew it was useless.

His fingers knotted in the bed sheets. "Look at me, Beth."

She did, her eyes smoky and dazed. "Levi?" she whispered.

He drove into her, unable to reply.

"I'm going to come again, too."

That did it, especially with the way her voice caught on the last word, the way she moaned and tensed and twisted beneath him.

He took her mouth, devouring her, their groans mingling together, so much a part of her that he knew sex with any other woman would never compare.

Spent, Levi relaxed his weight down onto her. He felt Beth's mouth touch his sweaty shoulder, felt her legs slide away from him.

Damn it. He couldn't take much more of this without her acknowledging their future together. Levi rolled to the side of her, staring at the ceiling, so aware of Beth that he felt her in his heart. Cool air wafted over his sweat-damp skin, but not for long. Beth curled into him and sighed.

Levi waited.

"It keeps getting better and better."

He smiled, ready to point out how great it'd be in a few years. But Beth wasn't finished.

"I keep saying this, but . . . could we talk in the morning?" She gave him a halfhearted pat on his chest. "I'm fading fast. You've worn me out with the chase and the capture and the awesome way you just made me feel."

Because she sounded sincere, and she ended that statement on a deep yawn, Levi relented. "Sure. Go to sleep, honey. I'll be here when you wake up."

"I know." She snuggled closer. "Because I'm not letting you go."

Levi's heart nearly stopped, then went into a fury of pounding that might have bruised his ribs. *She wasn't letting him go?*

After several moments of stunned silence, he lifted his head to look at her. "Beth?"

Her deep, even breaths gave the only reply. Well, hell. How could she make a statement like that and then just nod off? Did she mean what she said? Was she delirious? Too tired to think straight?

Confusing him with someone else?

No, not that.

Levi slid his arm out from under her and left the bed. Beth didn't stir so much as an eyelash. Feeling disgruntled, he went into the bathroom to dispose of the condom. When he returned, she didn't awaken but she did immediately settle back against him.

He understood her reserve, he really did. To go from being engaged to one man to marrying another in a matter of days wasn't an easy change to accept. But it was right. They were right together. This was their big opportunity at happily ever after, and Levi wasn't about to let her miss it.

Staring at the shadowy ceiling, Levi realized that he hadn't bothered to turn off the light. He looked at the lamp, but it was too far away from him to reach without getting up again.

He'd never get to sleep, damn it.

Confusion kept his thoughts churning for hours, but eventually the warmth and comfort of Beth's body wrapped close to his lulled him. He listened to her breathe while stroking his fingers over her supple waist and hip.

Finally, he drifted into a deep sleep.

He didn't stir once the rest of the night.

Grace hung up her sweater and then turned to the big bed she shared with her husband. She almost sighed. Noah was by far the most gorgeous man on the earth, and so wonderful that she often wanted to pinch herself to make sure it was all real.

Not that she ever doubted his love. Every day, in a dozen different ways, he made his feelings for her well known.

Grace enjoyed the sight of him a few moments more, then whispered, "Noah?"

Sprawled on the bed naked, Noah peeked open one eye. When he saw her in her undies, the other eye opened, too, and his gaze slid over her with heated appreciation. "Hmmm?"

Grace knew that look oh-so well—and she loved it. But wanting them to stay on track, she quickly pulled a nightshirt over her head before going to sit on the mattress beside him. "I'm curious about something."

His big warm hand settled heavily on her upper thigh, and he made a sound that showed she had his full attention.

As always.

To keep Noah's hand from roaming, Grace put hers over it. "What could Levi have done to Beth that she thought was so kinky?"

Startled, Noah gave up his perusal of her body and jerked his gaze up to her face. "What? Who says they did anything kinky?"

"Beth was embarrassed over what they'd done. She said she behaved like a sexual freak."

For a single moment, Noah looked horrified, then he gave a chagrined half laugh. "Hell, honey, I don't want to think about anything like that, much less talk about it. Beth's practically a sister. A baby sister." He shook his head. "Her sexual activities are definitely on my list of taboo subjects."

Grace wouldn't give up so easily. "Don't be ridiculous. She's only Ben's stepsister, and though neither of you show it nor acknowledge it, Ben's a half brother. That means Beth's not a blood relation to either of you, but she's even less of a real relative to you than she is to Ben."

Noah blinked at that long jumbled argument. "A brother is a brother and a sister is a sister. Doesn't matter how it comes about, it's still the same."

Grace frowned at him. "I could see if Ben was a little squeamish talking about Beth and Levi, but you—"

Noah shushed her with a groan. "Knowing Ben, he'd probably want details—so he'd have more reasons to demolish the guy. In case you didn't notice, Ben doesn't seem to like Levi much."

Grace waved that away. "Ben was just blustering, playing up that 'big brother' role. But we both know he wouldn't actually hurt Levi without good reason, and no reason exists, so it's not a problem."

"If you say so."

"I do." Grace bent to put a quick but interested peck on Noah's chest. "So, what do you think the two of them did?"

"I have no idea."

Grace bit her bottom lip. "Do you think they've done anything we haven't done?"

He made a sound that was half laugh, and half groan. "How the hell should I know?"

Grace huffed. Sitting straighter and frowning at Noah, she said, "Okay, let me rephrase this then. Is there anything we haven't done?"

Noah started to laugh, caught her frown, and changed his expression to one of serious consideration.

"You know what?" He hooked his arms around Grace, tumbled her down over him, and said, "Instead of talking about this, why don't I just run a few possibilities past you?"

It wasn't quite what she'd had in mind, but Grace gave into that suggestion with enthusiasm. "Now that you mention it, I like that idea even better." She put her arms around him. "Let's."

As Ben stepped out of the bathroom in the suite of rooms he shared with Sierra, she said, "We need to go shopping tomorrow. Can you free up some time?"

Still damp and busy drying, Ben glanced toward his wife where she sat cross-legged on the bed, a gift catalog opened over her lap. To his enjoyment, she wore only a ribbed undershirt and his favorite pair of pink and black barely-there panties.

Ben had bought her the underwear, and a dozen other pairs in a variety of styles, fabrics, and colors. When Sierra opened her Christmas presents this year, she'd have a dozen more.

He loved seeing her in sexy panties. They were such a contrast to her take-charge, tackle-any-job attitude and her sleek feminine muscles gained from hard work as a landscaper.

As he looked her over, his blood heated. "I can take the afternoon off. But what are we shopping for? I thought we'd finished our holiday gift buying." And he could definitely think of better ways to spend a free afternoon than shopping.

Without looking up, Sierra flipped the page. "We need something for Levi. The problem is that I don't know him that well. I guess I'll get something generic. You know, something all men enjoy."

"Like?" If Levi wasn't chasing Beth, Ben would suggest all types of things. But a man didn't make sexual jokes about a sister.

Sierra shook her head. "I don't know yet. I'm hoping to find some inspiration in this gift book."

After briskly drying his hair, Ben dropped the towel over the back of a chair and strode naked to the bed. "Maybe Levi won't be here that long and we won't have to worry about it. Christmas is still a few days away and Beth seems to want him long gone."

Although, Ben reminded himself, Beth had asked for one room.

But with two beds.

Very confusing. Except that damned Levi had seemed awfully sure of himself . . .

"She doesn't." Sierra continued with her perusal of holiday-inspired presents. "Want Levi gone, that is. She's in love with him."

Ben cocked a brow over that disclosure. "You really think so?"

"I know so." And then, distracted, "It's as obvious as it can be."

"I'll have to take your word for that." How was it that women always saw something different from what men saw?

"You are such a smart man." Sierra's mouth curved in a smile.

"Since Brandon's out of the picture, can't we just give his gift to Levi?"

Her smile lowered to a frown. "Of course not. All things considered, it wouldn't be right to give the man Beth will marry a gift that was meant for the man we thought she was going to marry."

Amused by that convoluted explanation, Ben stretched out beside her, took her catalog and dropped it on the nightstand.

It was Sierra's turn to raise a brow.

While looking at her breasts beneath the undershirt, Ben asked, "Am I supposed to understand what you just said?"

Sierra laid down on her side, facing him. "You could just trust me, I suppose."

"That I do, sweetheart." Leaning forward to kiss her, Ben growled, "I trust you to keep me in a fog of sexual satisfaction."

Sierra snorted. "You're so easy, that job's a piece of cake."

Dead serious, he said, "I'm easy for you, Sierra. No one else." Ben drew her down over him, and Sierra got to work.

Standing in front of her dressing-table mirror, wearing only a camisole and panties, Brooke removed her earrings and a delicate necklace.

As always, the sight of her charmed Kent. The way she moved, her posture, and the grace of her hands never failed to mesmerize him and turn him on.

Brooke caught his reflection in her mirror and smiled. "You look pensive, Kent. Are you thinking about Beth and that brazen new man of hers?"

Kent could have laughed, but he stifled his humor. "No." At that moment, with Brooke nearly ready for bed, the last thing on his mind was his daughter. "I think it'll work out just fine between the two of them."

After closing the jewelry box, Brooke turned to face him. "You do? Why?"

"Because Beth looks at that young man the way you always looked at me." The way Brooke *still* looked at him on occasion.

Laughing, Brooke reached up to take down her hair. "And how would that be?"

"With a little fear and a lot of fascination." As her silky hair tumbled free, Kent caught her around the hips and dragged her between his legs. "It's an incredible combination that gets to me every time."

"Fear?"

Nodding slowly, he let his hands slide down to cup her bottom. "Fear at being so fascinated."

Brooke laughed again. "I'd say it was more awe than fear. You are such a big, impressive man, and so blatantly sexual. I've never known anyone else like you."

Filling his palms with her lush, soft backside made it almost impossible for Kent to follow the conversation. "So you're in awe of me, huh?"

"What woman wouldn't be?" Inciting him with her gentleness, Brooke stroked her hands over his bare shoulders to his biceps. "Look at you."

"I'd rather look at you." Kent kissed her throat. "God woman, you are so hot."

Brooke cupped his face so she could see him. "And you think Beth feels about Levi the way I've always felt about you?"

His muscles tensed and heated. "This is not a good time to talk about my daughter."

Trailing one finger down the center of his chest, Brooke played coy and asked, "Why ever not?"

Kent growled, "Because I have a Jones, woman, that's why."

Her gaze dipped down his body and she smiled. "Well, my, my, my. I see that you do."

As if that wasn't reason enough, Kent rubbed his nose into the fragrant place between her breasts, whispering roughly, "And because you smell good and taste even better."

Brooke's fingers tunneled into his hair, drawing him closer to her.

Taking that as a sign of her readiness, Kent drew her down to the bed and turned her beneath him. "And because I know Beth can take care of herself."

After a deep breath, Brooke forced her eyes open. "I know you're right. And should she need anything, she does have Ben and Sierra in the hotel with her. It's not like she's alone—"

Kent silenced Brooke with a kiss meant to put her mind on the task at hand. He loved it that she cared so much for his daughter, and vice versa, but there was a time and a place for everything, and right now it was time to love his wife silly.

The second Kent nudged Brooke's legs open so he could settle between them, she gave in to him with familiar enthusiasm.

"That's better," Kent whispered to her. "Much, much better."

5

Watching Levi sleep proved an interesting pastime for Beth. He looked just as rugged and sexy in slumber as he did awake. Even a serious case of bed head that had his brown hair sticking up at odd angles didn't detract from his masculine impact.

Dark-beard shadow covered his jaw, and a low, even snore half mesmerized her.

Never had Beth been this fascinated watching Brandon sleep. In fact, Brandon had never really fascinated her in any way. Yet looking back, she realized that she'd always been intrigued by Levi, his connection with kids and his easy smiles, his sense of humor and his loyalty to friends.

She'd always liked being with him.

She'd always enjoyed talking to him.

Levi was a man's man, but ladies adored him, too. Only . . . he hadn't had a serious relationship with a woman in all the time she'd known him.

Maybe because of that, she'd never consciously considered him beyond a sexual fantasy. He hadn't struck her as the marrying kind, not when he seldom saw the same woman more than three times. To Beth, he was the quintessential bachelor—and that, along with his friendship to Brandon, had made him completely off limits for anything other than a very private fantasy.

Yet here she was, by her own volition, in bed with him. And he wanted to marry her, had all but insisted on it.

Out of guilt because he'd enjoyed making love with her? Or maybe out of that profound sense of responsibility, because she had been his best friend's fiancée and they would have eventually married.

Did he offer to marry her because he thought that's what she wanted? Or because he wanted it?

Did he hope to continue making love with her, except without the guilt?

There were too many questions, and not enough answers for Beth to consider marriage. The only thing she knew for certain was that she had it bad.

Unlike her mistaken feelings for Brandon, this was the genuine article. Love with a capital "L." The real McCoy. Everlasting, overshadowing, "till death do us part" love.

Now that she felt it, she knew how shallow and superficial her feelings for Brandon had been. At first, she'd have given anything to do over her wild weekend with Levi. Now she cherished the time she'd had with him. She wanted to do it over, again and again.

But . . . did Levi feel the same?

Her sigh roused him, and he began to stir. Stretching out his limbs while scrunching up his face a little, Levi flexed all those macho muscles that never failed to make her giddy. His biceps bulged, his abdomen drew into a tight, sexy six-pack, and a deep rumble came from his chest.

Leaning over him, Beth put a peck on his mouth and whispered, "Good morning, Levi."

He froze in a comical pose. His movements halted, his breath caught. Suddenly his eyes popped open. When he saw her face so close to his, bewilderment darkened his green gaze. Without moving anything but his eyes, he searched the position of her body over him, then the room, and then her face again.

Alert and wary, he murmured, "Good morning."

God, he even *sounded* wonderful to her now-enlightened ears. "You look incredibly sexy in the morning, Levi Masterson."

Keeping his gaze glued to hers, he asked, "I do?"

Beth nodded. "I've been awake for an hour."

His brows pinched in a frown. "You should have nudged me or something."

"No, it's all right." She glanced down his body, but that took her thoughts in a dangerous direction so she quickly took her attention back to his face. "I stayed busy watching you sleep."

A new awareness came over Levi. His gaze grew piercing. "Busy how?"

"Just thinking."

His eyes narrowed. "About?"

Beth hated the watchfulness that tightened his expression. She'd been so unfair to him that he didn't know if he should expect rejection or interest.

She drew a deep breath for courage. "Levi, from now on I want to be as honest with you as I can be."

Relaxing into his pillow, he said, "So you're admitting that you haven't been honest?"

"Not with myself and not with you." Rather than explain that she hadn't misled him on purpose, Beth said, "I'm sorry about that."

"You're forgiven."

Knowing he waited for an answer to his question, Beth gathered her nerve. "Since I woke up and found you asleep, I've been thinking about how nice it was to be this close to you without you pressuring me, or me molesting you."

The corners of his mouth quirked. "You can molest me any time you want, honey. I don't mind at all."

That reply proved a perfect example. "There, you see? Now you're awake, so the pressure starts again."

"It was just a joke, not a suggestion." He encouraged her to continue by saying, "Tell me what else you thought about."

"Everything." Daring and brave in light of her new attitude, Beth stroked a hand over his warm chest. She relished the feel of his crisp body hair, his strong muscles. And looking at his chest instead of into his eyes made it easier to say, "Mostly, I've thought about how foolish I've been."

Annoyance had Levi shoving upright. "Damn it, Beth—"

She threw herself over him, flattening him again. "I *have* been foolish." A finger over his mouth quieted his protests. "In lots of ways, but mostly for thinking myself in love with Brandon."

He bit her finger, and when she yanked it away, he caught her wrist and brought it back for an apologetic kiss that made her tingly.

"You *were* in love with him." Levi held her hand close. "Weren't you?"

She'd always thought so, but now that she could compare her feelings for Brandon with her feelings for Levi, she knew there was no comparison. "I was probably more in love with the idea of being in love with him. If that makes any sense."

Levi began kissing her fingertips one by one. "If you weren't in love with him, I'm glad, but yeah, it makes perfect sense. You're a mature, domestic, caring woman. You wanted to settle down."

"Gawd, I sound like a grandmother."

Taking her seriously, Levi said, "No, not grandmotherly at all. But you're not a partier, either, and you're not a woman who wants to spin her wheels on the dating scene. Like me, you value commitment and security."

"Yes." Beth wished that she'd realized sooner how much they had in common. "I'm trying to come to grips with some truths about myself." She looked at his mouth. "Another truth is that I enjoy you."

"Sexually?"

"Yes, definitely. But I enjoy your company, too."

"You always have."

Why did it sound as if he'd known that forever, when she was just figuring it out? "You're probably right."

Her easy admission had him staring hard at her again.

"Okay," Beth said, "so what are *you* thinking?"

"That I need up." Those words struck Levi funny, and he turned his head on a rough laugh. "Hell, what am I saying? I've been up since I opened my eyes and realized you were still here." He looked back at her. "In bed." His voice lowered. "With me."

"Of course I'm still here." Beth pretended affront. "I told you last night that we'd talk this morning."

"You also told me that you weren't letting me go. But you were half-asleep and I'd just given you an orgasm, so I wasn't sure how much stock to put into those words."

"You thought that maybe after everything we did last night, I'd freak out in the light of day and dodge you again?"

"That worry did keep me awake for a while."

They needed time to iron out all the misunderstandings and come to an agreement, one they could both deal with, Beth decided. "Well, we're here, and we're talking now."

Levi smiled. "And I'm thrilled, I really am. Except that before we get too involved, I'd like to hit the john, brush my teeth, shave—"

"Modesty?" Beth teased. "You want to greet me at your best?"

"You deserve the best."

He said that so seriously that she wanted to confess undying love. But before she did anything like that, she needed to figure out how Levi really felt, and why he wanted to marry her.

"I snuck into the bathroom without waking you." She brushed his mouth with hers in a feather-light kiss. "No morning breath for me."

His thumb skimmed her jaw. "No whiskers, either."

"I like your whiskers, Levi." What an understatement. She loved everything about him. "And your disheveled hair, and the warm, sleepy way you smell . . ." She put her nose to his neck and inhaled.

On a groan, Levi caught her upper arms, lifted her up and away from him and put her on her back beside him. "Do me a favor, will you, honey? Hold all those tantalizing thoughts while I do a rush job here, okay?"

Beth nodded.

His gaze dipped to her legs, exposed beneath the hem of her pajama top. Thanks to the cold, she'd buttoned up to keep her chest warm, but she hadn't bothered with her bottoms at all.

Levi slowly inhaled before visibly girding himself and, wonderfully naked, he strolled into the bathroom.

Beth watched him until he was out of sight, then she squeezed her eyes shut and hugged herself. Now that she'd accepted her involvement with Levi, things were easier.

And exciting beyond belief.

When she heard the water come on, she jumped out of the bed and called the front desk to request a pot of coffee and a basket of Danishes. Being Ben's stepsister got her priority service, and she barely had time to drag a brush through her hair and pull on her pajama bottoms before the knock sounded on the door.

Looking refreshed and resolute, Levi stuck his head out of the bathroom.

Beth deliberately confused him by grinning. "Unless you want to be seen in your birthday suit, you better duck back into bed."

"Breakfast?"

"Coffee at least."

"You're an angel." And with that, he stepped into jeans and went to the door for her. After signing the charge and slipping a few singles to the bellhop, he turned back to Beth, tray in hand.

Beth patted the bottom of the bed. "Put it here, and we can get comfortable together."

His jaw worked, but he gave in with a shrug. "If you say so."

Beth went about pouring coffee for them both. "I suppose you're wondering about my change in attitude, huh?"

"A little, yeah."

His dry tone made her chuckle. As she handed his coffee to him, she tried to explain. "Well, you know I talked with Grace and Sierra and Brooke last night?"

"Yeah." He took the cup from her and sipped.

"We talked about . . . us. You and me."

"I figured." He took another sip.

"I told them how I felt like a marauding sex fiend with you."

Levi choked. He looked at her, then sputtered and choked again. Quickly, he set the steaming cup of coffee back on the tray and stood.

"Are you all right?" Jumping to her feet, Beth went to the other side of the bed and started to pat his back.

Still coughing, Levi shot to the side to dodge her. "I'm okay," he wheezed.

"Are you sure?" He didn't sound all right.

Holding out a hand, he kept her at bay while he sucked in a few strangled breaths. When normal color returned to his face, he looked at her, put his hands on his hips and opened his mouth.

Beth blinked at him.

He said nothing. His mouth closed. He frowned.

"Did I embarrass you by telling them about us?"

He shook his head, more in confusion than denial. "Sex fiend?"

Maybe she shouldn't have shared that with him. "You have to admit that I'm not really myself with you."

"You're *exactly* yourself."

"I hadn't been that way before."

"Because you hadn't been with me before."

He sounded pretty confident about that. "It's not what I'm used to. It's not how I thought things should be."

"It's how I hope things will always be between us." Shaking his head, Levi said, "Forget what you told your family. I don't want to think about that."

"Not my whole family," Beth corrected. "Just the women."

"Ha." He shook his head again. "They probably made beelines to tell the men. They probably shared stories. Hell, they'll all be grinning at me this morning, you watch and see."

"They wouldn't do that!"

"No, you're right. Ben will probably want to kill me for debauching his little sister."

Beth rolled her eyes. "I'm not really his little sister, just a stepsister, and I seriously doubt that Sierra said anything to him."

"She's his wife. If she doesn't tell him everything, then she should."

Beth scowled. "So you're saying that you think she should have told him?"

Levi held his head. "I think you should have talked to me about this instead of telling them."

Damn it, Beth hated feeling guilt, and Levi had made her feel more guilt in a week than she'd felt in her entire life. "I'm sorry."

"Don't be." He dropped his hands. "We're here talking about it, and that's a big improvement to me chasing you. However we got to this point, I'm grateful." He came back to his seat. "So, you feel like a sex fiend, huh?"

Now he was smiling! Beth cleared her throat. "My point, before you started strangling to death, is that none of the women were surprised."

"You know why? Because what we did was perfectly normal."

"I didn't tell them anything we did."

"No?" He relaxed a little. "Then what did you tell them?"

"That it was more than I'd ever done before, and that it—*you*—made me feel so much more."

Levi absorbed all that before smiling again. "And they told you that was a good thing, right?"

"They told me to own up to my feelings, which is what I'm trying to do." To keep Levi from interrupting further, Beth shoved a cherry Danish toward him. "Now, since we've just established that I enjoy you, and you haven't denied enjoying me, I think we should continue to . . . enjoy each other."

Levi knew if he took a single bite of the Danish, he'd start choking again. He set it aside on one of the small plates that had come with the tray.

So, did Beth want to commit to him? Or just sleep with him?

It was a first, but damn it, he felt used. Insulted. He wanted everything, not just sexual satisfaction.

After a long look at Beth, he went to his overnight bag and withdrew a small wrapped package. "Here."

Rather than take it, Beth stared at the ribbon. "What is it?"

"A Christmas gift." Levi took her hand and pressed the package into it. "I know it's not Christmas yet, but close enough, so open it."

Excitement twinkled in her eyes. "Okay." Careful not to rip the shiny paper, Beth opened the present. "A CD? Oh, by my favorite artist! I was going to get this next month."

"I know. I heard you mention it. You'd already spent so much on Christmas shopping that something for yourself wasn't in the budget." He went back to his overnight bag and withdrew a larger gift. "Open this one, too."

"But—"

"Just open it, honey. Please."

Happy to oblige, Beth tore through the tissue paper. "The decorating book I mentioned."

He tossed the next present to her, and without argument, she opened it, and then laughed. "Socks?"

"Special socks to keep your feet warm."

"Because I'm always complaining of being cold?"

He nodded. "That's right." Digging deeper into his bag, he withdrew one more gift. "I wrapped this up after."

"After?"

He looked into her beautiful blue eyes and said, "After you were no longer Brandon's. After you were no longer off limits."

Her lips parted. "Levi . . ."

"After you became mine." He handed her a beautifully decorated, slender box.

For long moments, Beth just stared at the package. Finally, with infinite care, she opened the red-velvet ribbon, parted the silky paper, and lifted the lid.

"Oh Levi." In no more than an awed breath of sound, Beth lifted out the delicate bracelet with a dangling pearl held inside a three dimensional heart-shaped pendant. "This is the exact bracelet that I fell in love with last summer."

Levi crossed his arms over his chest. "I know. We were downtown for a play that Brandon wanted to see, and you stared at it in the jewelry window."

Slowly, Beth brought her gaze from the bracelet up to Levi. "You noticed that?"

"I notice everything about you. I always have. I just didn't let you or Brandon notice me noticing you."

Beth hugged the bracelet to her chest and gave a tremulous smile. "I've always noticed a lot about you, too."

"I know." He crossed the floor to sit beside her on the bed. "Sometimes it worried me, because I didn't want to be the cause of problems with you and Brandon. I kept wondering when the two of you would marry, and I didn't know how the hell I was going to handle it."

"Now you don't have to handle it, because Brandon and I are over and you had nothing to do with it."

Levi took her hands. "You like your gifts?"

"Yes, very much. All of them, but especially the bracelet."

"While you were still engaged to Brandon, I didn't dare give it to you. CDs and books were platonic enough, but jewelry . . ."

"It was so long ago, I'm surprised you were able to get it."

"After seeing you admire it, I bought it the very next day." He shrugged. "You wanted it, so I didn't want anyone else to have it. I'm glad I can finally give it to you."

Beth grinned. "It's so beautiful. Thank you." She reached for him.

He said, "Marry me, Beth."

She went still.

"You admitted to wanting me."

Nervousness replaced her elation. "I do."

"You admitted to liking my company."

"I don't think there's anyone I'd rather spend time with."

"Then marry me. Right now. The sooner the better."

She wavered. Levi could see it in her eyes. She wanted to say yes, but fear of condemnation held her back.

Tentatively, she asked, "Don't you think it's a little too soon for that?"

"Not for me."

"But . . . what will I say to everyone? I was just engaged to Brandon, and then poof—I'm marrying you."

"I don't care what anyone else thinks."

"Well, what about Brandon? Do you care what he thinks? How will he react to you, his best friend, wanting to marry me?"

Levi was about to reply to that when their phone rang. They looked at each other, Beth shrugged, and Levi reached out his arm to snatch up the receiver. "Hello?"

Beth watched him as he listened to the message from the front desk. Knowing she wouldn't like this new turn, but that perhaps it was for the best, he held her gaze.

"Okay, thanks. Tell Ben we'll be right there." Levi hung up the phone. "You're worried about Brandon's reaction? Well, now's our chance to find out what he thinks."

Beth's face went pale. "What do you mean?"

"Brandon's in the lobby, waiting for us."

"Oh no."

"Oh yes. And once again, your whole family is there. Seems they all came over to have breakfast with you. Only now they know that Brandon cheated on you."

"Oh no."

"Better yet, the desk clerk says it looks like Brandon tied one on last night, and he hasn't sobered up yet."

Beth rubbed her forehead. "Dad's reasonable enough. He won't meddle in my business."

"No? Well what about Ben and Noah?"

Beth jumped up from the bed and made a mad dash toward her clothes. "Hurry, Levi. Get dressed."

He narrowed his eyes and watched as she threw off her pajama bottoms and stepped into her jeans. He waited, but she turned her back to him before shrugging off her top and yanking on a sweatshirt.

"Are you so worried about Brandon's welfare?"

While stomping her feet into shoes, Beth scowled at him. "Don't be an idiot. I have no romantic feelings for Brandon anymore. It insults me for you to even suggest otherwise. But that doesn't mean I want someone else trying to punish him."

"You're sure about that?"

Beth stopped dressing long enough to stomp over to Levi, bend down close and snarl into his face, "I know I've been a little wishy-washy here, but don't insult my pride, damn it. Brandon burned his bridges as far as I'm concerned."

"And what about me?"

"I want you." Beth grabbed his ears and kissed him hard. "Only you."

His tension eased. "Okay then." In less than a minute, he'd pulled on a sweatshirt and socks, and tied up his boots. He took Beth by the hand. "Come on."

* * *

Before they reached the lobby, Levi could hear Brandon's loud drunken voice. The idiot. He picked one hell of a time to start drinking.

Worse, every word out of his mouth was an insult to Levi.

Looking down at Beth, Levi said, "Given his attitude, I'd say Brandon already knows about us."

"But how?"

"You spent a weekend with me, Beth. Plenty of people could have seen your car there."

She made a face. "Great."

"Did you tell anyone you were coming here?"

"My neighbors, so they would get my mail."

"And they would have told Brandon if he asked. And he would have seen my truck out front." So the cat was out of the bag. "Stay out of sight, honey."

"Why?"

"Because neither of us wants Brandon to say something stupid to you. If he does, your family will maim him."

"Oh, right." Beth stayed around the corner as Levi went into the lobby.

"You miserable bastard!" Brandon staggered toward him. "You fiancée-stealing ass. You pretended to be my friend."

Levi stepped in front of Brandon to keep his attention away from Beth. Normally well suited and groomed, Brandon looked like hell warmed over.

Levi felt sorry for him. After all, he'd just given up the very best thing in his life. "I am your friend, Brandon."

"Bullshit!" He almost fell over with that outburst. "You stabbed me in the back."

Levi glanced around and saw the fury gathering among Beth's relatives. "Why don't we take this someplace private?"

"After you just publicly took her from me? Why bother. Let's settle it right here, you traitor. You Benedict Arnold. You—"

"Just calm down, Brandon. Let me explain."

"Explain!" Being drunk didn't suit Brandon at all. "You're not good enough for her and you know it."

Levi stiffened. He could feel everyone looking at him.

"You're a gym teacher, for God's sake." Brandon stuck his nose in the air. "She was going to marry me, a doctor."

His anger sparked. "Until you cheated on her."

"One time! Just that one itty-bitty time." Brandon listed to the left, then caught himself. "It was only a little indiscretion. Marcia isn't anyone important. She didn't mean anything to me."

The females in attendance all grumbled over that.

Hoping to divert the topic, Levi said, "You didn't drive here drunk, did you?"

"Like you care?"

"Did you?"

Brandon hiccupped. "I came down here last night, but the desk clerk refused to tell me which room Beth was in. Then I saw your truck, and I remembered everyone saying that her car was at your place for the whole weekend." He stabbed a finger at Levi. "Then I started drinking."

Damned fool. "Because you thought that would somehow help?"

Brandon's face fell. "Tell me that you didn't touch her. Tell me, Levi."

Levi clenched his jaw, but said nothing.

Brandon howled. "Where is she? I need to talk to her."

"No. Not like this. Not while you're crocked."

"Beth still wants me, I know she does. She deserves a doctor. A man of money. An educated man." He curled his lip at Levi. "She deserves a man who can give her anything she wants."

She deserved love, but Brandon didn't understand that. "She's mine now, Brandon. Accept it."

Screeching like a wet cat and looking just as pathetic, Brandon took a half-hearted swing at Levi's head.

Levi dodged him, and then had to catch him so Brandon didn't land on his face.

Brandon shoved him away, or more to the point, he shoved himself away and into a wall. "What do you mean, she's yours?"

Levi stood over him and gave him the truth. "I'm going to marry her."

Brandon's mouth fell open. "But . . . she loves me!"

"No, she doesn't."

"You're lying. She won't marry you. You barely make a middle-class income. You live in a cracker box, not a real house, not the type of house I was going to buy for her."

"Shut up."

Everyone turned to look at Beth.

Her hands were fisted at her sides and she looked furious.

"Levi has a beautiful house, and a very important job, and he's a good man. An honorable man."

Levi felt the stares intensifying. True, he couldn't afford any of the luxuries that Brandon took for granted, but he knew those things weren't important to Beth.

He knew Beth better than Brandon knew her.

"It's all right, Beth."

"No," she said, "it is not."

Brandon's eyes narrowed with mean intent. "Did you go to bed with him, Beth?" His voice rose to a high pitch. "Did you?"

Levi said, "That's enough, Brandon."

"You did!" Incensed, he took two drunken, wobbly steps toward Beth. "Why you little—"

Levi pulled him back before he got close to her, but Ben and Noah, having seen enough, started forward.

In the awkward position of defending Brandon now, Levi said, "Come on, guys. He's had a hell of a blow."

Noah stared at Brandon. "He's a loud-mouthed idiot and he's causing a scene."

"And he's insulting Beth," Ben added. "Reason enough to toss his ass back outside. He can sober up in the snow."

Just what Levi didn't need: angry relatives. He glanced at Kent, but Beth's father looked ready to take Brandon apart himself. Shit. He could think of better ways to spend this morning.

To Noah and Ben, Levi said, "Back off, I've got it covered." His take-charge tone stalled everyone. "Look, Brandon messed up and he knows it. He lost Beth, and now she's with me. He doesn't usually drink, but you can see that he's so hammered, he doesn't even know what he's saying."

"I know the truth," Brandon slurred while struggling to stay on his feet. "And the truth is that Beth wanted to hurt me, so she crawled into bed with my *supposed* best friend."

On the surface, that was damn close to the mark. Levi leveled a warning look on him. "Shut up, Brandon."

"All this time," Brandon continued, too drunk to show common sense, "she's been pretending to be a goody-two-shoes but she's really no more than a—"

Levi slapped him. Hard.

Brandon's head snapped back, and as if in slow motion, he started to crumble.

Cursing to himself, Levi caught him by the shirt collar to keep him upright. "Drunk or not, Brandon, you won't insult her."

Practically on his knees, Brandon blinked at Levi. "You slapped me."

"Be glad I didn't break your damn nose."

Shrugging free of him, Brandon dropped to sit on his ass. "But you *slapped* me. Like a bitch."

Levi glanced at Beth, saw her reddened face and narrowed eyes, and wanted to choke Brandon for upsetting her. "Until you get over it, I'm sticking you in a room and by God, Brandon, you'll stay there until you're sober enough to make your apologies."

No one got in Levi's way as he more or less hauled Brandon with him to the front desk where a clerk quickly assigned him a room. By the time Levi actually got Brandon into the room, Brandon was dead on his feet. Levi let him fall onto the bed, and Brandon didn't move.

Levi pulled out his cell phone and dialed Beth. She answered on the first ring.

"Levi?"

"Yeah, it's me. You okay?"

"I'm fine. How's Brandon?"

Levi worked his jaw. "Passed out on the bed."

"Good. I hope he wakes up with a killer headache. He deserves it for being such a jerk."

"Look, honey, I want to talk to you. I want to be with you. But I don't dare leave him. If I do, he might end up right back in the thick of things—"

"No, I understand." There was a slight hesitation, and then Beth said, "Thank you, Levi."

"For what?"

"For being you."

She didn't elaborate on that, so Levi asked, "What do you have planned today?"

"Christmas shopping. I have to catch up to you."

He grinned. "Be careful. Think about my proposal."

"Levi."

"I'll see you later on." He hung up before she could say anything more, then looked again at Brandon. It didn't look like he'd be stirring any time soon, so Levi turned on the television.

It was going to be a long, miserable day.

He fell asleep.

Levi couldn't believe it when he opened his eyes and found the room empty. A glance at the clock showed it was time for dinner.

Damn, damn, damn.

He'd lost sleep the last few days, but that wasn't a good excuse. If Brandon had found Beth and upset her again . . .

Or worse, what if she forgave him? What if she reconsidered her position?

In record time, Levi was out of the room and heading for the diner. He walked in on a crowd of guests and family alike. Servers bustled back and forth. The clink of forks on plates mixed with the drone of multiple conversations. A quick glance around the congested room helped Levi to locate Beth at a far table with her family.

Brandon stood before them.

As Levi cut through the throng toward them, he saw Brandon gesturing, and Beth nodding.

Fury boiled up.

When he was within a few feet of them, he heard Brandon say, "I got spooked every time I thought of settling down forever. I mean . . . forever is a hell of a long time, and I'd spent my whole life working toward a goal. There wasn't time for fun, and finally when there was, everyone expected me to settle into married life."

Levi pulled up short behind him. So far, no one had noticed him. They were all too busy giving Brandon the floor. Somehow, without waking Levi, Brandon had washed and dressed and he looked more like his old stylish self now.

He looked like a very respectable doctor, like Beth's old fiancé.

Beth said, "Go on, Brandon."

"I know that what I did to you is unforgivable."

"Unforgettable, certainly," Beth said. "We can't go back, Brandon."

Stoic and proud, he nodded. "I understand."

"Is that all you have to say?"

"No." He cleared his throat. "No, of course not. I need to apologize for my display earlier, too. I've never before overindulged. It's unfortunate that I did this time."

"Very unfortunate," Kent said.

"From what I remember, which granted, isn't much, I was a total ass."

Ben and Noah nodded—until their wives elbowed them.

Brandon ran a hand through his hair, and then he straightened his shoulders and looked only at Beth.

"I'd like to say, with what little dignity I can muster, that I'm the one who was never good enough for you. In the long run, I'll make more money than Levi, but I don't have half his character, honor, or fortitude. In every way that counts, he's a much better man than me."

Shocked at hearing such a statement, especially when he'd expected Brandon to be schmoozing his way back into Beth's good graces, Levi snorted. "That's bullshit."

Brandon jerked around to face him. Beth and her family looked at him.

Shoving his hands into his pockets, Brandon said, "No, it's true, Levi. You've propped me up so damn many times I've lost count. But you've never needed propping. Not once."

"Levi is a rock," Beth said with a smile, and Brandon nodded.

"You've had your difficulties, Levi, but you always work through them." He pulled his hands from his pockets and held them out in a conciliatory way. "Not to get sappy, but I admire and respect you more than any man I know. If I have to lose Beth—"

Levi took a step forward. "You have to."

Noah and Ben chuckled at that.

"—then I'm glad I'm losing her to you. The one thing I remember saying that was true, is that she deserves the best." Brandon nodded. "That would be you."

Ben cursed, and when everyone looked at him, he shook his head. "I really wanted to hate the guy, you know? But I think his reasoning is starting to make sense to me."

Both Brandon and Levi grinned.

Turning back to Beth, Brandon said, "I think I knew all along that we weren't really meant to be. But you're a special woman, and even if I wasn't the right man, I hated to lose you."

"Too late," Levi said.

Brandon smiled, and turned back to Levi. "I concede the loss. And if you'll have me, that is, if Beth doesn't mind, I'd still like to be your best friend."

When Levi looked at Beth, she nodded.

He held out a hand to Brandon. "Still friends."

Brandon accepted the handshake with huge relief. "Not to push my luck, but I'd be honored to be the best man."

Levi grinned. "Your friends won't have a clue what to think."

"Yeah," Brandon agreed, a little sad, a little amused, and happy for them. "But who cares?"

Beth said, "Now wait a minute."

Levi cut her off, saying to one and all, "She's still resisting the idea of marrying me. But I love her enough that I won't give up."

Beth's mouth fell open. "What did you say?"

Levi cocked a brow. "I'm not giving up."

"No," she gasped out, "the other part. About loving me."

He shrugged. "I love you. But you already knew that."

She shook her head. "No. I knew you wanted to marry me. But I wasn't sure why—"

Rolling his eyes, Levi said, "Maybe it's time for us to have that long talk." He took Beth's hand and pulled her from her seat. To her family, he said, "Excuse us."

As Levi turned them away, Brandon dropped into her seat. Levi heard him say, "I know I don't deserve it, but I would sure love a cup of coffee."

Grinning, Levi tugged Beth through the mob of diners, out of the dining room, and down the hallway until he reached the privacy of their room.

Beth pulled back. "What are you doing?"

After unlocking the door, Levi urged her inside. "I'm going to convince you how much I love you."

Beth closed the door herself, and then licked her lips. Levi saw the start of a smile.

"How much?" she asked.

He cupped her face and held her still. "More than anything else in the whole world."

"Okay." She gave in to her smile. "Since when?"

"Since forever. Since I first met you."

"So even though we only got together because I offered myself to you—"

Levi shook his head in disbelief. "Think about it. Would I have run the risk of ruining a fifteen-year friendship just for a piece of ass?"

She started to chuckle. "Um—"

"And remember," Levi said, "at the time, I didn't even know what a hot piece you'd be."

"Levi!"

He laughed, too, knowing by the glow in her face and the love in her eyes that he'd won. "I did know, however, that you were smart and sweet and kind and caring and dependable and loyal—"

"Levi?"

"Yes?"

"I love you, too."

Finally, she admitted it. "I know."

Beth laughed. "And I'll marry you."

He slumped against her. " 'Bout damn time, woman."

Beth threw her arms around him. "I guess I get my do-over after all."

"Your do-over?"

"A chance to change the things I did wrong." She kissed him. "At first I wanted a chance to do over that weekend with you."

Levi frowned at her.

"But now I know that I get to do over a real mistake."

He crowded her back against the door. "Your engagement to the wrong man?"

"Yes."

He cupped her chin and turned her face up to his. "And marriage to the right man?"

She nodded. "Thank you, Levi, for the very best Christmas present ever."

Impatience rose up, nearly making his dark blond hair stand on end. "This is no time for games."

Oh, boy. And here she'd always thought preachers were supposed to be full of endless, unwavering forbearance. Such a contradiction. But Shay didn't scare easily. "I'll go with you. When I know your name." And then, to soften her insistence: "You can't expect me to just go traipsing off with a stranger."

"And hearing my name is all the reassurance you need?"

His disbelief and suspicion made Shay grin. "Yeah."

Rankled, he rubbed his jaw, dragged a hand over his damp hair. Then he stuck out his hand. "Bryan Kelly." No sooner did he say it than he looked poleaxed, like he wanted to turn around and walk away from her, or curse, or punch the brick wall.

Instead, he just stood there, frozen, his hand extended.

"Bryan." She tasted the name, watched him watching her, and closed her fingers around his. "I like it."

"I meant to say Bruce."

Shay blinked twice. "What?"

With her hand still held in his, he repeated, "I meant to say Bruce. Bryan's . . . my middle name."

"Bruce Bryan Kelly?" And she thought her own name was unique.

His scowl was back, blacker and meaner than ever. "I prefer you call me Preacher."

"Why?"

He appeared to be grinding his teeth. "Because that's what everyone calls me."

"So?"

"I can't show favoritism." He seemed satisfied with that explanation, enough to expound on it. "You can imagine how that'd look, all things considered."

It was difficult not to laugh. "Things being that I'm a prostitute and you're offering to protect me?"

If looks could hurt . . . "Exactly."

"I'll call you Bryan—but only when we're alone."

Seconds passed while he stared at her, probably trying to intimidate her. "Will you, now?"

She met him stare for stare. "Yes."

His eyes narrowed more, his lip curled, and he turned away. "Good thing we won't be alone much, then." He still had her hand caught in his, practically dragging her along, keeping close to the buildings and as far from the blowing rain as they could get.

Pulling the tiger's tail, Shay asked sweetly, "Don't you want to know my name?"

They walked another ten feet before he said in distraction, "What the hell? Go ahead and tell me."

His absent tone was tempered by the protective way he led her down the deserted street. For a preacher, he had incredible instincts, staying alert, constantly scanning the area. Had he maybe served in the service before choosing this vocation? Or was his edgy, suspicious nature just a basic part of the man?

Whatever the reasons for his unique attitudes, Shay liked them. She liked him.

It was the first time since her husband that a man had bothered to show interest in her for any reason other than her money. She was well used to men fawning over her, trying to ingratiate themselves into her life. She had connections and wealth, which meant she had power. The combination served as quite an inducement to most guys.

But Bryan Kelly was unaware of her assets; for heaven's sake, the man thought she was a common hooker in a dirty little neighborhood, desperate enough to be selling her wares on a night like this. It wasn't the most complimentary assumption ever made.

But it was better than being wanted for her money.

And for the moment, she preferred he go on thinking it. Which meant she couldn't give him her full name. "You can call me Shay."

"Shea what?"

No way would she give him her last name. After recent events, she'd suffered some truly awful publicity and he'd probably read most of it. Knowing how he felt about WAM, it wouldn't be a stretch to think he'd leave her standing in the street alone if he realized her identity. "Just Shay."

After a furtive glance, he asked, "Just Shea, like the stadium?" Amusement lightened his eyes. "Or just Shea, like Cher, important enough that you only need one name?"

Was he laughing at her? It didn't matter. Laughter was better than disdain any day. "Just Shay, as in short for Shaina." She spelled out her name for him. No one in the papers had known her full name. No one had called her Shaina since she'd been adopted.

He nodded, then said, "No last name, huh?"

"I like to protect my privacy."

After a look that could cut, he let it go, and for once, Shay was glad. If he didn't ask any other questions, she wouldn't have to outright lie to him.

He led her along until they came to a fully lit section, leaving the blackout behind. The buildings were close together, some rundown, some tidy, all of them showing signs of poverty.

He released her hand and pointed ahead. "See that tall,

skinny building at the end of the street? That's the safe house. You're welcome there any time."

"Thank you, Bryan."

His piercing gaze locked on hers, while one side of his mouth curled. It wasn't humor that put that half smile on his hard face. "You're a pushy broad, aren't you?"

Since Shay couldn't deny that, she only shrugged an apology. It was a rhetorical question anyway, given how he turned his attention away.

She liked holding his hand and walking beside him in the rain, feeling his attentiveness to his surroundings and listening to his deep voice and breathing his scent.

She'd like to get to know him better, too, to maybe work with him, maybe be . . . intimate with him.

Okay, so she'd jumped ahead with giant leaps on that one. The timing couldn't be more wrong, and considering that he was a preacher, those thoughts were even more inappropriate. But these things really didn't wait for perfect timing, she supposed.

It had been a long time in coming, and now that desire was finally hitting her again, it did so in full force. She felt it everywhere, such wonderful feelings. And they were intensifying with each second they spent together.

Watching Bryan's long-legged stride excited her. Hearing his deep-toned, rough voice made her insides swirl. Even his ears seemed sexy, and if that wasn't lust, she didn't know what to call it.

With his palm at the small of her back, he ushered her ahead of him. He was easily six feet tall, which left them nearly the same height. Bryan didn't seem intimidated by that. In fact, he didn't appear to notice. His inattention to her as a woman might be a problem, she decided.

He wrestled a set of keys out of a tight, damp jeans pocket and unlocked the door, then held it open for her. Lights were on inside, and though the room was shabby, it was clean and warm.

Furnished with multiple seating of mismatched couches and chairs and benches, it reminded her of a used furniture store. The scarred linoleum floor had a deep slope and was bare except for an occasional worn area rug. No dust collected in the corners, and no muddy tracks marred the floor. Somehow, the room appeared comfortably lived in, inviting and cozy.

As she slipped out of his now soaked jacket, she watched him. "Do you stay here, too, Bryan?"

"No." He had his back to her, snapping the door shut and turning all the locks to secure the house. With the brighter lighting, she could study him in more detail. His thickly lashed, dark eyes were made for seduction. His dark blond hair, straight and a tad too long, had lighter sun streaks, making an interesting contrast with his eyes.

"Why not?"

"Staying here wouldn't be appropriate, now would it? And you can just imagine how WAM would slant it. By the time they retold the circumstances, we'd all be involved in drunken orgies or worse."

He ran his hands through his wet hair to push it out of his face, and turned toward her. Shay held out his jacket—and he froze.

With his hands still in his hair, his gaze zeroed in on her body. Slowly, very slowly, he lowered his arms. His attention was nearly tactile, heating her, making her heart beat fast.

Belatedly, Shay remembered what he'd told her, that the rain had made her tailored, white silk dress transparent. Oh, no. With dread, she looked down, and almost collapsed with embarrassment.